ALSO BY

DARA HORN

A Guide for the Perplexed

All Other Nights

The World to Come

In the Image

MORE PRAISE FOR *ETERNAL LIFE*

"As a philosophical novel, *Eternal Life* asks the most fundamental of questions: What makes life meaningful? Is its traditional arc, from birth through family formation to death, necessary? Is it a blessing that we insufficiently appreciate?" —Julia M. Klein, *Forward*

"The chilling pathos of Dara Horn's *Eternal Life* is bound to turn every mortal reader into a philosopher of cosmic joy."
—Cynthia Ozick, author of *Foreign Bodies*

"A mature, wry, uniquely female take on the problem of immortality."
—Chelsea Leu, *Los Angeles Review of Books*

"Passionate, playful, and poignant." —*Parade*

"To an extent, it's the humor (and horror) of infinite diaper changes that drives this masterful page-turner. However, *Eternal Life* is at its core a serious meditation on the meaning of life and purpose of death." —Renee Ghert-Zand, *Times of Israel*

"An elegant musing on sacredness, history, and purpose that is, at the same time, a deliciously romantic, highly suspenseful page-turner."
—Geraldine Brooks, author of *The Secret Chord*

"Rachel speaks with the wisdom of the ancients when she observes that immortality offers no consolation for the death of others. 'Not dying doesn't make it better,' she says of all that sorrow. 'It only makes it take longer.'" —Sam Sachs, *Wall Street Journal*

"Horn does not hedge her bets, whipping up a Jewish telenovela of ancient-world drama and present-day complications. It'll put you off immortality for good." —Marion Winik, *Newsday*

“[Horn’s] lyrical sentences, sharp intellect and originality place her among the finest American Jewish novelists writing today.”

—Sandee Brawarsky, *Jewish Week*

“With Rachel’s life spanning Jewish societies—continually dying yet reborn after each disaster—from the Roman Empire to modern Israel, *Eternal Life* reads as a metaphor for Jewish history.”

—Marina Bolotnikova, *Harvard Magazine*

“In *Eternal Life*, the familiar account of the joys and sorrows of motherhood turns strange and mythical. Wisdom literature is a rare thing, and even rarer when it arrives, as it does here, in a story so passionate and playful.” —Joshua Ferris, author of *The Dinner Party*

“A real Jewish story slips in and out of time. That’s because our texts talk to each other through time. [A] Jewish story is one in which both authors and characters engage in a larger-than-life narrative. Horn’s characters speak to us in larger-than-life time.”

—*Jewish Herald-Voice*

“Horn . . . is interested in ‘the story’ itself, not an alternative narrative driven by a contemporary agenda. Her characters may be mischievous or impious, but she does not seek to upend tradition; she seeks to understand it and bring it to life. . . . Parenthood, Judaism, and even the novel itself are places where past and future meet and reveal their interdependence. In this way, the elaborate fictional conceit of *Eternal Life* reveals something we could have, or should have, known all along.” —Sarah Rindner, *Jewish Review of Books*

“*Eternal Life* takes the psychological novel to places I’ve never seen before. Through the meticulously, humorously, and humanely-rendered psyche of a two-thousand-year-old woman, we get a unique view on the historical constants and variables of the lives of women. . . . The writing is so assured, and the observations ring so true, that at times I forgot it was a novel, and felt like I was really reading the thoughts of someone viewing the world through two millennia of life experience. Riveting, startling, hilarious, and sad—I've never read anything like it."

—Elif Batuman, author of *The Idiot*

"Horn has taken on a challenging project here with a light hand, crisscrossing strands of plot and a timeline stretching from the era of the Second Temple to the present day, or rather the day after today. . . . Although the story is fantastical, Horn buttresses her fiction with historical and biblical research."

—Frances Brent, *Moment*

"By musing on sacredness, history, and purpose, Horn is able to give us a romantic, funny, witty, and suspenseful look at how we live. We, along with Rachel, meditate on the meaning of life while at the same time explore the future and memory. Bravo!"

—Amos Lassen, *Judaica*

"A dramatic and intelligent mix of historical fiction and fantasy, combined in an involving story as [Horn] examines philosophical issues and questions surrounding the meaning of life."

—Gila Wertheimer, *Chicago Jewish Star*

"A surprisingly fun read, and one that'll stay on your mind even after the turn of the last page." —Evan Pille, *Daily Nebraskan*

"*Eternal Life* combines elements of Jewish history and folktale with speculative fiction, which . . . results in an absorbing and thought-provoking look at living, dying, and love of all kinds."

—Sarah Rachel Egelman, *Bookreporter*

ETERNAL LIFE

A

N O V E L

. . .

DARA HORN

W. W. NORTON & COMPANY

Independent Publishers Since 1923

NEW YORK LONDON

This is a work of fiction. Names, characters, places, and incidents are the products of the author's imagination or are used fictitiously. Any resemblance to actual events, locales, or persons, living or dead, is entirely coincidental.

Printed in the United States of America
First published as a Norton paperback 2019

For information about permission to reproduce selections from this book, write to Permissions, W. W. Norton & Company, Inc., 500 Fifth Avenue, New York, NY 10110

For information about special discounts for bulk purchases, please contact W. W. Norton Special Sales at specialsales@wwnorton.com or 800-233-4830

Manufacturing by LSC Communications, Harrisonburg
Book design by Barbara Bachman
Production manager: Beth Steidle

Library of Congress Cataloging-in-Publication Data

Names: Horn, Dara, 1977– author.
Title: Eternal life : a novel / Dara Horn.
Description: First edition. | New York, NY : W. W. Norton & Company, Inc., [2018]
Identifiers: LCCN 2017044684 | ISBN 9780393608533 (hardcover)
Subjects: LCSH: Idea (Philosophy)—Fiction. | Immortality—Fiction. | GSAFD: Humorous fiction.
Classification: LCC PS3608.O76 E85 2018 | DDC 813/.6—dc23
LC record available at https://lccn.loc.gov/2017044684

ISBN 978-0-393-35656-4 pbk.

W. W. Norton & Company, Inc.
500 Fifth Avenue, New York, N.Y. 10110
www.wwnorton.com

W. W. Norton & Company Ltd.
15 Carlisle Street, London W1D 3BS

1 2 3 4 5 6 7 8 9 0

For my parents,

Susan and Matthew Horn,

and their grandchildren:

Maya, Ari, Eli, Ronen, Zev, Rami, Lila, Gabriella,

Eliana, Orli, Abigail, Aliza, Yael, and Asher.

(My parents made it look easy.)

And for Brendan Schulman,

again and again and again.

ETERNAL LIFE

CHAPTER

1

#CRAZYOLDLADY

. . .

Either everything matters, or everything is an outrageous waste of time. That's what she would have said, if anyone had asked her. But no one asks crazy old ladies for their opinions.

If her father had described it—it was his job to write, or at least to copy, though he liked to add his own details—he might have written: *These are the generations of Rachel, keeper of vows, who bargained with God and lived.* If her son had written it—her first son, the wise one, the reason for everything that followed—he would have put it differently. *If all the heavens were parchment, and all the seas ink, such would not suffice to record the days of Rachel, whose years are no more than an eyeblink of the Master of the World.* If her twentieth son had written it—he was a panderer, a bootlicker, but that had been worth something then—he would have sprinkled it with rose petals until it reeked. *O mother of thousands, she who escaped the sword; most loved, most honored, most blessed of the Lord!* Or something equally trite. He was no poet, but the delusion had been harmless. Her sixty-third son, who was one of her favorites, would have written something else, in a different language this time, though still the same alphabet: *If you like, dear reader, I'll tell you a story you'll never forget for as long as you live, about how my mother once made a promise she forever regretted. Just don't tell anyone I told you.*

This latest granddaughter had reminded her of that sixty-third son: quiet, with a simple smile that hid a voracious intellect. With that sixty-third son's wild brothers, she had lost her temper frequently, though the sixty-third son had been silent, almost ignored. Then one day he had stood up on a chair during a meal and declaimed a rhymed alphabetical list of all the curses she had hurled at him and his brothers, and she had laughed until her insides ached. Even now she felt a lightness when she thought of the books he wrote later, which still made her laugh. She had almost told him, but hadn't in the end. He would have thought she was joking.

But this was the longest she had stayed anywhere, and these were the oldest grandchildren she had ever dared to know. The youngest one, sitting at the table before her—the one she had kept in reserve in her mind for years, just as she always chose one, the one she thought she could trust—that one was already over thirty, with children of her own. Perhaps she would tell that granddaughter. Or not, and simply leave without a word, as she usually did. Either way, she couldn't stay much longer.

The day's meeting had been awkward. Just getting into the office above the store had meant crossing through a line of seven people holding signs. The signs said "Boycott Zakkai Gemstones" and "Divest from Zionist Occupiers." It was odd, she thought. She wasn't Israeli, at least not the way these people thought. Or rather, she was, in exactly the way these people thought. In either case, it made no sense. Her grandchildren upstairs had an explanation, though not a good one.

"They've got the wrong store," one announced. "They think we're the Bukharian guy."

No one named the Bukharian guy. It was company policy never to name the Bukharian guy.

"If they think we're the Bukharian guy, they'll be pretty disappointed when all we have to divest is eighty-five cents," another added.

"What do we do to get rid of them?"

"Give them time to get bored. They'll leave."

"They'll leave faster if we give them the Bukharian guy's address."

"Who do you think sent them here in the first place? The Bukharian guy."

"Crazy shit, Gram. Crazy shit."

She rolled her eyes, a gesture she had picked up along with English, years ago, and everyone laughed. As the meeting proceeded, she looked around the table at them: her children, her grandchildren, familiar faces, repeating faces, with only one son rebelliously absent—but one wasn't bad, considering. She had done well, she thought, in this version. "Version" was the word she used when thinking of it—*nusach*, the liturgical term, like a melodic variation on a theme. That's what they were, these different versions: different tones, different moods, melancholic, joyful, anxious, calm, hectic, fast, slow. This version was one of the best, the happiest, which was why she hadn't wanted to leave. But she couldn't stay forever. And that one son lingered in her mind, a fifty-six-year-old disaster. Or, as she preferred to think of him, a challenge.

She ran the meeting strictly, as she had for the past few years since Mort had died. Trivial details flowed through her days. Long ago, when the details were different, she had wondered if those details that filled every minute of every day were actually concealing something, something large and still and sacred. Many days and years and people had passed before she understood that the details themselves were the still and sacred things, that there was nothing else, that the curtain of daily life itself was holy, that behind it was only a void. Yet some days she still wondered.

As she rose to leave, one son surprised her with a personal matter.

"Mom, before you go," he said. She glanced back at the table, alarmed to see that everyone else was still seated, watching her. The thought crossed her mind that they had planned this. "The new lawyer suggested a few modifications to the will," he said slowly. "Nothing major, but he noticed that nothing's been signed."

They had been through this before, many times. But this felt different. She paused, leaning on the table, refusing to sit down. And then she spoke.

"I'm not signing."

One daughter drew in her breath, prepared to spit fire. "Dad would have signed. He would have signed years ago."

"I'm sure he would have," she answered, her tone firm, closing a door. "But I'm not him. And I'm not ready to sign yet."

"Mom, you're eighty-four years old. I'll be sixty-two next week," her oldest son said. Her oldest son, she thought, and smirked. "We all know you're well now. Honestly, I wish I felt half as good as you do," he added. "And none of us want to say this to you. But no one lives forever."

The youngest granddaughter had been fiddling with her phone under the table, but now she looked up, smiling at her uncle. "Um, haven't you noticed? Gram is the exception to that rule. She might as well sell her plot. It's not like she's going to use it."

Still standing, Rachel turned to her granddaughter and grinned. "Exactly," she announced. "I'm the head of this company, and I've made an executive decision not to die." And then she walked out of the room.

What haunted her most about the children was how many times they died. Every day of raising a child brought a rush of unwanted mourning. New parents think of each day as a cascade of beginnings:

the first time she smiled, the first time she rolled over, her first steps, her first words, her first day of school. But old parents like her saw only endings: the last time she crawled, the last time she spoke in a pure raw sound unsculpted into the words of others, the last time she stood before the world in braids and laughed when she shouldn't have, not knowing. Each child died before the person did, a small rehearsal for the future.

She raised her children, all of them. She raised them, nurtured them, watched them love or hate or succeed or fail, gave each of them her private excesses of possibilities, observed, sometimes from afar, what they did with them, watched her own ideas wither or grow. Then she finally watched her children die, and she was jealous.

She would tell that granddaughter, she decided as she left the building, passing by the protestors. Yet it was this granddaughter, of all of her articulate descendants, who announced online to the universe:

> My grandmother just told us she can't sign off on her will because she CAN'T DIE. #crazyoldlady

Oh child, she thought, you have no idea just how crazy I am.

CHAPTER

2

THE INVENTION OF REGRET

. . .

She didn't know exactly when she had first felt the sensation of regret. It was a physical sensation, a shudder that began deep in the stomach and traveled up through the throat; it was distinct from remorse, which one felt first in the throat and only later in the gut. Yet it was regret that she couldn't handle. She did anything she could to avoid it—including the initial bargain, the one that began everything. And now this one.

Meet me in twenty minutes, the text on her phone read. *You know where.*

She knew, of course. *No*, she tapped back. *Not now.*

Now, the text replied.

This was the problem, always. And all this time she had never found a way out. More words appeared on the phone's screen, unbidden: *Unless you want me to come to you.*

No thank you, she responded. *Wait for me. I'll come.* She always did.

HE HAD FOUND HER coming out of the office one cold evening when she had been working alone. Mort was dead three years already, the business was just beginning to fail, and she was thinking about leaving. But she couldn't leave just then, just when everyone and everything was poised at the edge of ruin; she couldn't do that to them. She would wait another year or two or three, she'd thought—just until the business got a bit more stable, just until she could convince Rocky, her youngest son (her youngest son, ha), to stop with the stupid digital currency, "mining" digital currency, panning for digital gold. Rocky was a terror, a whirlwind of wonder and anguish that had started the day he was born and would clearly only stop with his death. She never understood her children, not ever, not even her very first son. He had been the first one to replace the real with the virtual, the one who turned two thousand years of otherworldly power into a metaphor. What it came down to was that children were stupid. She had been stupid too, of course, once. But only once.

All this clouded her mind as she emerged from the building that cold evening and bumped into him—actually bumped into his ramrod-straight body, torso to torso, so that he caught her in his arms. Cities forced intimacy on everyone, the same way they had for centuries; the ancient solution was to avoid eye contact. Flustered, she mumbled excuses and began to push by, just as she had that first time, long ago, so long ago that it was sometimes the only thing she could remember. He liked to lie in wait for her. It was how they first met.

"Excuse me, sir, pardon an old lady," she said with a smile, talking to a stranger. She enjoyed playing the old lady card, she had noticed over the last few versions. Youth was no doubt wasted on the young, but only she knew how much of old age was wasted on those near death. The man blocking her way was young, she noted, or if not young, then at least younger than her children. It was safe to assume he was stupid.

The man rudely stepped right into her path, just as she turned around after locking the door. People were rude, she had learned that, and she'd be a fool to be any more polite than anyone else. The man was only slightly taller than she was, she saw in that half-second glance—very short for a man these days, though she remembered when men were like that. Even a tall man like her father would have been dwarfed by the giants people had recently become. The man blocking her path had olive skin like hers, a dark beard, a long dark coat over his narrow body, and an old-fashioned hat on his head. A nobody. She tried to duck out of his way.

The man stepped toward her instead of away from her. "Madam, I pardon everyone, old and young," he announced, with an accent she couldn't place. "I am the master of forgiveness."

This city really was full of crazy people. Her grandchildren knew it better than she did. She glanced at the man's face again, still trying to push past. Then she saw his eyes, green eyes in his tan-skinned face—Phoenician eyes, her mother had called them. *That wild boy; do you know where he comes from? His mother worked on the docks before she came here. You think he knows who his father is? Ha! Don't you dare believe a word he says!* He looked at her and the wind rushed from her lungs.

"Elazar," she whispered.

"Rachel." He said her name not as her children and grandchildren did, but with its guttural intact, the name her father had given her. He said her name again and again, an incantation. "Rachel, Rachel—"

He was reaching for her, but she held her body rigid, unwilling to lean toward him. She stepped back toward the door and tried to keep her eyes on the ground. But she couldn't help looking.

"How did you find me?" she finally asked.

He laughed. "Are you really asking me that? It's always a matter of time."

Cold air blew across her face. It had taken longer than usual this time, and that had made it harder, the waiting. During the waiting—years and years of waiting—she had found herself wanting him to come. To get it over with, she told herself, to leave less to endure until the next time, the next stretch of freedom. But now that he was before her, she knew she hadn't wanted to get it over with. She had wanted him here.

"No one's hard to find anymore," he said. "Not even you. 'Zakkai Gemstones.' You hung the name right on the wall." He laughed again. Her legs shook. "I remember how much you cared about names. We last said goodbye at Azaria's bookshop. You named that one too."

She pressed her hands against the brick wall behind her, and glanced past his shoulder, feeling her eyes filling with tears. Dusk had fallen, and cars blinked their headlights on as an old man hailed a cab around the corner. The world was so large, she thought. How could it contain only the two of them, as if there were no one else? She thought back again to that very first regret, turned the thought in her mind like a thumbscrew, twisting her soul. "Look at you, the big American," he was saying. He had shifted to the language they both remembered. "You did the right thing, Rachel. Married the right man this time, it seems. He must have been kind, to let you name the business yourself. You deserved someone kind."

She breathed in, her lips tight. He deserved nothing, she reminded herself, as she always reminded herself. Worse, there was no future in this. She already knew it. Don't touch him, she told herself. How could she make the same mistake again and again and again? But he looked at her now with his eyebrows raised, humbled. He had come home.

"Where were you?" she asked.

He smiled. "I'm happy to tell you everything, Rachel. But not here. Come with me. There's a place where we can talk."

"My granddaughter is expecting me in an hour," she mumbled.

He laughed out loud. He liked to laugh; she had noticed that about him from the beginning. "Come now, or don't come now. If you don't come now, I'll wait for you until you do. *Mai nafka mina?*" he asked. It was a legal term, the sort of thing her very first son would say: *What practical difference does it make?* Inside the question was an urge to make things matter, not in the abstract but in this world, now. The question still scared her. "Waiting for you is one of my greatest pleasures, Rachel. It always has been," Elazar said softly. "You're the only thing worth waiting for. And I have all the time in the world."

He put out his hand to her. To her eternal regret, she took it.

SHE WAS GRATEFUL WHEN he didn't lead her to his apartment (did he have one? did it matter?) but to the Metropolitan Museum. She went inside with him, immune now to grandiose fake classical columns and other stupidities that had galled her long ago. She was relieved when he walked her to the Egyptian galleries, sitting down with her on a bench in a quiet room surrounded by glass cases of papyri and broken idols.

"You would laugh at me, but I've begun to really like museums," he said, dropping English words between the others. Languages came quickly to him; he put them on and took them off like clothes. The gallery was empty, dim and carpeted, warmed by the intimacy of his voice. "Not all of them. Actually not most of them. I just like these museums of ancient times. Real ancient times. It's nice to be in a place you don't remember. This must be how other people feel all the time, every time they walk into an old building or see a little piece of something from before they were born. No memories, no grief. Can you imagine? It's like a pleasant dream."

"I've often thought that," she said, her voice softer than she expected. She looked around the room and thought of taking her children, the recent children, to these same galleries years ago. She remembered that unexpected sense of comfort in standing among these ruins, an inexpressible relief that she couldn't explain even to herself. Naturally Elazar understood it immediately. He always noticed patterns, and their absence. He used to open up her father's scrolls in front of her, noting oddities. *Why did he write here that there were seven of every clean animal in the ark, but in the previous column he wrote that there were only two? A simple mistake like that, can't he change it? Tell him we want a corrected copy.* She would read over his shoulder, follow, argue. *You want it to be perfect, but that's not the point*, she would insist, but still she brought the scrolls and questions back to her father. *It's not my job to change it*, her father would mutter—though she knew he did change things sometimes, when he felt he had to. *And not his either. Go tell him to learn from his own father. He's inheriting a far more important job than mine.* Her father was right about that, of course: deeply, profoundly right. Until he wasn't. And then, sometimes, she would change the scrolls herself.

"I should have come here long ago," Elazar said. She glanced at the gallery, at the unfurled Book of the Dead and the treasures destined for the underworld, and knew he meant something larger. He was facing her now, hopeful. "I should have followed you to New York," he continued. "When you left with—what was your husband's name?"

She pretended she had to think to remember, but she didn't. She remembered all of them. She knew he did too. "Hirshl," she conceded. "But here they called him Harold."

"Yes, Hirshl. Not too bright, was he? All the teachers hated him. I remember you tutored him yourself. That was impressive, Rachel. But you're always impressive."

She suppressed a smile. "You're the only one who ever noticed," she said.

Elazar laughed. "I'm not the only one. But him? Of all the people to marry! He was so ashamed to be with you, a woman smarter than he was." He switched languages again, imitating the man he remembered. " 'In America they appreciate *real* talent. You'll see what happens when a man puts down his books and uses his brains.' Really, Rachel! I hope at least it went well for him."

She grimaced. "He died two years after we arrived." Killed himself, she remembered, when they ran out of money and the landlord was going to throw them out on the street. He had killed her too, or so he thought, leaving the gas on in their apartment while she was sleeping, pregnant. She had lost that pregnancy in a flood of tears. It never got easier. But here again was Elazar. Elazar! Everything changed, but what left her awestruck was how nothing changed.

"When you left with him, I should have followed you," he said, his voice lower. "You made the right choice, as usual. I was a fool."

"You are the opposite of a fool," she said. She let herself look at his face. He had hidden himself well under his beard. The skin around his eyes was unwrinkled, yet his eyes seemed sunken, sagging. Then she understood that he was no longer sleeping. "Don't tell me you stayed in Poland."

He looked at her. "I stayed in Poland." Then he shrugged, and smiled. "They burned everyone, so it was easy to start over. Over and over again. You wouldn't believe how many times."

She stared at him. "You're disgusting."

He sat straighter, glaring at her as he defended himself. "I had a wife there, you know. Actually three."

"At the same time?"

"Don't talk that way. It was real for them."

"But not for you. It's never real for you."

His jaw slackened. "How could it be, when I know you are wandering the world—and when I know someday you'll come back? Rachel, please, have mercy on me."

She drew back, facing him. "Why should I?" she replied. "Have you ever had mercy on me?"

"Yes, Rachel, I have. I could have come much sooner, but I found out you were married. Not to Hirshl, but to the next one—or the one after that—well, it doesn't matter."

She bit her lip, feeling his eyes on her. "It matters to me."

"I know it does. I had mercy on you. I waited for him to die. And now here I am."

They sat for a moment in silence. She looked at his hands, at the black hair and dark veins on the backs of his hands, then up at his chest, then at last at his face, at his strange green eyes. Was her mother right about him? How could she believe anything he said? How could she still not know?

"Afterward I went to Palestine, as they called it then," he continued. He picked up where he had left off, as he always did. As they both did. It amazed her how much his voice alone affected her, the boyish quiver in his stories, the old dead words alive in his mouth. "All those terrified people, trying so hard to start new lives. It's easy to forget how hard that is."

"Maybe you forget," she said. "I don't."

He smiled. "Of course I don't either. I wish I could." For all his flaws, he had never lied to her. At least not recently. She listened. "I spent the past forty years in Jerusalem. In the Old City, as they call it now. Lord of the World, what it's like just to be there. It never occurred to me that I wouldn't find you there. I was sure you would come. Every year, every day I was looking for you."

"I've been a few times," she said softly.

"'A few times'? Are you serious? How? Looking out the window of a tour bus?"

She remembered, her throat constricting. When she had taken her family for the first time in 1968, she hadn't known how she would feel. She had seen the Western Wall and had crumpled into hysterical, gagging, wrenching sobs. To be so close, and to still be trapped! Her husband and children were embarrassed. They made up stories for the tour guide about how she had been religious as a child, while the tour guide cracked English jokes about the Wailing Wall. Later her family asked her what was wrong. She did not tell them.

"How could you not live there? Why didn't you come? Was it

because of me? Surely that wouldn't have stopped you. Wasn't it at least worth trying?"

She looked down. "I was here for fifty years already then. It was impossible with the children—"

"The children, the children, the children. The children are always your excuse for not living."

"The children are my only reason for living."

"Since you were—how old were you, sixteen?"

"No one was counting then."

"Three years at the monthly women's bath already. That's how old. I remember you told me that, that night in the tunnel. Most girls didn't go to the baths until they were married, but your father held some minority opinion."

She felt her skin growing hot.

"You're so beautiful, Rachel. I couldn't wait to marry you. How could anyone wait to marry you?"

"Fuck you," she said in English.

He laughed again, but she saw him shrink. She could wound him, and he knew it. "After all this time, you're still angry," he said softly. "You'll never stop being angry. Anger eats people alive, you know."

"If only," she said.

"You know that if someone asks for forgiveness three times, and the offended person still refuses to forgive, the Holy One forgives instead. I've asked you hundreds of times, Rachel. But at least I know I'm forgiven." Often when he spoke, she heard his father's voice in his, echoing off a wide stone courtyard as he recited his incantations, roaring them aloud to the crowds of thousands: *Forgiven!* Within every person were so many other people; was there even room for a person's own soul? "I'm forgiven, with you or without you."

"I'm sure that fact has helped you sleep at night," she said. She avoided his eyes, staring at a miniature golden calf on a shelf across the room. She felt the rage rising within her. It was an old and familiar rage, fire flaming through her body. For the first time since Mort died, she felt absolutely alive.

"I want to help you, Rachel," he told her, and reached for her hand again. Again she let him take it. "You need me now."

"You'd like to think that," she said. His hand covered hers, wrapping her fingers in light.

"It's actually true. You need me. You just don't know it yet." His eyebrows rose. "Tell me this, Rachel. How old do they think you are now?"

Rachel hunched her shoulders in. "Eighty?" she tried. "Something like that."

"You're not going to be able to keep this up much longer."

Rachel sighed, and said, "When I have to go, I'll go." She tried to sound casual, but her voice was too loud. This time, for the first time, she did not want to go.

Elazar laughed. "You're saying that because you think it will be like all the other times. Burn, then run to the next town or the next province or the next country, and no one will know. But that won't work anymore. You only don't know because you haven't tried it yet. When was the last time you left?"

She tried to think of it. She remembered all the people, but dates meant nothing to her. "Maybe seventy years ago?" she muttered.

"Exactly," Elazar grinned. "Seventy years ago—before you needed any identification for anything, when you could be paid for any job with money you could touch, when no one ever asked you to prove who you were. But this is the fifty-eighth century, Rachel." He still counted time like they always had, according to scrolls.

"Or the twenty-first."

"Fine. The point is, it's not a *gezerah shavah*." *A valid analogy*. It was what her first son used to say as he dug through the holy books, looking for ways to turn reality into a metaphor, to prove that he was right. "If you leave now," Elazar continued, "it isn't going to be like before. You're going to need things that aren't easy to get. And I know you won't do the things you'll need to do in order to get them. I know you, Rachel. You won't. Only a person like your son Rocky would."

Rachel sucked in her breath. "How do you know Rocky?"

Elazar smiled. "Oh yes, Rocky," he repeated, with a perfect American "R." Elazar was a chameleon, blending in, clutching at branches. "I can't imagine why you named him that."

"His real name is Rachmiel," she admitted, the guttural "ch" natural in her throat. *Divine mercy.*

He snorted, one grunt short of a laugh. "You try everything. Even giving your children prayers for names."

She wouldn't tolerate this. "What are you doing with Rocky?"

"Mining currency," Elazar said happily. "People used to do it with pans in a river, but this is so much easier. All you need are machines, money, brains and time. And when necessary, a total willingness to disregard the rules, whatever those rules are—a willingness I have myself, as you know. Rocky is a fine young man. Or a fine old man, I suppose."

Years of scenes flooded her mind—meetings with Rocky's teachers, angry door-knocking from Rocky's classmates' mothers, painful phone calls from Rocky's children, sobbing visits from Rocky's ex-wives. *He has so much potential. Did he tell you what he did? Make him tell you! I know he didn't mean it. At least he's bright, so he has that going for him. He's a good guy, really he is. He means well. He just. He only. If only if only if only.* She clenched her teeth. "Stay away from him."

"He's never even seen me. We've only met in the imaginary world." He used the term her father used, *olam hadimyon*. When her father said it, he meant this world, the physical world, as opposed to the true world: the world of the dead. Was her entire life imaginary?

Elazar touched his beard, then looked back at her. His face alone comforted her. He was here, which meant she was real.

"All I mean to say is that leaving is going to require some unpleasant work this time, and a lot more lying than before," he said. "And working with people like your fine son. Or if not him, someone like him. I happen to know that you would never do that, not on your own. That's why you need my help." He paused, his presence heavy with expectation. "And Rocky needs my help as well."

Rachel shook her head, and pulled her hand away. "I won't be in your debt."

"It's I who owe you," Elazar replied, his voice low. "You trusted me first. Remember?"

He had come to it at last: the beginning and end of everything, the shameful fact upon which the world hung, suspended over a meaningless void. "No, Elazar," she said. "You owe me because you sold my husband."

He leaned back, stunned. It had been a long time since she had accused him like this, so directly, to his face. She had watched her daughters in recent years and had grown bold. His lips were quivering. She had almost never seen him flustered before. She rallied inside, enjoying the triumph.

"I never sold anyone," he stammered. "You don't know—"

The fire raged within her. "Tell me they didn't pay you," she spat. "Because if they didn't pay you, you're even more repulsive than I ever imagined."

He tried to smile, and failed. "Everyone does things they regret, Rachel. Even you." He knew how to make her feel dirty. "And if I had known what would happen—"

"You knew exactly what would happen."

"I had other people to think about then. I had you to think about then. I had Yochanan to think about then."

"I never want to hear that name," she said. "If you ever want to see me again—"

He laughed out loud. "Don't worry, Rachel. I'll always see you again. I'm the one thing you can always believe in."

The gallery was empty. He leaned toward her, and she tried to turn away. But when he kissed her, the absolute loneliness, the bottomless homesick loneliness of years upon years of lies, the deep cold void of a loneliness no mortal can imagine, finally drained from her soul. She was alive, inhaling beauty. She kissed him back with pure relief as he embraced her breathing, beating body—her body that was still eighteen years old, and always would be.

CHAPTER

3

CONSULTATIONS

. . .

It wasn't exactly true that she had never told anyone. She had tried. Oh, how she had tried. In every age some new solace was on offer. In every home she'd ever lived in, she always had a little hiding place—a bathroom drawer, a wooden box, a leather pouch, a sheepskin sack. Inside it she kept the things people had given her, or that she had stolen from people who claimed to have special knowledge: carved bones, vials of poison, molten gold, spells and curses written out in various languages, parchments and papers blessed by holy men. The problem was that the cures were all predicated on belief in the cures. And she and Elazar were beyond believing.

Her most recent attempt was the most pathetic. Her granddaughter Hannah—the name was all wrong, of course, pronounced nothing like her mother's name, although her son had supposedly named the girl for her "great-grandmother"—had first told her about the psychiatrist. Hannah was Rocky's daughter, which was punishment enough for a lifetime. In her twenties, she had been a little quivering thing, a brilliant woman so silent that her silence frightened Rachel, because Rachel heard in that silence the girl she herself once was, the girl who didn't know how to say yes or no, the girl for whom regret was waiting. Rachel was right. Hannah fell headlong into a marriage to the worst kind of man: handsome, manipulative, desperate—like her father, but without the brains. Rachel couldn't bear to watch. It was as if she were forced to observe herself again, seeing herself from the outside making all the same mistakes and powerless to change them. But within a year Hannah extricated herself, and did so as a completely different woman from the one she had been: a proud, brave woman, resilient, outspoken, independent. Rachel watched all this and felt as if she stood at the parting of the sea, stunned by the impossible. One day, years later, when Hannah had already married again and was pregnant with her second child, Rachel dared to ask her how she had done it. She barely expected an answer. But Hannah answered immediately: "Dr. Moskowitz."

"Dr. Moskowitz?"

"My psychiatrist. She's amazing."

Rachel had heard such blather from husbands and children before, with only the slightest changes in details: *My doctor. He told me to buy a juicer, and it changed my life. The lady at the settlement house. Just meet her, and you'll become a different person—she'll teach you English in three weeks! My rebbe. When he teaches, I feel as though I were seared by holy fire. The rav, the greatest of our generation. The divine law comes alive through him, you can feel it. The priest. The first time you bring a sacrifice, you'll understand—your soul makes contact with the Most High, and you'll never be the same. Trust me.* People she otherwise respected said such things regularly. Was she really such an exception to human rules?

"What did she do?" Rachel asked. "Give you pills?"

"She could have, but she said I didn't need them."

"So you just . . . talked to her?"

"She does a combination of cognitive behavioral therapy and old-fashioned analysis."

Old-fashioned might work for me, Rachel thought. "What's cognitive—what's that?"

"It's about recognizing and redirecting negative thoughts. Breaking old negative behavior patterns, patterns that are very destructive."

Breaking old negative behavior patterns could work for me too, Rachel thought. "But how does she do that?"

Hannah laughed. "She's like your brain's cleaning lady. You dump all the garbage in your head, and she takes it out to the curb. I swear, in six months I became a new person."

Rachel needed to become a new person, and not in her usual way. And when she found out that Dr. Moskowitz didn't mind being paid in cash, she gave herself a new name and made an appointment.

Dr. Moskowitz was a small thin woman in her forties, with short black hair and a long narrow face that reminded Rachel of one of her daughters—her fifty-second daughter, the one she had left behind in Poland, abandoning her at about Dr. Moskowitz's age. That daughter had died over a century ago. But might Dr. Moskowitz be one of her great-great-grandchildren? It sometimes seemed to Rachel that her descendants surrounded her, that by now she had populated the world. Except that so many of them had died. Again and again and again.

"It's a pleasure to meet you, Rachel," Dr. Moskowitz said, and shook her hand firmly before they both sat down. Rachel said a silent thank-you to her long-dead parents for giving her a name that survived so many years. She couldn't remember what surname she had given herself this time, but hopefully it wouldn't matter. "What brings you here today?"

Rachel paused, arranging herself in the seat as she remembered the line she had rehearsed in the waiting room. "I think I'm depressed," she said carefully. In every setting, one had to speak the right language. "I'm repeating old negative behavior patterns, and I feel it's very destructive."

Dr. Moskowitz's eyes locked on Rachel's. Rachel looked at this small woman who so resembled that fifty-second daughter and saw her face open, an expression of actual compassion. Rachel knew she shouldn't buy it. This woman was being paid to be kind. But that fifty-second daughter had been so loving, so overflowing with debilitating empathy, that Rachel couldn't help imagining being in her presence. *Mama, I found this blind kitten behind the bathhouse and I just had to take him home. I'll take care of him myself, don't worry. Mama, Rivka's mother died last night. She's supposed to go to her uncle and aunt in Lublin, but she's never even met them. Can she come live with us, just for a while? Yes, Mama, Ronya and her kids are staying with me, for as long as they need to. Her husband broke her arm! How could I say no?* She had died in her forties, that daughter. But what could one expect of a saint?

"I want to hear more," Dr. Moskowitz said, "but I have to ask you a clinical question before we go further. Do you ever have thoughts of killing yourself?"

Rachel nodded. "All the time, but it won't work."

Dr. Moskowitz pursed her lips. "What do you mean, it won't work?"

"I mean there's no point in trying. It's just a fantasy."

Dr. Moskowitz made a note on the clipboarded paper propped in front of her. She seemed relieved. "It's very common to have suicidal ideation without ever acting on those thoughts," Dr. Moskowitz said. "You're very brave to share that with me."

Either brave or stupid, Rachel thought. Of course, everything brave was also stupid. Sadly the same could not be said of the reverse.

"So tell me about this—this negative behavior pattern," Dr. Moskowitz said.

Rachel drew in a breath. "Well, I was widowed a few years ago," she began.

Dr. Moskowitz held her pen still. "I'm so sorry," she said. "Grief can be devastating."

"Oh, it's nothing," Rachel muttered. The doctor looked alarmed. "I mean, that's not my"—what was the term on the form in the waiting room?—"my chief complaint."

Dr. Moskowitz tipped her head, as if listening to the wind. If only all these people knew how familiar they look, how unoriginal they are, Rachel thought—and if only they knew how miraculous that was, how they lived and lived again, how no one ever really died, how no one was ever alone. But Dr. Moskowitz was still waiting, listening.

"After my husband died, a man came to see me—a man I knew from before I met my husband. An—an old flame, as they used to say." She winced, trying to remember what she had chosen as her birthdate on the intake form. She had made herself about sixty, she recalled. It was irritating, constantly adjusting herself—her clothes, her hair, her words, her ideas, everything that was supposedly a personal choice. No one had any idea of how thick a layer of arbitrary conventions enshrouded a naked soul.

The pause as Rachel thought this through was apparently some sort of clinical indicator. "People often feel they need permission to move beyond their grief," Dr. Moskowitz prompted. "I don't know you yet, so I shouldn't say this, but I see you're struggling, so I want to start off by saying that it's very normal."

Rachel shook her head. There would be a lot of garbage to unload before this woman could scrub down her brain. "My problem isn't that," she said. "He and I—"

"I'm sorry to interrupt," Dr. Moskowitz said, "but can you give me this man's name? It will make it easier to talk about it, going forward."

Rachel considered coming up with a fake name, but the name burned through her throat, searing her lips. "Elazar," she said, and shivered. It was the first time she had said his name out loud to anyone but him in over a hundred years.

"I've never heard that name before," Dr. Moskowitz mused. "Is it Spanish?"

"Yes," Rachel lied. She was still shuddering.

Dr. Moskowitz noticed. "I can see he means a lot to you."

"He and I have a—a history."

"Tell me."

"Isn't this is a fifty-minute appointment?"

Dr. Moskowitz laughed. "Just give me the highlights then. When did you first meet?"

Rachel bit her lip, as she did every time she heard a question beginning with the word *when*. "Oh, a long time ago," she muttered. "I don't know, exactly."

"Well, how old were you, about?"

About was right, Rachel thought. Who was counting? Elazar was. *Three years at the women's baths*, she heard Elazar say. *That's how old.* "About sixteen," she answered.

"Oh my. That is a long time," Dr. Moskowitz said. "So you were high school sweethearts?"

Rachel laughed. "Something like that," she said.

Dr. Moskowitz nodded, taking notes. "And I'm guessing you were in love with him at the time?"

Rachel dropped her eyes to her lap, to the skirt made of some bizarre material someone had concocted in a laboratory, and suddenly remembered the day her mother heard and believed a rumor, how her mother, before beating her with a leather strap, had forced her to sit on the floor, where Rachel had stared down at her own dirty skirt—pure linen then, never mixed with wool, and woven with her own hands—while her mother spat venom, shouted until her little nephews and the two house slaves gathered to listen: *Are you going to tell me that you love him? What does that even mean? Do you love him the way you love God? Who commanded you to love him? You can't be his wife, so you want to be his concubine? How can you love someone without a contract? Are you crazy? Don't you understand what he can do to you?* To think how irrelevant that fury was, how commonplace love had become, a box you checked on a form. Now no one but a psychiatrist would even have a reason to care. Rachel said nothing.

"I understand this is difficult," Dr. Moskowitz said when Rachel remained silent for too long. "We're often shaped by our early experiences, more than we might want to admit. And there's no need to go into detail now. But keeping in mind that those early relationships can be very, very intense, full of wild emotions and complicated sexual dynamics and probably also full of mistakes and regrets, would you say that this was a normal teenage romance?"

Rachel felt herself peering down at her lap again, a habit of centuries. But then she looked back at Dr. Moskowitz and spoke. "If a normal teenage romance involves me giving birth to his child, and then him having my husband murdered, then yes, this was a normal teenage romance."

Dr. Moskowitz stared, slack-jawed. Her pen fell to the floor. "Wait. What?"

Rachel waved a hand. "He didn't murder my husband who just died. I was married before."

"Wait, stop. This man—Elazar—he *murdered* someone?"

"He didn't do it himself, he just turned him in to the authorities. He said he didn't know it would happen that way. But it was obvious. It was obvious!"

"Wait." Dr. Moskowitz folded and floundered like a fish caught on a line, keeping her eyes on Rachel as she bent over and desperately felt the carpet for her pen. "This was—where did this happen?"

Obfuscation came easily to Rachel. "Overseas."

Dr. Moskowitz glanced at the paper in her lap. "In Latin America? I'm guessing—during a junta or something like that?"

What's a hunta? Rachel wondered as she nodded.

Dr. Moskowitz had gathered herself now. Rachel could see her settling back in her chair, resuming her professional pose. "I understand this is painful. You said you have—" Dr. Moskowitz tried to say.

But Rachel had more mental garbage to unload. Hannah was right: there was something beautiful about dumping it all. "He denied he did anything wrong," she continued. "He still denies it, even now, even when everyone is dead. I should have listened to my mother. My mother knew who he really was—she told me he was a bastard, and that bastards always have something to prove."

"Wait, wait. You said you and he have a child?"

Rachel swallowed. "A son."

"And your son is—does he—"

"He died a long time ago."

Dr. Moskowitz didn't even mumble a consolation this time. She tipped her head back, like a little girl looking for a lost balloon in the sky.

"See, there's no one else left in the world who knew me then," Rachel said. "Not even a child. Everyone from then is gone except for him. He's the only thing I have. And he ruined my life." Rachel heard her own words and felt like she had turned into one of her grandchildren, those insanely selfish creatures who actually believed they had lives independent of anyone else's. *He ruined my life*. The idea was ridiculous, indulgent, insulting. Her mother would have laughed, a long cruel laugh. She felt like laughing at herself. But she needed to tell someone. "I know people often complain about other people ruining their lives," she continued. "But no one in the world has done what he did to me. He didn't just ruin my life. If he had just ruined my life, at least my life would have eventually ended."

"Everything eventually ends, Rachel," Dr. Moskowitz said in a quiet voice. Rachel thought again of that long-ago daughter, the one touched by an inhuman kindness. "It may seem like a curse, but it's also a great mercy."

Rachel nodded. "Exactly," she said, and clutched the armrest of the chair. "That's the mercy I need. I need this to end. But the only way it can end is if I die."

"It can feel that way, in the moment," Dr. Moskowitz said. "And it can be very, very hard to see beyond that moment. But there really is something beyond that moment, and you can get there."

Rachel could almost feel that lost daughter touching her, gentle fingers clutching her arm. But she needed to be free, and the last thing she needed were those stupid gentle fingers holding her back. "No, Dr. Moskowitz, I need you to listen to me. My problem is that I can't die."

Dr. Moskowitz leaned back, her pen poised above the paper. "Tell me what you mean by that."

Rachel took a breath. "I mean that I can't die. At first I didn't know. I just thought I was lucky." She paused, thinking of how to continue.

"Everyone feels invincible when they're young," Dr. Moskowitz offered. "It's often only when someone our own age dies that mortality feels real."

But Rachel was no longer listening. "I just thought I was lucky," she said again. "It wasn't obvious, at least not right away. I still got hungry and thirsty every day like everyone else; I still had the same body, the same feelings. Years passed, and I even looked older, my face sagged, my skin loosened, my hair got lighter and thinner—maybe just from being exposed to the sun, or maybe it was more from suffering than from age, I don't know. It was enough that no one who knew me noticed anything strange, and at first I didn't either. But nothing else changed at all. Illnesses didn't matter, injuries didn't matter. Then there was a plague, whole neighborhoods were wiped out, but nothing happened to me, or to him. And then years after that, the city was besieged and everyone starved, but for us it was irrelevant. When the city finally burned I saw that it wasn't my imagination. I stepped through the fires and walked out the city gates."

Dr. Moskowitz tried to speak, but Rachel would not let her. "Later I understood that it was the opposite of luck," she said quickly, "and that was when I started trying. I've tried over and over again, everything you could imagine. The only thing that works is if I'm burned alive, but even then I just wake up somewhere a few miles away, with a fresher face. That's my only way out. Then I can flee, I can change countries, I can at least pretend to start a new life, but only until he appears again." Dr. Moskowitz, Rachel saw, was furiously taking notes. She felt buoyed by Dr. Moskowitz's moving pen. "That's the negative behavior pattern I meant," Rachel added. "I always go back to him. Every time. He offers me money or help and I take it; he offers me comfort and I take it. I can't stop myself. No one else in the world knows what I've suffered, no one else in the world understands. He's the most awful person in the world, and I'm as much in love with him now as I was when I was a girl."

Rachel was surprised to find herself fighting back tears. "Dr. Moskowitz, please, please help me," she begged. "I need you to make me stop loving him, and I need you to make me die."

Dr. Moskowitz looked up from her papers, her face still the same open maw of pity. But this time her voice was careful, contained, pressed wine dripping from the stomping trough down to the vessel below it.

"Rachel, you've been through a lot, and you're obviously a very brave woman," she said. "But grief can be very damaging, and in some cases it can even be deranging. Especially when people blame themselves." The doctor rearranged her papers on her lap, pulling out a small bluish pad and scribbling numbers and illegible words. "I'm putting you on lithium," she said. "It's a low dose to start, just to see how you respond to it, but I think we'll raise it within the next few weeks." She tore off the page and handed it to Rachel, an offering. "I think it will bring you some relief. Once you've got that relief, we can work together on these—these challenges you're facing. You're at a stage in life that's very difficult, when it's very hard to change. Here's your receipt too, for insurance. I'd like to see you again next week."

Rachel took the papers mindlessly. On the second page, Dr. Moskowitz had checked a box next to *Bipolar Affective Disorder*, and another next to *Psychotic Disorder, NOS*. Rachel laughed out loud. "I feel better already," she said.

Dr. Moskowitz looked confused as Rachel left. When Rachel got home, she slipped the papers into the back of her bathroom drawer, where they belonged, the same sort of spot where she once had kept bones and vials and parchments from holy men.

The following week, when she dropped off Hannah's sons at her house, she mentioned it. "I saw Dr. Moskowitz a few days ago," she said with a smile.

"Really? Are you okay, Gram?"

"I am," she said. "I'm just old. And that means it's very hard to change."

And then she went to see Elazar.

CHAPTER

4

MORTALITY

. . .

What reasons are there for being alive?

The more Rachel considered it over the centuries, the fewer she could think of—and those she did think of were contradictory at best:

To love the Lord your God with all your heart, with all your soul, and with all your might. She did, once. She remembered being a little girl, when the world was full of the weight of God's presence, bowing down and pressing her forehead against a stone floor, imagining her future children promised to the service of the Lord. She remembered opening her eyes after an illness as a child and feeling each limb of her body pulsing with life, her mother's words in her ear: "God has healed you." She recalled seeing her oldest sister, the one who had died young, slipping into her room one night years after her death, promising Rachel that God would bless her; Rachel had risen from her mat on the floor and followed her out of the room only to lose sight of her, but then awoke with a feeling of invincibility, a certainty of a shining future. She remembered the first rains after a drought, dancing on dry ground with her mouth opened toward the skies as fresh cool raindrops pitted the dust, hearing the raucous songs of everyone around her thanking God for their rescue. She had once given all her heart and soul and might to that love, knowing there was nothing else. She still knew, when she walked through the woods and climbed up to sit on rocks older than she, that there was nothing else. And she knew it, too, because of Elazar. But in the years since those times, that love had too often seemed sadomasochistic: seductive, cruel, and irresistible. In other words, like Elazar.

To serve others. This was a somewhat more compelling reason for living, and in any case it was the default for anyone with as many children as she. She had spent endless years, genuinely endless years, doing nothing else, swallowing bile every time she heard a supposedly older woman say, "Enjoy them; it goes by so fast!" At one point she tried to estimate how many thousands of times she had nursed an infant, how many meals she had cooked for others, how many spoons of medicine she had raised to other people's lips, how many withered hands she had held at bedsides, how many bodies she had buried in the earth. The sacrifice was bottomless, heavy labor cast into a void. Often she felt like a bridge that stretched between two worlds, bearing the weight of those who passed from one to the other. But what was the point of being that bridge when she was never able to cross over herself?

To experience joy. A nice idea, that pursuit of happiness. When people first started considering it, just a few recent centuries ago, it had the advantage of novelty. Why not experience joy? That first morning of flowers blooming in a garden, that first touch of someone's lips on yours, or that first moment of holding your child, when your body became the gateway to the world, and from it, pure light. The problem was that those moments unraveled before you, the petals dropped to the ground, the children and lovers grew older and older until they inevitably drifted away, and then you wondered why you had bothered, if all was destined for the void. The lovers repeated, and she loved them all the same, deeply and honestly, with variations so minor that only those living for less than a century could see them as important. This one was all tenderness; that one preferred to pounce. This one hung around like a stray starving puppy; that one kept leaving the room or the house, needing to be alone. This one was faithful; that one a craven cheat. After hundreds of years, these details that most people spent their lives exploring were only details. Every man was finally just a man, then bones, then dust. And the children repeated, which haunted her most of all. You could have sworn you had had this same wild son or this same hotheaded daughter before, maybe more than once, wearing different clothes. But you could never tell them.

To build for the future. She remembered finding this compelling, once. She recalled one of her father's heroes, a crazy sage named Honi the Circle-maker, who once drew a circle on the earth, stood inside it, and told God that he would not leave his circle unless it rained—and it did. That legend was silly enough, but what disturbed her was the story of how Honi once saw a man planting a carob tree, a tree that wouldn't bear fruit for seventy years. When Honi asked the man why he was bothering, the man said, "I myself found fully grown carob trees in the world, and as my parents once planted for me, so I will plant for my children." A fine idea, Rachel had thought long ago. As one of her bumbling recent grandchildren put it, *I just want to feel like I'm leaving the world a better place than how I found it.* A fine idea, if one is planning on leaving. In fact, that was Honi's problem. In the next part of the story, which she remembered her father copying down long ago, Honi fell into a deep sleep and woke up seventy years later, to find a man harvesting the carob tree's fruit. Honi asked the man, "Did you plant this tree?" The man answered that his grandfather had. But then the story took a turn for the worse. Honi went back to his own house and discovered that his children had died, and only his grandchildren were there, none of whom would believe he was Honi. His students at the academy where he had taught were likewise dead. The new students enjoyed quoting his ideas, but they too were annoyed by this crazy person claiming to be Honi. Eventually Honi asked God to kill him, because he realized he had become superfluous. Which in fact was the entire purpose of life, to live in such a way that one made oneself superfluous. And therein lay the root of the problem. There was no point in any of it, none at all, unless one had plans to leave.

Very occasionally, every century or two, she saw glimmers of answers.

She remembered once, in Alexandria—or Aleppo?—she had a daughter who had refused to learn to read. "No other girls read, Mama," the curly-headed child had whined. The girl was intelligent, Rachel had noticed. Even as an infant she had spoken quickly, singing songs, understanding every word. But now she was seven, and petulant. She had seen her friends' older sisters painting their eyelids. "When I'm grown up, I'll have a husband who can read letters and things. What's wrong with that? Why can't I be like the other girls?"

"Because the other girls are slaves," Rachel told her. As they worked in the flour mill, Rachel kept drawing letters in the flour, never stopping until the girl repeated them back, her little voice rich with resentment. In the blink of an eye the girl was sixteen and married to a fat merchant who went back and forth to India. Under the wedding canopy, the girl, still a child, stuck her tongue out at Rachel before turning her kohl-eyed face toward the groom. Rachel would have laughed if she hadn't been crying.

Years later, Rachel came back to the city—young once more, with her own merchant husband, veiled and pregnant and clutching the little wrist of her three-year-old boy. As they moved through the marketplace, her husband hurried them toward a busy stall, where a gray-haired woman wearing a widow's scarf was furiously recording sales, a long line of customers before her. "She's the one we need to meet," Rachel's husband told her, his voice an urgent whisper.

"She handles every silk order for the entire province. And woe to anyone who writes her a bad contract! She'll correct it until it drips with gall, and then forget about ever meeting her again."

It took some time before Rachel and her pregnant belly made it through the crowds to the woman's table. Behind tall piles of documents and coins, she saw the face she knew she would see, etched with age and framed with gray curls, her gnarled hands scribbling sense on scored parchment, a pillar of calm confidence crowning every letter. But what made Rachel shiver was the little girl at the old woman's side. As the old woman amended detail after detail on the contract with a long gray quill, the girl tugged at her sleeve. "Grandma, this is boring," she moaned. "I want to play with Miriam and her sisters. Please let me go!"

Rachel watched as the old woman signed her name, a wild wet flourish. Then, ignoring Rachel's husband as he puffed his chest in front of her, she turned to the girl. "Dear one," she said, "you are staying right here until you learn every word I'm writing. Then you'll be free to go wherever you want, for as long as you live."

Rachel breathed in, a sudden sublime harmony vibrating within her, attuned to the music of an unknown world. But then her little boy broke free from her grip. She whirled around and he was gone, lost in the crowd. And off she went chasing him, running after another reason for living.

Sometimes Rachel lay half-asleep and imagined her own death, the way it was described in the scrolls her father copied. She imagined being asked at the gates of the next world whether she had been honest in business, whether she had married, whether she had set time aside for studying holy writings, whether she had done good works. Her hundreds of children paraded before her like sheep herded by a shepherd, and she remembered all of them. She saw the children of those children, too, but she also saw the trees they planted, the houses they built, the machines they invented, the books they wrote, the people they taught or helped or healed—and also the people they betrayed or disappointed or ignored, the marriages they wrecked, the houses they burned, the people they killed or merely destroyed. No matter how good, how evil, or how indifferent her children's lives had been, there was a stunning majesty in seeing it all, in looking back on their years and being able to judge them.

She wanted to be judged.

Then there were other reasons for living too, ones that mortals rarely thought of but that raged like fires in Rachel's mind:

To correct mistakes.

To avoid regret.

To accept regret.

To change.

But none of these seemed possible either.

RACHEL AS A GIRL was a messenger. Her father was a scribe, and her mother had a market stall selling parchment and ink. She had no brothers, only sisters—so many of them that two were already married before she was even born. By the time she was born, her mother was old, and she was the last. It was good, being the last: her parents were tired, and needed her more than she needed them. Because her father did not trust the household slaves, and because she was the last, a scrap of a girl left like a bare bone at the bottom of a stewpot, she became her father's messenger, running through the city between houses and cisterns, through markets and synagogues and pagan basilicas, between courtrooms and palaces and workshops and jails, a one-girl postal service delivering messages and scrolls her father had copied and written in Hebrew and Aramaic and Greek and Latin, depending on what his customers told him to do. And because she was the last, her father hadn't cared when she sat at his side as he copied the scrolls and chanted them aloud, so she sat and watched and listened, matching letter with sound until the words rose from the parchments up into her mind. The fact that her parents let her run through the neighborhoods on her own like a boy gave her a reputation, and she was aware of the raised eyebrows that often followed her—and by the time she was sixteen, the leers of the Roman soldiers. Her mother knew that marrying her off wouldn't be easy like it had been with her sisters, and frequently she expended her frustration and rage on Rachel herself. But her father relied on her and was in no hurry to be rid of her. As for Rachel, she enjoyed a trifold blessing that the other girls of Jerusalem could only dream of: no one cared where she went, no one asked where she had been, and no one noticed when she was gone.

Sometimes she carried scrolls to the Temple. Not to the sanctuary itself, the colossal building that towered over the city and shimmered with plates of silver and gold, the House of God that contained the innermost room at the center of the world, the Holy of Holies—the *sanctum sanctorum*, as the Romans called it when they tried to put a statue of their emperor inside it. Only the high priest could enter that room, once a year. Rachel didn't go to the inner court either, where the priests offered their sacrifices each day, or even to the women's court just beyond it, except on festivals when she lined up with her mother and sisters to bow before God. For her deliveries, Rachel never made it past the outer court, but that was close enough. Up the stone steps, she would pass through the gates and colonnades and already be there, seeing the priests in their vestments washing their bare feet in the water channels, the bound animals ready for the priest's knives on their necks, the golden bowls of water and meal and wine and grain offerings filled to overflowing, the thick haze of incense entering her body through her nose, infusing her with divine power. The priests themselves were part of the scenery, their elaborate robes and silent gestures making them seem less like people than like living Temple tools, knives and firepans with faces. Young priests would take her father's scrolls from her in the outer court and turn quickly away. They never looked her in the eye, never even touched her hands, lest her impurity infect them. Not once had any of them spoken to her. Until one day when a priest stood in the corner of the outer court, as if waiting for someone, someone other than her. She saw him out of the corner of her eye, noticing how his eyes followed her as she hurried toward the gate. She was used to this, and kept walking.

"Wait, Daughter of Azaria. I have a message for your father."

She turned. The young priest in his white vestments stood before her, holding a tightly rolled scroll. She looked down and presented her hands, waiting to feel parchment on skin. When no parchment fell, she raised her eyes and saw the priest looking right at her.

"The message comes with a question," he said. "You are to deliver the question to your father as well."

He was young, she noticed, not much older than she, with a sparse black beard and, most strange, eyes that were nearly green, as if borrowed from someone else's face. "The high priest asked about one of the scrolls delivered for the New Year's public readings," he said. He spoke in a monotone, as if reciting a text. But his eyes remained on her. "In the story about Abraham's attempt to sacrifice Isaac," he continued, "there appeared to be a line removed. There was a dark area at the bottom of the column. The story still seemed complete, so it's possible it was merely water damage or a darker patch of parchment. But the high priest wanted to know if there was an error."

Rachel looked down at her bare dirty feet, horrified. Her father's project of adjusting scrolls—it was part of his work, making sense of all the dozens of existing versions of every chapter and verse—had lately become bolder, more inventive. It was as if her father, growing older, no longer cared about his livelihood as much as he cared about his own sense of truth. This was the first time she had dared to make a change, the only time. She never dreamed she would be caught.

"My father made the error," she said softly. "But I—I—I corrected it." She was shocked to hear her own voice. Later she would imagine over and over again how things might have gone differently if she had been just the slightest bit older and smarter, if she hadn't answered him, or if she had lied—how that tiny change in that single moment might have altered everything that followed. But she hadn't yet learned how to lie.

"*You* corrected it?"

It was unnerving, this young man watching her. She glanced around, suddenly fearful. They were behind the main row of merchants and moneychangers in the outer court. No one noticed them. Her father had taught her to be cautious with everyone, especially priests. Her father was not terribly fond of priests.

"Please, please don't tell anyone," she begged, trying to keep her voice low. "My father will kill me. Please, please don't tell."

The young priest was silent for a moment. She looked down at his feet, clean hairy skin beside her dirty toes. "What was the error?" he asked. His voice was light, friendly, she noticed, like a curious child's.

She still didn't dare to raise her face to his. "My father doesn't like the ending to that story," she said. Her voice shook, but she could not stop herself. "He thinks having Abraham attempt to kill the child was a mistake, maybe a mistake made by an earlier scribe. He wanted Abraham to change his mind."

"If only," the priest said.

Now she looked up. To her astonishment, he was smiling, his face crinkled into a laugh. "So what was the error?" he asked again.

She stared at him. Was he testing her? If he was surprised that she knew how to read, he didn't show it. "It wasn't an error. He just added a few words, that's all," she said quickly. "Right after 'And Abraham stretched forth his hand and took the knife to slaughter his son,' and right before 'And then an angel of the Lord called to him.'

In between, he wrote, 'And then Abraham turned the knife toward his own throat.' "

The priest looked at her, his mouth slightly open. "That's—that's beautiful," he stammered.

Rachel lowered her eyes. "I erased it."

"What?"

"I stained it with water until it wasn't legible anymore. I was hoping no one would notice." Stupid, she now realized. How could anyone not notice?

"But why?"

She glanced around the courtyard again. Boys in white were escorting dozens of sheep and rams to the inner court, shouting as they prodded the animals with sticks, the youngest boys focused on collecting dung.

"I liked the story better the other way, when Abraham tried to go ahead with it," she said softly. "It was easier to believe."

The young priest, too, she saw, checked the courtyard, making sure no one saw how long they had been standing there. No one did. "Why is that easier to believe?" he asked. "Wouldn't most parents give up their own lives for their children?"

No one had ever asked Rachel an intellectual question before; people only spoke to her to issue demands. The priest's question was like hearing her own thoughts in someone else's voice. The thrill of it welled within her body as she watched him. But now he was waiting for her answer. She considered, debating with herself as she thought of her own parents: her worn mother who openly resented having yet another unmarried daughter at home, her father who was done caring about his household and cared only about the stories he copied, in scroll after scroll. "I think parents actually look for reasons to give up on their children," she said. "I don't blame them, either. They've done enough." She glanced around the courtyard once more, listening to the shouts of the Roman soldiers down below the retaining wall, and said, "Sometimes I wonder if God feels the same way about us." Suddenly the import of what she had done clouded her mind. "Please, please don't tell anyone," she begged him again. "My father will kill me."

The young man was silent for a moment. Finally he asked, "What is your name?"

"Daughter of Azaria," she said.

He snorted, an awkward noise that erupted from his young nose. How strange, she thought, to hear a priest snort. She wondered: Did priests also do all the other things mortals do? Did they yawn, piss, fart? She knew they did, but she still found it difficult to believe. "I know you're Daughter of Azaria," the young priest said. "Everyone knows you're Daughter of Azaria. The priests all say it like an incantation. 'Give this to Daughter of Azaria.' 'Send for Daughter of Azaria.' 'Wait for Daughter of Azaria.' You're like one of the heavenly host. But what's your name?"

For the first time in a man's presence, Rachel sensed an odd solidity rising within her, a pillar of unexpected strength. A moment passed before she recognized it: pride. She looked down again, not wanting him to see her smile. "My name is Rachel," she said softly. "Rachel, daughter of Azaria." Then she added, "Who wants to know?"

"Me. Elazar, son of Hanania."

She drew in her breath. Hanania was the high priest, the only person who could enter the Holy of Holies, the person on whom the redemption of the people depended. This snorting boy was his son? She stared at his barely-grown beard, his odd green eyes, his smile. It was impossible to believe. "Does that mean you'll be the high priest one day?"

Elazar laughed. So priests laughed too, she thought. Then they surely pissed and yawned and farted as well. "Probably not," he said. "I have three older brothers, so if someone from our family were appointed again, it's not likely to be me. And I'm also not fit for service, honestly. Not particularly pure, if you know what I mean."

Rachel didn't know what he meant, but she saw that the sleeves of his robe were stained with something brown. Mud, maybe, or dried animal blood. "It must be difficult to wear white all the time," she said.

"Very difficult," he replied, then lowered his voice. Even his lowered voice seemed to contain a laugh. "Sometimes I sneak out of the Temple. Not sometimes—often. Every three days or so, I realize that I just can't bear the smell. I need to get away."

This alarmed her. Did priests even exist outside the Temple? Who was this snorting, laughing priest who needed to get away? "What do you mean, sneak out?"

"I leave the priests' quarters, without anyone knowing I've left," he said. "If I walk through the streets around the Temple mount, people recognize me, even in different robes. So I've found another way. I take the water tunnel. I come out a bit wet on the other end, but it's worth it."

Rachel couldn't suppress a grin. A boy priest who sneaked out of the Temple—through a water tunnel? Surely he was joking. "Isn't it hard to squeeze through there?"

"I don't take the Canaanite tunnel. I take the wider one."

She dared to look at his face, trying to judge if he was serious. "The Babylonian tunnel," she said.

Elazar smiled. "The Babylonians didn't dig that tunnel."

His smile disarmed her. "Of course they did," she said. "Everyone knows that." She hesitated, glancing down again at her bare and dirty feet. In her house, among the sages, some of the sages' wives liked to share their opinions, to report what they knew, to challenge the men. Her mother did it often. This was different, Rachel knew. She had already said far too much, and to a stranger. But she saw his eyes on hers, and felt a sudden urge welling within her. Her voice flowed like water. “My father says that’s the one thing we have to thank the Babylonians for,” she continued. “They burned the first Temple and destroyed the city six hundred years ago, but at least they carved out a water tunnel through the mountain to put out the fires.”

“In the Book of Kings it says it was dug by King Hezekiah.”

Rachel tried not to smirk. “That may be what my father copied, but even he knows that’s impossible. Some scribe before him just wanted to give the Judean kings the credit. My father says that the Babylonians were as good at building as the Romans, but we only built a Temple, and then palaces of words.” Her father, she recalled, had said this with tremendous pride.

Elazar was still looking at her. He said, “Your father is wrong.”

Rachel stood taller. The boy may have been a priest, but this was an insult. “My father is never wrong.”

“Of course he is, and you know it. You changed his scroll yourself.”

Rachel felt her face growing warm. Stupid, she scolded herself. Why had she put herself at this boy priest’s mercy? “Please, please don’t tell,” she repeated.

He laughed again. “It’s always worth correcting errors. In this case, your father is absolutely wrong, and I can prove it.”

Rachel folded her arms across the breasts she still wasn’t used to. This was far too long to be talking to a man, even if he was only a boy. She tried to think of how to end the conversation kindly, without simply walking away.

He saw her hesitation, and pounced. “I can show you, if you want. You’ll see, it’s something special. Something very ancient. You’ll be surprised. Actually, your father would love to see it. He’s probably one of the only people in the city who could read it, besides the priests.”

This intrigued her. “What do you mean, read it?”

Elazar smiled, but didn’t answer her question. “Here’s what you must do. Before sunset, go to the pool by the old palace, then wait by the entrance to the water tunnel. Call my name, and I'll send a signal."

This was outrageous. "What signal?" she asked.

He ignored her. "When the signal comes, start walking up."

"Up?"

"Up into the tunnel."

Rachel laughed. "I'd drown!"

"Not at this time of year. The water level is low right now. Even in the winter, it never gets higher than your legs. I promise you, it's worth it."

"Wouldn't I need a lamp?"

"You don't need a lamp. You need me."

"Why would I need you?"

"You need me. You just don't know it yet."

Some of the moneychangers had closed down their booths and were turning toward them, laughing as they talked about a customer. The Temple, her father often scoffed, had become the country's central bank. The thought entered her mind of how many people here might know her parents. The unsavoriness of how long she and the young priest had been speaking seeped into her mind once more, staining the moment like spreading ink. "I have to go now," she told him, and turned toward the gate.

"You forgot my message," Elazar said.

If she could have ignored him, she would have. But she knew her place. She turned back, bowed her head and put her hands before her, out of habit. As he placed the scroll in her hands, he brushed a finger across her palm. "It's urgent," he said, his voice almost a laugh. And then he walked away.

As she hurried through the gates and down the Temple steps, she decided to open the scroll. She untied the bit of gut string and unfurled the page, then nearly tripped down the last of the steps. The scroll was blank.

SHE KNEW SHE SHOULDN'T GO. It was time to go home, she told herself as she finished her rounds toward sunset; her mother would be back from the marketplace and would notice that Rachel hadn't returned. But even as she told herself this, she knew it wasn't true. Half of Rachel's deliveries involved her standing around waiting for some householder or official or tradesman to arrive, sometimes for hours. No one would notice if she stopped by the tunnel on the way. She could even bring a bucket of cool water back to the house. Her mother would be grateful. And what would happen if she didn't go, and the young priest told someone what her father had done? Before she knew it, her feet had taken her to the reservoir pool where the tunnel emptied.

She waited by the pool. It was late in the day. The blind and the lame water-carriers who usually crowded the pool hoping for odd jobs and small coins had already given up and left. Getting to the tunnel's entrance was easier than she expected. She lifted her robe to just above her ankles, and waded in along the pool's submerged stone steps. The cool water sent a ripple through her body, a feeling she didn't recognize. As she approached the tunnel entrance, balancing herself along the step's narrowing edge, she felt the water's gentle current and saw her dark bare feet just below its clear surface. The rush against her ankles made her nervous. Still, she approached the tunnel entrance until she was able to wedge herself into it, her body blocking off the last of the light. It was like looking down a throat. She braced her arms against the walls of the tunnel and called, "Elazar, son of Hanania?" Her voice was larger than she was.

No one answered. Embarrassed, she glanced behind her, but no one was there, just the still mirror of the pool at twilight, stray cats sipping at its surface. She looked again into the dark throat of the tunnel, feeling like a fool. She thought of calling again, but then something small rippled through the water, flowing down along the dark sluice. She caught it just as it passed between her ankles: a lit oil lamp, floating on a tiny reed raft. Wonder coursed through her chilled legs as she raised the lamp and began walking into the tunnel, leaving the last dregs of daylight behind her.

INSIDE, IT WAS DIFFICULT to climb. The stone floor was worn smooth, and the current against her feet pushed her back, as if some ancient presence had come to redirect her back to safety. She gripped at the damp rough-hewn walls with her free hand, finding toeholds in the smooth stone beneath her feet, putting one cold foot in front of the other up the tunnel's gentle slope until she had reached the point where daylight no longer streaked in at her back. The tunnel's aperture closed behind her like an eyelid falling shut. And then she was alone inside the mountain.

Her oil lamp glowed brightly against the wet walls, her gripping hand the same color as the carved stone. The light danced on the walls as her hand trembled. But her fear ebbed as she went deeper into the tunnel, carried away with the water at her feet as she marveled at what her lamp revealed. Her father was right, she saw with her own eyes: the Babylonians were amazing builders. The water tunnel went directly into the mountain, swerving here and there, but its surfaces remained uniform, each of the thousands of chisel marks equidistant from the ones around it. She felt as though she were moving through time instead of rock. Her fingers traced the marks in the walls and she imagined the Babylonian foremen shouting their commands, measuring and marking rock as they went, whipping their slaves, cursing the Hebrew god for surrounding his holy city with solid limestone mountains. It must have taken years. She thought of the Babylonians and began humming the mournful psalm about the city's destruction. Her voice echoed through the tunnel, and the sound startled her. She swallowed the sound, embarrassed—but then, who was here to hear her? The thought set her voice free, and the music rose high in her throat and reverberated along the water.

"Rachel, daughter of Azaria!"

She stopped singing, and nearly dropped the lamp. She lifted the lamp higher, afraid to speak again. But she didn't need to. "I can already see your light," the voice called. "You're almost there."

Almost where? The tunnel bent upward, then turned sharply to the right, and the next few steps were difficult to scale. But when she did, she saw another flame dancing in the darkness ahead of her, moving much more quickly than hers. A moment later the hand holding it emerged, and then the body. Standing before her was Elazar.

He looked different, and not only because of the dimness of the light. His linen robes were hoisted nearly to his knees, and she could see the dark hair on his legs, like a Roman soldier's. His dirty white tunic was even dirtier than before, and he had pushed his sleeves past his elbows, which were scratched and scraped and surprisingly pale. But what amazed her most was his face. In his eyes was an expression she hadn't seen on a man or boy's face since she was a very small child: pure wonder.

"I didn't think you'd come," he said.

Rachel had never before been alone with a man, or even a boy. The awe on his face soothed her. She felt as though she were with an old friend, someone she had known since she was small, someone who, like her, was really still a child. He lifted his lamp high, and his face fell into darkness as he turned toward the tunnel's wall. His turn away from her seemed casual, comfortable, brushing back her unnamed fears. They were two children on an adventure. "It's here somewhere," he said.

What was he looking for? She followed the lamp as it bobbed and swooped along the tunnel's wall. After a moment she raised hers as well, wondering what could possibly be of interest on a rock surface inside a mountain. Once her lamp was up, she immediately saw it: a solid block of limestone implanted in the wall, engraved with words in an ancient script.

"There it is," he said, the triumph in his voice held in by a quiet awe. "Can you read it?"

The two lamps flickered side by side as Rachel moved a step closer to Elazar, straining to see the carvings.

"It's in the old script," he said, "from the time of the First Kingdom. In the Temple they teach us how to read it, even though no one uses it anymore."

He paused, and turned toward her.

"I knew you could read," he said quietly. "I've seen you on the steps before, checking the scrolls the priests send out with you. You always open them after you leave the courtyard, behind the water basins. I've been watching you for weeks. And not just because you're beautiful."

Rachel had been looking at the inscription, but now she stared at Elazar, silent and stunned.

"At first I couldn't believe you were really reading. But then I started waiting for you, watching you read. You never noticed me. You just stood in the corner facing the wall, with your lips moving. It was like you were praying." He blinked at the oil lamp's smoke. "Three days I watched you before I understood it. You were doing the same thing I do when I come here. I saw you and knew I was seeing a free person."

Wonder lapped at Rachel's feet. The tunnel seemed too narrow, its walls constricting like tightened lungs. Elazar turned the lamp back toward the inscription. "Can you read the old script too?"

She swallowed before speaking, relieved at the distraction. "Just a few letters," she said, pointing to the first word. "There's a hey, and there's a nun."

Elazar's face glowed. "You're right," he told her, his voice gilded with a childish joy. "The first few words are hard to see, but then there's the hey and nun. I'll read it to you. It says, 'The tunnel was completed today. And this is the story of the tunnel. When the axes were against each other and when three cubits were left to cut, the men on one side heard the voice of a man on the other side, and each man called to his counterpart, for there was a cleft in the rock on the right and on the left. And on the day the tunnel was finished, the stonecutters struck each man toward his counterpart, axe against axe, and water flowed from the source to the pool for one thousand two hundred cubits, and one hundred cubits was the height over the head of the stonecutters.'" He paused. "That's all," he said, then paused again, a gap in time filled with rushing water at her ankles. "That means we're a hundred cubits below the ground."

She felt his eyes on her as she marveled, tracing the words with her fingers. "It's in the old script," she repeated, like an imbecile. "But that means—"

"That means this tunnel is eight hundred years old, not six hundred. And it was dug by King Hezekiah, just like your father copied, even though he didn't believe it was true. Your father was wrong."

She tried to laugh. "Not for the first time," she said.

"I promise I won't tell," Elazar grinned. "I really don't want him to kill you."

He lowered his lamp and rested it on a tiny ledge below the carved stone, so that he and the stone both fell into shadow. In an instant the flame expired, transformed into a tiny curl of damp smoke. Then he bowed before her, breathed a smooth puff of air, and blew her lamp out.

For a moment she stood alone in a void, a sliver of girl stuck in the world's dark throat. Cold water rushed between her feet as she groped for the damp stone walls. She opened her mouth, prepared to gulp down darkness. Instead warm lips pressed against hers, moist and sudden and alive and marvelous, her back against the cold carved stone as ropy hands slid over her wet robes and water streamed over their bare feet. She trembled as he paused, his lips still against hers, holding her steady, holding his breath. They held still, alive inside a void. Then they laughed and laughed like happy children as they fumbled down together toward the pool, released into a starlit night, each knowing as they parted in that doomed city that nothing lasts forever, and each praying that it would never, ever end.

CHAPTER

5

TO ANNUL A VOW

. . .

Some time around the ninth century, or perhaps centuries before that, someone—perhaps a poet, or a scholar, or a lawmaker, or a genius—came up with a way to absolve people of their vows to God. Not to absolve vows between people: there was no way out of those, other than the popular tactic of becoming a weasel or a worm. No, this solution was strictly for the kind of vows one made in absolute desperation, when catastrophe or stupidity or some other smallness of the imagination had made life unbearable, when one needed to break the laws of the universe and saw no other way but to sign over a first-born child or a first-true-love or one's ability to enjoy being alive. The solution, this genius understood, was not to break the vows after they were made, for then there could be no vows at all. The solution was to break the vows *before* they were made: to protect people, as any good contract should, from the consequences of their own stupidity, by preventing them from making vows to God to begin with. And so the formula was enacted: "All our vows—prohibitions, oaths, consecrations, or equivalent terms that we may vow, swear, consecrate, or prohibit upon ourselves—from this Day of Atonement until the next Day of Atonement (may it come upon us for good), may hereby be regarded as null and void, idle and invalid, not final and not binding. These vows are not vows, these promises are not promises." Or in other words: *Forgive us, God, for we are alive, and despite what we tell our children about how to be alive, we still have no idea what we are doing, and likely never will.*

One can see the appeal. A ceremony grew around it: scrolls of the law held aloft, a convening of at least three men to represent a panel of judges, the hour appointed just on the cusp of twilight before the Eve of Atonement fell, the melody long and loud and aching and repeated, and of course, the standing presence of every person in the nation, to the extent that even today, in the most nonbelieving American suburbs where hardly a soul has ever spent a split second considering whether any of this is real, thousands upon thousands flock to otherwise empty synagogues for no reason other than to gather at that moment and recite the genius's words. But only Rachel and Elazar understand the power of the vow.

RACHEL'S PARENTS HAD MADE VOWS, of course, before this forgotten genius lived: *Please, God, give me sons, and I will bring double the number of sacrifices. Please, God, bring my daughter a worthy husband, and her firstborn son will serve a year in the holy house.* Elazar's parents made vows too, of course, especially his father: *Please, God, protect your holy house, and I will pay any tax to the Romans, whether gold or blood.* But Rachel made no vows as she began climbing up into the tunnel every few days at twilight. She only prayed: *Please, God, let him hold me just a bit longer. Please, let no one find us. Please, let my father and mother never guess where I've gone. Please, let the wool and vinegar work this time. Please, let me not be pregnant.* But she never offered anything to God in exchange. Instead, she lit a lamp deep within the earth, shocked each time by how the world was filled beneath its surface with secret joy.

Then came her mother's discovery, the rumor that made its way back about Rachel's too-frequent exchanges with the young priest at the outer court—and then the beating, and the silences. Her mother wouldn't tell her father what she had heard, out of bottomless shame, so Rachel could still sometimes run to the tunnel, evading her mother's spies around the city. But then Zakkai arrived, and everything changed.

Zakkai came from Tekoa, a few days' journey to the south. He was the eighth of his father's children, and by that time the family olive groves had been so subdivided, and his oldest brother had swindled so many local merchants, that his depleted father had to send Zakkai off to Jerusalem to learn a trade. That was how he ended up living in Rachel's father's house, indentured as an apprentice to the master scribe.

Zakkai was young and thin, with a scraggly black beard, dark eyes, knobby wrists and a visible lump in his neck that quivered when he spoke. He was short, hairy and loud, reciting verses in a perfect chant as he copied scroll after scroll. He was supposed to simply copy, Rachel knew, an extra pair of eyes and hands to speed her father's work. But Zakkai never just copied. Instead he asked questions, many questions.

"In this verse about the urim and tumim, the oracle in the high priest's breastplate, the Greek translation calls them 'light' and 'truth,'" he would say to Rachel's father, with far more knowledge than he needed to copy the text. "But wouldn't 'cursed' and 'innocent' make more sense, for an oracle? If you just repeat the letter reysh in urim, then it's a curse. What do you think, master? Is it a light, or a curse?"

"Find the other places it appears and see," her father muttered, still writing. "If it fits, change it."

"But then you'd have to change the actual oracles in the Temple too," Zakkai said. His voice was always too loud. "How can you be sure if—"

"Don't change it, then," her father would spit. Then he would hand Rachel a stack of scrolls and send her out, still trying to shut Zakkai up as Rachel made for the door.

One warm evening after Rachel had completed her rounds of the city, along with a visit to the tunnel, she went up to the roof of the house to collect the laundry that had been put out to dry. She noticed Zakkai seated on the ledge of the stone roof, his head bent toward a scroll in his lap. He had become a fixture in the house, like an awkward piece of furniture for which there was never enough room. He didn't look up. She ignored him and began taking down the laundry as she thought of Elazar, blood humming through her veins. She imagined the rush of joy as he came around the curve of the tunnel, trying to relive it as dry linens flapped in her face. Was there any reason that it couldn't last forever?

"Urim and tumim," Zakkai chanted, "urim and tumim." At first she thought he was just reading aloud, an annoying scribal habit. But then she heard him mutter, "It just doesn't make sense."

Rachel sighed, and finally put down the blanket she was folding. "It's a curse," she said.

Zakkai glanced up, startled. "What?"

"The oracle, the signs in the high priest's breastplate. You were right, it's not light. It's a curse. It doesn't make sense the other way."

Zakkai looked bewildered. It occurred to her that he had never heard her speak before. His mouth hung slightly open.

"'Light' and 'truth' aren't opposites," she continued. "What would it tell anyone, if the high priest were just throwing dice for 'light' and 'truth'? How would that show anyone anything about God's judgment?"

Zakkai was staring at her now, brushing his thick hair away from his eyes. There was something sweet about him, she noticed, an innocence in his face. "Your father said there was no point in asking about things like that," he said.

"My father can be wrong," Rachel smiled. "And I thought it was a good question."

"Girls in Tekoa don't ask questions," Zakkai murmured.

The words seemed rude, but Zakkai was watching her, marveling.

"This isn't Tekoa," Rachel answered. "In any case, it was your question, not mine. And it was worth asking." She placed a folded cloth into her basket.

He looked at the laundry, then at her. His clothes were old and dirty, she noticed, or perhaps she was spoiled by Elazar's rich white robes. Zakkai's eyes were hungry, starved for affection. She felt a sudden desire to reach for him, to do something kind.

"Your robe needs to be washed," she told him gently. "I can clean it for you if you like."

Zakkai clutched his scroll. Affection was so rare that it confused him. "Now?" he asked.

She smiled. This boy was so honest, so innocent. Elazar could eat him alive, she thought. An urge rose within her to be more like Elazar, to prove something to him, even if he was only present in her mind. "Yes, now," she said to Zakkai with a grin, and put out a hand. "I'll clean your clothes for you right now. Just take them off and give them to me."

Zakkai stumbled to his feet, and glanced anxiously at his sleeves. "But—"

Rachel laughed out loud. "I was joking," she said.

Zakkai's tan skin turned a dark red as he stared at the roof's floor.

Rachel felt as though she had just dropped a jug of water in the summertime, life spilled on dry earth.

"I guess girls in Tekoa don't joke either," she tried.

She tried to smile at him, but the boy had lowered his eyes. "I was the butt of every joke in Tekoa," he said.

Rachel looked down at her feet, shame seeping through her hands as she folded another cloth. She watched him as he lowered himself back down to sit on the ledge, twisting his scroll in his hands. "In Tekoa, if you can't pull a plow or tell exactly when an olive is ripe, you're nothing," he said. "After my grandfather died, I was the only person within a three days' walk who could read." He looked at the scroll in his lap. "I wish I had been born a priest. Then maybe there would be some purpose to knowing what I know. But my only purpose now is to pay off my brother's debts."

A wave of heat passed through Rachel, burning her cheeks. *Sometimes I can't stand being at the Temple*, she heard Elazar repeat in her mind. Why wasn't anyone born as who they should be? She looked at the sad young man before her. Suddenly the strange thought crossed her mind that perhaps he wasn't just a man, but something more than human, a messenger of some kind, whether from another world or from the future, placed here on this roof as some kind of test. The evening had turned still, the laundry hanging motionless as though time had ebbed to a stop.

"You're here now," Rachel said, "and you're asking good questions."

Zakkai smiled a small sad smile, his face illuminated by the setting sun. "So maybe it's a blessing that I wasn't born a priest," he said, "because priests don't ask questions. That's something they have in common with girls in Tekoa."

Rachel's skin crawled as she folded more cloth. Zakkai shook his head quickly, as if emptying out an impossible thought, and opened the scroll in his lap. "So it should be arurim, not urim," he said, "with an extra letter reysh. I'll fix it."

Rachel put her basket down on the ledge beside him. "Don't fix it," she said.

He looked at her again. "Why not? You told me you thought that was right."

"That doesn't mean you should change it. Why not change the next word too, and the next and the next, and explain it all?"

"Well, why not?"

"Because then you're taking away the questions," Rachel said.

Zakkai was still watching her, but Rachel suddenly felt the floor burning beneath her feet. She pulled down the last of the laundry and hurried down into the house. As she left Zakkai behind, she was surprised to find herself filled with a deep and strange foreboding—as though she had sensed something behind a curtain, something large and still and eternal.

ZAKKAI WAS CURIOUS; questions kept him up at night. When Rachel would return in the evenings after her deliveries were done, her body still singing and her feet still damp from the cold water in the mountain, he somehow managed to be wherever she was, following her around the house as she carded wool or mended clothes, asking more and more questions.

"Do you think God really needs sacrifices? Why does the creator of the world need so many dead goats?"

"I don't know, Zakkai."

"When the text says 'Don't cook a kid in its mother's milk,' wouldn't it make more sense to say 'Don't cook a kid in its mother's fat'? 'Fat' and 'milk' are spelled exactly the same. You know how to cook. Isn't meat usually cooked in fat?"

"Maybe, Zakkai."

"The prophets I'm copying now keep saying we're supposed to destroy idols. So why aren't we destroying the Roman ones?"

"Because we'd be crucified, Zakkai."

"When God tests Abraham by telling him to sacrifice his son, but then God stops him, does that mean Abraham passed the test, or failed?"

"Ask my father, Zakkai."

"Did you ever notice that when you read the same book again and again, the book doesn't change, but you do?"

"Not until now, Zakkai."

"Why do you always come home so late, Rachel?"

"You're annoying me, Zakkai."

Zakkai slept in the wine cellar with the house slaves, but when Rachel's last sister married and Rachel's bed was suddenly hers alone, he began to peek into her alcove at night, watching her sleep. She wasn't sleeping, of course, only pretending, sweating on sheepskin as she thought of Elazar. Zakkai would draw back the curtain, watching her. With Elazar she felt alive in every limb of her body, molten silver flowing through her veins. But in this darkened room under Zakkai's silent gaze, she felt strangely removed from her body—as though Zakkai were not looking at her, but reading her, like one of her father's scrolls. She rolled toward the wall and continued not sleeping, her skin inscribed with imaginary words.

Zakkai was honest; he never touched her, though her parents slept deeply; no one would have stopped him. The house slaves gossiped. He surely knew what people in the city thought of the wild Daughter of Azaria, knew why she was still unmarried, knew why her parents had failed to find a man for her, knew, standing at that curtain, that he could have done as he pleased. Zakkai was holy; he would never touch a woman without a contract. Zakkai was indispensable; it was Rachel's father who thought of the ingenious way to keep Zakkai in his household even after his debts were repaid. Zakkai was respectful; he made sure that Rachel herself said yes, though he failed to see that there was no realistic possibility of her saying no. When the marriage contract was signed and the dowry handed over, her father was overjoyed, her mother relieved. Rachel put on her bridal veil as though it were a shroud. Zakkai was wise; when she failed to bleed in the bridal chamber, Zakkai said nothing. And when she failed to bleed in the weeks after that, Rachel said nothing. Except to Elazar.

They met in the tunnel less often now, even though Elazar had still managed to evade his father's proposals of the daughters of other priests; he was young, and a boy, and could avoid choosing a bride for at least another year. But Rachel was a married woman with her hair bound beneath a veil. One late afternoon when Zakkai went to read his scrolls before the High Court, Rachel hurried to the priests' quarters, left a blank scroll for Elazar, and hid inside the mountain. After dark cold hours, Elazar waded toward her in the dark and held her as she sobbed.

"Rachel, you were just married. Everyone will think it's Zakkai's baby. And will they be wrong? Maybe it is Zakkai's baby after all." He tapped her flat belly, and her flesh tingled. "Hello, Son-of-Zakkai! O great Son-of-Zakkai, nine months hence your father shall welcome you into the covenant!"

He wanted her to laugh. She couldn't. "I know it's not Zakkai's baby," she said. "Even Zakkai will know it's not Zakkai's baby. I'm terrified."

"Rachel, no one will know. There's nothing to be afraid of."

"What will happen if the baby has green eyes?"

Elazar sighed, scooping up a handful of water and letting it dribble idly between his fingers. "Let me tell you exactly what will happen if the baby has green eyes," he said. He took her lamp from her, putting it down on an indentation below the carved stone. "Imagine that by some miracle, Zakkai actually notices the baby's eye color. He won't, of course, because no man has ever noticed anyone's eyes except for those of the woman he loves. But let's imagine against all reason that he notices. He will accuse you of adultery. And then he will bring you to the Temple, to my father, to find out if he is right."

"He'll be right," Rachel whispered.

Elazar touched her hand. "My father will write the curses about adultery on parchment and dissolve the ink from them in water, and then Zakkai will bring you before my father and the other priests. They'll uncover your hair"—he fingered the edges of the scarf tied around her head, coaxing it along her neck until his wet fingertips slid into her hair beneath it— "and then they will make you drink the water and ink. And if you really are an adulteress, then you will immediately fall ill, your belly will instantly distend, your body will sag, your children will fall from your womb, and you will die." He withdrew his hand and laughed out loud. The sound echoed in the tunnel, slapping wet stone.

"Why are you laughing?"

"Because I've seen that ceremony at the Temple a hundred times. I've even dissolved the ink myself. And I will tell you right now that not a single one of those women ever dropped dead on the Temple steps. No one's belly stretched, no one's body drooped, no one's womb bled on the floor. Not once."

Rachel gaped at him, then felt like a fool. "Maybe you just never saw—"

"I never saw it because it never happened. And trust me, that wasn't because all those women were innocent."

Cold water flowed around her ankles. "You're a heretic," she breathed. "A hypocrite priest, just like the sages say. You're all corrupt."

Elazar laughed again. "Obviously I'm corrupt."

"But—but—how can you not believe? Your father—"

"It's not a matter of believing. It's simply that the ceremony's power doesn't require anyone to sicken or die."

Rachel was baffled. "Why not?"

"Because those sages your father loves are right. When someone drains the blood from a person's face by making that person turn pale with shame, it's as if they spilled that person's blood. The humiliation for the woman and her husband, and the mistrust between them, is far worse than her death. That is the Temple's divine power. To make people die without dying." She listened as Elazar breathed. "But if it were to happen to you, it wouldn't matter. You wouldn't care what others thought of you."

"Zakkai would care. And he would be right to care. He—he's a righteous person." She stumbled over the word.

Elazar frowned. "Zakkai is a person who lives in his head. He's above the world of mortals. And we're a hundred cubits below it."

He seemed relieved to see her smile, pausing before speaking again. The pause made Rachel uneasy. "You should know that things are changing among the priests," he said at last. "Just yesterday I heard of a priest who's going to marry a girl without a single priest in her family. If the girl's family is well connected, it's worth it now. The Romans are at everyone's throats."

"Elazar, I'm married. Stop talking like this."

He took her hands in his. "I wouldn't talk like this if you weren't the most important thing in the world, Rachel. But you are, and this is your only life. It's true, Zakkai is a righteous person. But does Zakkai think you're the most important thing in the world?"

Rachel was silent. The tunnel air chilled her skin.

"You need to think about the future. This marriage of yours, it isn't a death sentence."

"Of course it is," she said. "I'm dedicated to him forever, according to the law. Unless he wants to offer me a divorce—which he would never do, not with a thousand bastard children. And in any case, a priest can't marry a divorced woman, only a virgin or a widow."

Elazar ran his fingers through her hair. She could tell he was thinking, deciding what to tell her. "Sometimes I think you read too much," he finally said. "You and Zakkai and your father, you all care far too much about the law. The law of the land is Roman law, whether we like it or not. And there are plenty of ways for Zakkai to run afoul of Roman law."

Rachel watched as Elazar smiled, a frightening smile. She stared at him. "Zakkai is the last person in this city who would break any law," she said.

"I've heard him reading documents with your father at the High Court, and talking with the judges. Zakkai is no lover of the Romans."

"Who is?"

"Most of us keep our mouths shut. Even your father's sages say we should keep our mouths shut. But Zakkai speaks out against them. Everyone knows it. He wants people to destroy the statues of the emperor."

"He would never say that in public. Maybe in meetings with other scribes—"

"Meetings with informants in attendance. I'm simply saying, he's the sort of man who gets in trouble. It wouldn't take much. Not much at all." Elazar let the water flow against their feet, pausing as he did before a bound animal, holding the knife still at its neck. "Rachel, there's hope. I know you feel trapped right now, but there could be a very long future ahead of us. In fact, I'm sure there will be."

He leaned his face toward hers as his lamp flickered. But she turned away, looking down into the tunnel shaft. The future was suddenly clear.

"Elazar, I can't come here anymore."

"Why not?"

"I don't want to drink ink and die, for one thing."

He laughed again.

"Truth, Elazar. This child is our punishment. Just like it was for King David a thousand years ago."

"Rachel, don't say that."

"I will say it, because it is true. I will never see you again. I hardly could if I wanted to. Our life is over, Elazar."

She knew that if she stayed, listened to him argue, let him kiss away her horror, she would stay forever. So she turned away and hurried down through the tunnel. She was relieved beyond imagining when he did not follow her. As she passed into the tunnel's curve, she heard his voice behind her. "Our life isn't over, Rachel. Our life has just begun."

She ignored him and continued down into the pool.

THE BABY WAS BORN A BOY—tiny and, to Rachel's joy, dark-eyed. Relief engulfed her, disguised as happiness. She brought him to her breast and poured pure light into the child, into the world. Zakkai rose like a pillar, an accomplished man, drinking wine and accepting blessings. On the baby's eighth day Zakkai circumcised him and named him Yochanan.

Yochanan grew wildly, and before he was weaned he could already speak. Rachel often placed him on her father's knees, and her father sang verses at him. The boy sang them back in his baby voice until he got stuck and repeated a word or a phrase, unable to continue: "In the beginning God created the heavens and the earth. And the earth was FORMLESS AND VOID! FORMLESS AND VOID! FORMLESS AND VOID! FORMLESS AND VOID!" He kept repeating the words until Rachel bound him to her back and returned to her chores. Even then the baby would continue singing at her—"FORMLESS AND VOID! FORMLESS AND VOID! FORMLESS AND VOID!"—until his heavy sturdy body clawed its way out of her swaddled robes and he was free, running madly away from her and out into the street so that she was chasing him as he continued singing: "FORMLESS AND VOID! FORMLESS

AND VOID! FORMLESS AND VOID!" She had to remind herself that he didn't know what the words meant, and then she had to remind herself, as she heard the words rendered into pure nonsense, that she didn't quite know either. But meaning did not matter when it came to Yochanan. He stumbled through the streets with his mother behind him, barreling naked and barefoot, singing over and over again, "FORMLESS AND VOID! FORMLESS AND VOID!" Until one morning he would not sing. Then the next morning he would not run, and then the next morning he would not walk. And the next morning he would not sit on anyone's knees. He curled on a sheepskin mat, one finger lodged in his mouth, and withered.

First the women healers came, then the sages, then the market magicians whom her father so disdained, then even a Roman doctor who spoke to them in stilted Greek. Each brought pouches of herbs, rubbed powders into the child's skin, forced liquids down his throat. Zakkai brought sacrifice after sacrifice to the Temple. But Rachel knew nothing would help.

One day her mother understood. "Go, my daughter," she said. "Go. You need to see something beyond the walls of this house." Did her mother know? Surely she did. Rachel didn't object. She grabbed a blank scroll from her mother's cart and ran to the Temple, dropping her signal into the hands of a young priest and telling him to bring it to Elazar, before returning to the tunnel. She no longer cared what anyone thought.

It had been over two years since she had spoken to Elazar. He knew about Yochanan; the priests had heard of Azaria's heir, had seen Zakkai bringing offerings of thanksgiving. And Elazar had seen her and the baby: she still delivered her father's scrolls to the Temple, now with the child on her back. Many times Elazar had lain in wait for her, watching her; she had seen him in the corners of the outer court. A few times she had even delivered scrolls into his hands, feeling the trace of his fingers on her palm. Once he even dared to compliment the child's beauty, and asked the child's name. But never had she been back to the tunnel, until now.

She waited for a long time under the ancient carving, one hundred cubits below the surface of the earth. The light that approached brought her no comfort. Elazar took her in his arms eagerly, covering her face with kisses. She sobbed aloud, and he stopped.

"He's dying, Elazar."

"What? Who?"

"Yochanan. He's ill. We've tried everything. Offerings, poultices, every remedy in the world. Elazar, he's dying." She gagged. "And you know why," she wailed. "It happened to King David a thousand years ago. The child he had with his lover died, and everyone knew why." She pulled herself away from him.

Elazar looked at her. "He won't die, Rachel," he said softly. "He'll recover. I promise you he will."

"Don't insult me, Elazar. What are you, a witch?"

"No. But I'm the son of the high priest. And there is a way." His voice made her feel like a child, as though someone were holding her hand. "We'll make vows," he said. "More than vows. We'll become Nazirites."

Why hadn't she thought of it? The Nazirite vow was for just such a situation, for repentant sinners. To become a Nazirite, one only had to declare one's vow and then abstain from cutting one's hair, drinking wine, and touching the dead. After thirty days, one went to the Temple, cut off one's hair, and offered it on the altar along with many sacrifices, including one for one's sins. Everyone knew that God forgave Nazirites. Rachel listened to the rushing waters and felt protected, immersed in a priestly blessing. But nothing was simple anymore.

"Zakkai will know that I'm a Nazirite. He'll suspect." Suspect what, exactly? she wondered. It hardly mattered. Her entire life had become a maze of lies.

Elazar laughed, and reached under her veil. She thought to stop him, but couldn't. He tugged at her bound braid and wound her long black hair around his hand, pulling her breath from her lungs. "People notice when men become Nazirites, not women. No one will notice if you drink only water. If no one in your family dies in the next thirty days, you won't touch a corpse either. And no one will notice if you don't cut your beautiful hair, at least until the end when they shave your head at the Temple. If he notices then, what of it? You were trying to save his boy." Elazar's smile was painful to endure.

Rachel remembered the sages in her house, debating whether such vows were acceptable. "But at the end of the vow we would each have to bring a lamb, a ewe, and a ram, and then unleavened bread, and grain, and on and on," she said. "Zakkai is already making too many sacrifices for us to afford. How could I sacrifice all of that? We aren't rich."

"Fortunately, you have a rich and priestly friend." Elazar took her hand as she shuddered. "It will work, Rachel. The power of the Temple is to make people die without dying," he said softly. "Without the Temple we would have to wait until death to be judged or forgiven by God. But we don't have to wait until death. We can speak to God now. We don't even need more witnesses. We can make the vow right here."

To her surprise, the urgency had left Elazar's body. He spoke calmly, without passion. He knew what she needed. She looked up at the carved stone, thinking of the ancient kings who dug their way through a mountain. "Speak the vow with me," Elazar said. "'Let me be a Nazirite.'"

"Let me be a Nazirite," she repeated.

He smiled at her, and she was overwhelmed with relief. "Now go home and care for the boy. And meet me in thirty days on the Temple steps. The boy will get better."

THE BOY DID NOT get better.

Each day his complexion changed slightly in color, becoming first pale, then yellowish, then finally darkening, as though his body were bruised. Sores opened on his skin. By the second week of her vow he could barely even cry; by the third, he struggled to keep down food. On the thirtieth day, she told her mother she had to leave, that she would be back before nightfall. "Don't go now, Rachel. Your child needs you."

"I have to."

Her mother was too weak to stop her. Yochanan lay in her mother's arms, his breaths swelling like a mist.

She went to the ritual bath first, stripping and immersing herself as quickly as possible before dressing again and ascending the Temple steps. One of the priests' wives met her at the gate, took her to a corner of the women's court, and removed her veil. Rachel had not expected to feel so embarrassed. The woman took a razor and hacked off her hair in thick long clumps, until Rachel felt a cool breeze against the skin of her scalp. The men in the courtyard stared. In another corner of the immense plaza, she saw Elazar kneeling before another priest, bowing his shaven head.

The woman bundled the hair into a thick rope and placed it in Rachel's hands. Then she signaled a different priest, a man even younger than Elazar, who came leading the three animals by leather cords. Behind him, a boy priest carried the meal and grain and water offerings. Rachel followed the two across the women's court and up the fifteen stone steps to the threshold of an open gate she had never approached before, the entrance to the inner court.

The smell overwhelmed her. She breathed in and gagged, tasting burning incense and roasting animal flesh. The odors made her vision blur, but she still saw the altar with its perpetually burning fire, the penned rows of calves and rams and goats, the golden bowls and other implements for tending to ash and blood, the intricately fitted multicolored stone tiles that covered the floor. Towering before her was the colossal edifice of the sanctuary itself, the shrine containing the Holy of Holies, its walls gleaming with plates of silver and gold, its massive bronze and cedar doors closed tight. Her eyes had barely focused before a man came around the altar and stood before her, a man in a tall cloth hat like a crown, wearing a golden breastplate adorned with twelve glowing jewels. Hanania, the high priest, Elazar's father. She knelt on stone.

Hanania signaled the young priests, who brought the animals to the altar. They dispatched them quickly, efficiently, and the animals barely moaned. Soon their burning flesh mingled with the other smells, the unleavened bread offerings and the meal offerings and the water offerings, blood and water draining into golden bowls and through channels in the floor as smoke rose in columns toward the bright blue sky. Rachel could hear the smell of the smoke rising up like thin lyre music, impossibly high-pitched, like a newborn's wail. She felt weak, and pressed her face to the floor. When she heard the young priests' footsteps hurrying away, she opened her eyes and cautiously rose to her feet, wondering if she was finished. But she was still holding her hair in her hands, and now Hanania moved.

Hanania's breastplate was thick, raised from his chest like a golden box. He opened it as she watched, and took out what appeared to be two circles made of slices of bone. He threw them on the floor before her, where they rattled and spun and dropped. One fell down blank, a circle of solid white. The other fell with a word carved on it: *Urim*. She heard Zakkai's voice in her head: *Is it a light, or is it a curse?*

"You are here for a child," Hanania said.

She looked at him, uncertain of whether to answer. "Yes," she said at last.

Hanania looked at the bones on the ground. "Your Nazirite vow has failed."

Rachel stared at him, speechless. If she were a man, a sage, practiced in the art of arguing, she might have challenged him: *How can it have failed? I offered a sin offering! You haven't even burnt my hair! Isn't*

God all-merciful, abounding in lovingkindness? Isn't the Temple where one can die without dying? Save my child! But she was a woman, and young, and gutted. She held out her hair. The smoke piqued her eyes, bringing forth hot tears.

"Vows fail when something more is required of us," the priest said. Rachel shuddered, feeling accused. But Hanania's voice was gentle. "We are living in perilous times. Everything here is in danger." Rachel glanced up at the massive façade of the sanctuary, God's eternal home on earth. What danger? "If all this is destroyed, it will take uncommon wisdom to find a path to holiness beyond it," Hanania said. "Not every child has that capacity for wisdom."

Rachel listened, confused. Was he talking about her baby?

"There remains one possibility for you," he said slowly. "A new vow."

"The same vow, again?" she finally asked, when he remained silent too long. She did not meet his eyes. She had heard of people renewing Nazirite vows, or failing to keep them and trying again. But the high priest's face seemed far too grave.

"No. Something else, a new vow, an eternal bond between you and God. You may reject it, but if you do, your child will die."

Now she raised her face to look at Hanania. The high priest himself: was he even human? He was: a thickset man with a graying beard and grizzled bags beneath his eyes. His eyes were black, but his eyebrows arched upward like his son's. She had the sickening thought that she was staring not at divine redemption but rather at her own future, at her lover grown old. She winced and looked away. "What eternal bond?"

"Not a temporary vow like the one you made."

"A lifelong vow?" she asked. Now she was frightened. She had heard of lifelong Nazirites, forbidden forever from touching the dead. Did that mean she couldn't bury her parents?

"A lifelong vow is also temporary," he said. "I am speaking of an eternal vow. This vow will make you die without dying. If you make this vow, your son will live, but so will you."

Rachel stared at him. "I don't understand."

"Your child will live through this illness, but there is a price."

"You mean a sacrifice." She steeled her nerves. Would Elazar give her more animals? He would give her anything. But she hated asking.

"Yes, but not one you can touch. The sacrifice must come from you."

She drew in her breath. "What do you mean?"

He looked at the bones on the ground. "The price is your death."

She followed his gaze to the bones, then looked back at Hanania's face. A wave of strength rushed through her, inhaled with the stench of entrails and blood. The words she erased from her father's scroll rose within her mind. "I would gladly die for my son," she said, with an unfamiliar pride.

Hanania touched the red stone on the breastplate on his chest. "No. You will live for him."

Rachel almost smiled. "I'm already living for him. All mothers live for their children."

Hanania spoke slowly, as if struggling to form the words. "To make this vow, you must live for all your children, forever," he said. "You must sacrifice your own death for him to live." He breathed, thick audible breaths, still staring at the bones. "You need to understand what this means, my daughter." *My daughter.* Did he know? She raised her face again and looked into the deep black of his eyes. He knew. "It means that your child will live, but you will never die."

Rachel remembered the verses about the first people ever created, the ones who had eaten the fruit from the Tree of Knowledge: *And God said, Now that man has become like us, knowing good and evil, what if he stretches out his hand and also takes from the fruit of the Tree of Life, and lives forever?* "That's impossible," Rachel said. "The Tree of Life is protected by a revolving sword."

Hanania smiled at her. "Your father taught you well." To him, she was still Daughter of Azaria. "The Torah is our contract with God, and it is also the Tree of Life. The Master of the World has planted it in our midst. But this vow would be a new contract with God, undertaken only by you. You and the child's father."

He did not say *you and your husband*. Rachel inhaled the stench of burning animal flesh. "Are there people who have upheld this—this contract?"

Hanania touched a finger to his beard. "I know of no others who have made this vow. It has been offered, but no one has ever accepted. Not once in a thousand years."

"Why not?"

Hanania sighed, a long deep sigh. "Someone as young as you could never understand that," he said. "You are young, my daughter. Don't do something you will regret. You will have more children."

Rachel glanced over her shoulder, as though she could see Yochanan behind her. The Yochanan she saw in her mind was not the one whose body was covered with sores, who was too weak to speak or move. She saw instead the little boy reciting verses, ensnared in the final words. *I set before you life and death, the blessing and the curse*, her tiny, healthy, black-eyed Yochanan sang, perfectly imitating his grandfather's lilt. *Choose life, so you and your children may live, may live, may live, may live.*

"I only want this child."

Hanania looked at the bones. "Then you must make him matter," he said. "Are you ready?"

"Yes."

"Then bow."

She knelt on the stone floor. Hanania lowered himself alongside her and whispered in her ear, telling her what to say. He rose, placed her cut-off braid in her open hands, and placed his empty hand on her head.

She spoke, surprised by how loud her voice sounded against the stone walls. "I give up my own death in exchange for the life of my son, Yochanan son of—"

She hesitated. For centuries upon centuries, she would remember that pause: the silence in the court, the smoke and smells blowing in and out of her body with each breath, the weight of the hand of Yochanan's grandfather against her bared head.

"Elazar," the high priest whispered.

"Yochanan son of Elazar," she spoke aloud. The name rose from her lips, riding a crest of incense. "For this child's life, I give up my own death. This I swear, I swear, I swear, by the holy name."

She pronounced the name of God and felt the warmth of hot stone against her knees as her hair burnt before her, a smell she would inhale again and again in the years to come, every time she burned herself alive.

CHAPTER

6

COIN COLLECTION

. . .

When he was six years old, Rocky began collecting coins. He started with pennies, looking for Indian heads and then trying to find at least one specimen from every year. Soon he moved on to more obscure coins, saving money from walking neighbors' dogs and shoveling snow and then "borrowing" more from his mother so that he could order them from catalogues that came in the mail. This baffled Rachel.

"Why would you spend real money to buy fake money?" she once asked.

"These aren't fake money," he told her in his ten-year-old soprano voice. "They're investments."

Everything with Rocky was an investment: a weird, illogical, eternal faith in the future—for which only Rachel, his prime investor, seemed obliged to pay. She was still paying. More than anyone else, he reminded her of Yochanan.

Rocky had been small as a boy but was large as a man, a hulking six foot three, with a broad chest and, even in middle age, a full head of hair—lustrous black hair whose refusal to recede had made her nervous as he grew older, since any sign of her children not aging induced in her an existential panic. Over the past ten years she had noticed him graying a bit at his temples, which brought her immense relief. He would die after all. But not yet, apparently. Now he was fifty-six years old and still collecting coins. This time he was doing it in her basement. That was familiar too.

One late afternoon, not long after his wife had kicked him out and Rachel had taken him in, Rachel cornered him there. He sat crouched over a laptop on her husband's old desk, which was now buried under a snowdrift of Rocky's insurance records, legal notices and bills. It was incongruous with the rest of the windowless room, which was filled with several generations of toys to occupy great-grandchildren. Rocky had only been living with her for two months and already his mess had followed him, overdue papers and unfulfilled obligations swirling around him like a visible manifestation of his harried soul. He hunched over the keyboard in his dead father's rumpled pajamas with his unshaven jaw hanging open before the screen, several feet away from three large bins of wooden blocks and Legos. Rachel approached him slowly, watching the thick ropes of veins twitching on his dark-haired hands as his fingers rattled the keys. She always felt unsettled when she caught her grown children engrossed in something: it evoked the eternally disturbing sensation that this creature who once lived with her, once lived within her, was in fact a stranger.

"What are you doing down here all this time?" she asked the side of Rocky's head.

"Mining money," he told her. He didn't look up.

As had been true for centuries, she had no idea what her child was talking about. None of the children ever made any sense to her, not even Yochanan—especially not Yochanan, who threw away two thousand years of civilization in exchange for some pathetic shadow version of it, trading in all those rituals that had formed a connection to God for the chance to study and discuss and write about all those rituals that had formed a connection to God. Kind of like what Rocky was doing right now: spending real money on a coin collection. Again.

"Is that legal?"

"Would I be doing it in your basement if it weren't legal?"

Rachel did not know the answer to this question. She recalled several visits to the police station when Rocky was a teenager, and two separate bail hearings in his twenties, none of which Rocky seemed to remember anymore. "Mom, seriously, that was a long time ago," he would mumble on the rare occasions when she dared to mention them. As if he knew anything about a long time ago.

"How can you mine money on a computer?"

He glanced up briefly, a fake smile on his face. "I run SHA256 double round hash verification processes to validate transactions and add them to the blockchain," he said, "though I'm thinking of switching over to Scrypt." Then he turned back to the screen.

He was trying to intimidate her. It had been years since anyone had intimidated her. "What's a blockchain?"

Rocky's eyes illuminated. He swiveled toward her on his dead father's office chair, his face radiant with a sudden thrill. "It's only the most amazing thing that's happened in technology in the past twenty years."

She always had one like this, Rachel noticed: the child awed by the future, the one convinced that whatever old people were doing right now was absurd. She remembered a child who insisted on finding a new way of polishing gems, another who disputed everything the barber-surgeon said and finally started bottling her own healing herbs, and another who was convinced that everyone in town was an idiot and only read newspapers from abroad. One son once told her with a smirk that anyone with any sense was reading books now, that only fools still read from scrolls. She remembered her father and objected. *But books make people into fools*, she insisted. *With books, readers skip around, they leave out chapter 3 and go straight to chapter 9, they don't bother remembering the beginning because they can always go back and see what happened, they only read the exciting parts and miss the important parts, they skip to the end. With scrolls, readers have no choice but to be diligent, they have to read carefully, they have to remember the beginning when they reach the end, they can't be fools. Books are made for fools!* He had listened to her, still smirking. *Exactly, Mother*, he had told her, and opened a bindery, which thrived until his grandson ran it into the ground. Those future-facing children, Rachel knew, were the most insufferable of all children—disrespectful, arrogant, dismissive, ungrateful, impossible to raise. Worst of all, they were invariably right.

"The blockchain is the foundation for an entirely new internet," Rocky was saying. He was speaking quickly now, electrified as he always was by something new. He had talked the same way about the company he started five years ago, and the one he started ten years before that, and on back for the past thirty years. It always began and ended the same way: Rocky invented something, or claimed to have invented something, and then some business partner "stole" it from him, and before he knew it, either the company collapsed or his partners kicked him out. His life was littered with failed apps, underfunded websites, computer chip variants that violated some obscure patent, brokerage systems that bent some inconvenient federal law, an archaeology of almosts thirty years deep, starting with his very first telecom jobs, when he already couldn't get along with a boss. Sometimes he made it out of his mistakes with money, occasionally quite a bit—though more often he lost money, and typically a wife along with it. Thirty years later, Rocky was still all potential. Rachel heard that familiar electricity in his voice and stifled a groan.

"Right now the internet is based on trust," he was saying. "It's supposedly this decentralized democratic thing, but it's not, because almost all your data is stored by a few very large companies. You give your private information or financial details to all these central institutions, and then you just have to hope that they don't abuse it. The blockchain gets rid of all that."

"So who's running it instead?"

"That's the beauty of it. No one is."

"No one?"

"Yeah. Isn't that beautiful?"

Rachel could recall several situations in the past several centuries in which no one was running things. None of them had ended well. "So what's a blockchain?" she heard herself ask.

"It's like a ledger, basically the record of every transaction that's ever happened in the system. It's a permanent record of the past that can never change, and it happens without trusting anyone at all."

Like me, Rachel thought. Rocky smiled, and a wave of warmth ran through her, an alertness in her body to the presence of her child—her middle-aged, spent, grizzled, pathetic child, but still her child. Here he was, despite all reason, trying to achieve what his mother already had: a permanent record of the past that can never change, without trusting anyone at all. But that was a live wire she could not touch. Instead she said, "Sounds like a great way to buy drugs."

"That was true until a big bust years ago. Honestly, if I wanted to buy drugs I'd be better off with dollars. I read somewhere that half the physical bills in the United States carry trace amounts of cocaine." He shrugged and turned back to the screen.

"So all this money-making, or money-mining, or whatever it is—it's all happening on your laptop?"

"No. This is just keeping track of the process. I bought shares in a mining rig."

"A mining rig?"

"It's a giant hardware system that uses enormous amounts of power. It overheats so easily that it has to sit in a bath of cooling fluids." He turned to her with a grin. "Aren't you glad it's not in your house?"

"Where is it?"

"Some guy on the network runs it. I guess it's in his basement instead of yours. I bought the shares from him."

A dead weight fell in Rachel's gut. "Do you know who he is? How can you trust that he even has these machines?" The fact that she knew the answers did not prevent her from asking the questions.

"God, Mom, you're so damn nosy. What the hell do you care?"

She gave an indignant huff, hiding her own fear. It was amazing how easy that was to do with children, no matter how old they were. Even grown children never expected their parents to be afraid. "I care because I don't need the FBI raiding my house," she said, summoning as much resentment as she could muster. "And because I don't need you dropping money you don't have on things that don't exist."

Rocky grunted. His annoyance relieved her. "Here it is, okay?" He banged on the keyboard, typing faster than she would have thought possible. "Look, an actual photo. There's your mining rig. And there's the guy who owns it. Notice that they both exist."

He turned the screen toward her. Most of the picture was filled with dozens of enormous hard drives lined up on metal racks, their bases bathed in blue fluid. Wires grew out of them, burgeoning in bunches like thick black uncut hair. It was astonishingly ugly, almost deliberately so. It reminded her of the mechanical water-clock one of her sons had built once, a mess of wooden gears and axles that somehow calculated when to add an extra month to the lunar year. *The moon is so beautiful and your machine is so ugly*, she had told him. He had grinned at her. *But it works, Mother! So what if no one is going to write a poem about it!* Yet this time the machines weren't what caught her eye. In the corner of the photo, a short man who was obviously holding the camera had tipped his face into the frame, one olive-skinned hand held out toward the wires with a salesman's flourish. Her stomach sank like a stone.

"See how he exists?" Rocky grinned, tapping the screen. A shiver ran through Rachel's body. "And he's some Arab or Spanish guy or whatever, so think about it—if the FBI comes after someone, it's going to be him, not me. You know, this digital currency probably has the most potential in failed states anyway, or places where the regular currency can't be trusted. Maybe he's got contacts in places like that. Supposedly in Argentina it's a going concern, since their normal money routinely falls down the toilet."

"What makes you think he's Arab or Spanish," she said, in order to say something, though she failed to make it a question. It was hard enough to keep the quaver out of her voice.

"My general racism regarding tan people," he said, and kept typing. He had inherited her dead husband's pallor, though he had her thick dark hair.

"Tan people like me?" she asked. "Maybe he's just Jewish."

Rocky rolled his eyes. "Yeah, except his online handle is @highpriest. So, no, I don't think so." He talked and typed simultaneously. "Anyway, who gives a crap. The guy exists, case closed."

Rachel breathed as he clicked the photograph away. The man's face lingered in her mind, a tiny opening in the veil between her and the abyss. The only way to close it again was to change the subject.

"Do you ever hear from Judy anymore?" she asked.

She regretted the question immediately. Judy was Rocky's latest ex-wife—or rather, his almost-ex-wife—and the source of his most recent financial woes. She had asked hoping for good news, finality, but that was ridiculous. Nothing ever ended, and you could never expect good news from Rocky.

"Judy is eating me alive," he moaned. "She took my house, she took my car, she emptied the accounts, and now her lawyer calls me every day. She thinks I'm hiding assets somewhere."

"Are you?"

"Would I be here if I were?" He pulled a face like the child he once was, and still was. "It's her fault that I'm even doing the mining. Or her *inspiration*, let's call it. Three months ago she hacked into my computer and held it for ransom."

Judy was the receptionist at Rocky's last company, a college dropout who had worked at a hair salon before a friend got her the job. "That seems a bit beyond her ability," Rachel said.

"Nothing is beyond that bitch's ability," Rocky seethed. "So she paid someone to do it. What's the difference? The point is, my computer was frozen and some asshole made me pay a thousand bucks to get it back."

"You actually paid?"

"Of course I paid. What was I going to do, prosecute? But here's the thing. They made me pay in Bitcoin. 'Digital currency only.' They even gave me a list of preferred vendors for the exchange! I go to one of the vendors, and they make me hand over every ID known to man. Not just my photo ID, but a photo of me *holding* my photo ID. So I got to thinking, this could happen again any time, it could happen to anyone, it's only going to happen more and more, there are obviously whole office parks full of people in Latvia or wherever doing this every day—so let's cut out the middleman. That's when I decided to invest in the rig. There's gotta be a future here, right?"

There's always a future, Rachel thought. Unfortunately. "If you're betting on the future of crime, I would say that's a winning bet."

"It's not crime, it's everything. I'm telling you, the blockchain is—"

"Rocky, of all the smart people I know, you may be the dumbest."

He turned back to his screen. Rachel stared at her son, at his fully grown body, the back of his thick head. The sight of him hunched over in her basement, three feet from the blocks he had once played with, made her suddenly ill, as though he and his childhood and adulthood were already buried together underground. She thought of him as a boy, lurking in the basement with his blocks—and all the other centuries of boys lurking in basements, building futures. The girls sometimes looked back, but only rarely. The boys never did.

"I can't believe you're still hovering over me like I'm a teenager," he muttered.

"I can't believe I'm still letting you live here when you're fifty-six years old. If you don't want me hovering, feel free to get out of my house."

She saw him flinch. The typing slowed, and finally stopped. He spun on the chair toward her. In his weary unshaven face, in her husband's pajamas, she saw his father—years of mornings, caresses, kindnesses, lies, arguments, comforts, all of it now dust. One day, not that many years from now, her son too would be part of the soil, part of the plants, part of food, part of her.

"Mom, I'm just trying to get back on my feet, okay? In a few months I'll cash out of this, I'll be out of your house, out of your life. This thing is going to take off. Then you'll never have to think about me ever again. I'll even pay for your retirement. I swear to God."

"Don't swear," she said. It was an old reflex, translated country by country, as though each successive life offered her some way to prevent future regret. She buried the idea quickly, smothering it in words. "I really just came down to remind you that it's Friday, and Hannah and her family are coming over for dinner in an hour," she said. "You might want to put on some clothes."

Hannah's name made Rocky snap the laptop shut. Seeing his eagerness made Rachel feel lighter, happier. But she was already on her way upstairs, turning away from him.

Elazar's face on her son's computer screen had shaken her. As she hurried to finish cooking the meal, she could not loosen his image from her mind. What could he possibly be doing there, on Rocky's laptop? She didn't know what he was plotting, but clearly it was something, and the details were changeable and therefore meaningless, as they always were. Elazar had only one reason for living. Her own thousands of reasons for living, including Rocky himself, mattered not at all.

HANNAH MADE A POINT, as children of screwed-up parents like Rocky often do, of being ambitiously, relentlessly normal, grinding her way to conventional success. She had plowed through school, and even her first wrong-turn marriage hadn't stopped her from collecting every academic accolade in her path. Now she was some kind of medical researcher, doing work Rachel couldn't even pretend to understand. Her current husband, Daniel, was some sort of technology journalist—and also Hannah's lover, partner, and best friend, always laughing with her at their two gorgeous children. Imagine if I had had *that*, Rachel thought every time their miniature family graced her doorstep, each member of that perfect square of people always mid-laugh, a palpable intimacy between them. Not that she hadn't had families—dozens!—or lovers who had brought her happiness—more than anyone deserved! But that total honesty, that completely shared life, that sense of pristine partnership and common purpose—Rachel ached whenever she saw it, and ached even more knowing how it would end, even if they didn't know it yet. Even the children exuded purposeful ambition. The older son was six, blond, silent and obsessive, never objecting to anything but doing what he wanted anyway, reading fantasy novels under the table and playing chess against himself. But the younger son, five years old, stirred Rachel with a familiar feeling she couldn't quite name. He barreled into Rachel's house with his black curls flying, wearing a superhero cape.

"I'm the Amazing Jumping Man!" he screeched. "Watch me JUMP!" In an instant he had scaled a floor-to-ceiling bookcase and was careening toward a chandelier.

"Ezra, get DOWN!" his mother thundered, as his father grabbed at his legs. The boy managed to swing by one arm from the chandelier before his synchronized parents succeeded in yanking him back to earth. Even the parents' exasperation left Rachel in awe, the perfect union of purpose as they wrestled the boy to the table with his older brother in tow. Once the appropriate dinner table blessings had been recited—the ones Rachel had first heard from Yochanan—both boys consumed their food as quickly as possible and immediately raced down to the basement to play, to everyone's relief.

"Everything is delicious, Gram," Hannah said as Rachel passed around a dish of noodle kugel. It annoyed Rachel how perfect Hannah was, how openly she tried to compensate for her father. She glanced at Rocky, who didn't look up from his plate. Rachel was pleased to see that he had shaved.

"Eating here always reminds me of my own grandmother," Daniel added. "She made everything the old-fashioned way, just like this. It really is true that smell and taste are connected to memory. Thank you for bringing her back to life!"

Rachel smiled to hide a grimace. She had thought she was cooking new things; everything on the table was something she had only learned to cook in the past two hundred years. Was it true that smell and taste were connected to memory? For a century or two, of course. But after that the smells expired, vanished from the world. It wasn't even possible to cook her childhood foods anymore. They required clay ovens, copper heating coils, inverted iron bowls over open fires, grains that no longer existed, animals whose parts were no longer for sale. Once, about seventy years ago, she had seen a jug of olive oil in a store, for the first time in over a century: ages had passed since she had lived anywhere near where olives grew, or near where anyone might buy them. Olive oil! She had felt a thrill when she bought it. But at home she had discovered that there was nothing to eat it with, and when she tasted it, the flavorless slick on her tongue bore no resemblance at all to what she remembered. She was newly married to a wonderful man then, in a brand-new purpose-built suburb deliberately designed for forgetting, and it had been a long time since she had cried. But that day she did, alone in her chrome-lined electric kitchen. She felt pathetic, like a grown-up trying to play with a doll.

"So what's going on with you, overachiever?" Rocky asked his daughter. In Hannah's presence, Rocky seemed at least ten years younger.

"Not much," Hannah murmured.

Her husband butted in. "Hannah's too modest to tell you, so I have to brag for her. She and her lab just won a major grant from Google."

Rachel was relieved to see the joy on Rocky's face. "Wow! What's the grant for?"

Hannah smiled. "Basically, I'm trying to solve the problem of death."

A trapdoor opened under the heap of years beneath Rachel's chair. She felt, physically, her knees against a warm stone floor as the air filled with fragrant smoke. She opened her eyes wide, struggling to see what was in front of her, to distinguish it from the reality beneath her. Her granddaughter sat smiling across the table, unwrinkled and innocent. Rachel took hold of her wineglass and forced herself to concentrate on the sensation of its smooth round bowl, its weight in her hand, the dark-haired actual girl across the table, the one who looked like hundreds of other daughters and granddaughters but who also looked the most like her. *Stay here*, she told herself. *Stay here*. She took a deep swig of wine and asked, "Is death a problem?"

"Well, Google thinks it is."

Rocky looked up from his food. "So how do you solve it?" he asked. "Fill me in. I'm in the market for a new lease on life."

Hannah gave a little sigh, which Daniel echoed. Clearly they were both bored by telling the same story again and again. Rachel had no patience for other people's boredom. "Okay, short version," Hannah began. "So everyone's got chromosomes, right? That's where the DNA are, they're in every cell in an organism, every cell in you. And they all contain the entire genetic code for the organism. Now the genes on the DNA, they're the rungs in the double-helix ladder. My group is researching the telomeres, which are the nucleotide sequences—"

Daniel smiled at her. "Can you say that in English?"

"That's all right," Rachel said. "I'm so old that I'm fluent in Latin and Greek."

Everyone laughed, except for Rachel.

"And tenth-grade biology was the best three years of my life," Rocky said.

Everyone laughed, except for Rachel.

"Proteins, okay?" Hannah explained. "Proteins that act like protective caps on the genes. They prevent the genes from degrading near the ends of the chromosomes, by allowing their ends to shorten. The problem is that telomeres divide, and eventually they get reduced, which speeds up the deterioration of the genes. The thinking is, that's why we die. It's really just decomposition."

Rachel's food became tasteless in her mouth. She remembered a son in Poland, the one who had abruptly become an atheist after his father's death, while the son was still a teenager. They had fought endlessly, she and he, she constantly trying to force him back into the yeshiva, he constantly getting himself expelled, until he left home to go to the university in Lemberg—which she suspected required a baptismal certificate, though of course she never asked. Seven years later he had returned home with a little girl, explaining to his mother that his young wife had dropped dead.

"Papa, what happens to people when they die?" the little girl had asked that first evening at Rachel's house.

Her father had stared right at her, smiled, and said, "They decompose."

Rachel looked at his smiling face and slapped it. Her son walked out the next morning and never returned. Only later did Rachel realize that that was the reason he had come home, that her slap had been her granddaughter's blessing. She raised that little girl too.

"So there's an enzyme, telomerase, that might be able to maintain telomere length," Hannah was saying. "And if we can maintain telomere length, then no one would have to die."

Rachel reached for her water and began drinking, pouring it down her throat without pausing as she heard her mother's voice. *Stop guzzling, stupid girl! It's summertime! Where do you think you are, some rich place with a river like Egypt? Babylon? Rome? You think we have endless water? Nothing is endless, stupid girl! Stupid girl, you'll kill us all!*

Rocky leaned forward with his fork in his hand. "That sounds excellent. Sign me up!"

"That's what everyone says," Daniel put in.

"Don't get too excited," Hannah said. "First of all, telomerase can also cause cancer, so it's not exactly a magic bullet. And anyway it'll be a while before we make it to human trials, if we ever do. Right now we're doing work on planaria."

"What's planaria?" Rocky asked.

"They're everyone's favorite microscopic organism," Daniel groaned, still grinning.

Rachel took refuge in the conversation's eddy. It still astounded her, after all these years, how much more there still was left to learn, how it never ended. I should be a scientist in the next version, she thought in passing—the same way she thought of everything else her children or grandchildren did. I should be a writer, she had thought before. Or a musician. Or an artist. Or I should be—except then someone might notice her.

"They're microscopic parasites, and what's special about them is that you can't kill them," Hannah explained. "They just regenerate over and over again. That's the model we're trying to follow."

Rocky pointed a fork at his daughter. "So let me get this straight. You're trying to figure out how to make people live forever, and the way you're doing it is by figuring out how to imitate parasites."

Hannah looked at her father. "Yup."

"Like I said, sign me up. I'm already your ideal subject. Just ask Gram over here. I've been a parasite for years!"

Everyone turned to Rachel, who failed to smile. A shadow fell across the table as one candle's flame guttered and died. Rachel tried to say something trivial, but couldn't. She hoped someone else would speak, but the three of them were watching her, waiting. *Stay here*, she told herself again. *Stay here*.

"I'm confused about why someone would want to live forever," she finally said.

Hannah answered analytically, like someone who had only read about life in a book. "It's not about living forever, exactly. The idea is to stop the aging process. Which I think we can all agree would be a good thing. I mean, no matter how long you live, no one wants to deteriorate physically or mentally, right? But yes, ultimately what we're trying to achieve is an indefinite lifespan."

Daniel grinned. "This is what I keep asking her," he said. "We seem to have a fundamental disagreement about whether this would be a good thing. I even started a discussion about it online. It's 'hashtag eternal life,' if you want to take a look. A lot of people participate."

"What do they say?" Rocky asked.

Hannah rolled her eyes. "Daniel thinks it's some fascinating conversation. But it's actually just filled with trolls."

Daniel frowned. "That's a matter of opinion."

"Someone who constantly posts about kale smoothies as the key to immortality counts as a troll," Hannah said.

"In your opinion," Daniel replied. "Isn't caloric restriction the only thing that actually slows down aging?"

"Someone who constantly posts about how the research is all a corporate plot counts as a troll."

"In your opinion. Honestly, Hannah, you're sponsored by Google."

"Someone who constantly posts about the Rapture counts as a troll."

"In your opinion. Google would probably prefer to call it the Singularity."

"How about someone who constantly posts about how he's already immortal, but he doesn't recommend it, because after twenty centuries he still can't get together with the immortal girl of his dreams?"

Daniel laughed. "Okay, that guy really is a troll."

Ice cracked through Rachel's veins. But Hannah finally laughed, a laugh that escalated until she leaned against the table, barely able to get out the words. "He—he—he's like, 'What do I have to do to get her to take me back? I saved her kids from the Black Plague, wasn't that enough?' "

Daniel continued, "And then all she says is, 'No thanks, I'd rather be with a guy who will actually die and leave me alone.' "

Hannah was still gasping. "Can you blame her?"

"And then he's like, 'But why won't she remember the good times? We had so much fun under the Romans! And remember that time when the Crusaders burned us alive?' "

Rachel's hands shook under the table. She tried to rise from her seat, to flee the room, but she found she could not move. Now Rocky was laughing too. Hannah caught her breath, wiping tears. "Dad, remind me to show you. It's like Mel Brooks."

Daniel settled down, holding Hannah's hand. "But it's not totally a joke either."

Hannah smirked at him. "Um, yes, Daniel. It is totally a joke."

"I don't mean there's really some guy out there who's immortal. I mean that the points he's making aren't completely ridiculous. There are a lot of major downsides to eternal life. Think of your bad high school boyfriend or girlfriend who never goes away. Now imagine that they *really* never go away. Honestly, I kind of want to kill myself just thinking about it."

Rachel looked at her empty glass and barely breathed.

"The online conversation is fun," Hannah said. "But the reality is that most people in it just want to sign up."

Rocky laughed. "Like I said, count me in. I'm already the bad boyfriend who never goes away, so I've got nothing to lose."

"Actually, the only human participants we need now are people who are old already."

"Sign me up!" Rocky repeated. "I'm already getting junk mail from AARP."

"Well," Hannah hesitated, "right now we're collecting DNA samples from people who are aging well."

Rocky laughed again. "Okay, I guess I don't count then. I'm definitely not aging well."

"You don't count because you're only fifty-six," Hannah said. Then she turned in her seat, and swiveled her beautiful young face toward Rachel. "But you do."

Rachel sensed the black hole closing in on her, the void that separated her from every other person on the planet. It often occurred to her that she was no longer human, that she was something else, something no other being on earth could imagine. Except for one. *The bad boyfriend who never goes away.*

"No thanks," she finally croaked.

Daniel laughed. "You've already solved the problem of death. What are you, eighty-four? You sure don't look it."

Rachel forced a smile. "I guess I'm just a parasite."

Hannah had turned serious now. She narrowed her eyes at Rachel as though examining a specimen. Rachel suppressed a shudder. This was hardly the first time a child or grandchild had eyeballed her, marveling. But she knew where it went from here, since the time she had made the catastrophic mistake of demonstrating the truth.

You don't believe me? Then watch, she had threatened a daughter, long ago, before she had lived long enough to know.

That daughter, another Hannah, was an angry person—a girl with two murdered brothers and a reeling mind, a girl brimming with fury, desperate for vengeance against the world and God. One night after a brutal fight with Rachel, that ancient Hannah came out with the long-awaited words: *I wish you were dead.*

At first Rachel laughed. *Not as much as I do.*

But then the words came back at her, fierce and wounding. *I mean it, Mother.* She saw the anger in her daughter's eyes and could not believe the intensity, the pure molten rage, as though the universe and eternity contained nothing but the two of them. The power of Hannah's fury, and the bottled-up energy of keeping her own secret for fifty years (fifty years! Who cared about fifty years! How little Rachel knew then!) made Rachel a living powder keg, ready to explode. Rachel was only on her second version then: too young to know better.

You wish I were dead? she screamed. *You think that's even possible for me? I've been alive a hundred and forty years, Hannah. I saw the Temple burn. I can't die. I never will.*

You're crazy, her daughter roared. *If I were a boy, I would run right out of this house. I'd let the Romans flay me alive, just like they did to Azaria and Simeon. Anything's better than being here. But now all I can do is wait for you to die. Crazy old lady!*

You'll wait forever, Rachel said, *and I'll prove it right now.*

While the angry Hannah watched, Rachel took the oil lamp she was holding and set the neckline of her own robe ablaze. In an instant her face ignited, her body alive and burning. She was sure her daughter would witness it, dumbfounded, as she suffered and then rose again. But instead that Hannah screamed as though she herself were on fire. She pounced on top of Rachel, screaming for her mother, and died from the flames. Rachel threw the memories into a deep pool in her mind, and heard the thunk as they sank like stones.

"Eighty-four, and no health problems at all, right, Gram?" Hannah announced. The question strummed through Hannah's voice like a plucked string. Rachel's insides burned. "No cancer, no heart disease, no memory loss—"

"You'd be surprised by what I've lost," Rachel said softly.

"Gram, seriously. It's harder than you'd think to find participants who actually meet the standard. I would love to have a sample from you. All it takes is a cheek swab. You wouldn't even need to come to the lab."

Rachel tried her best to smile. "Sorry," she said, "but I'm at an age where I've finally learned to say no."

Rocky was jubilant. "Come on, Mom. Give it a try! Then we really can live forever, instead of just laughing about it."

Rachel looked at her son across the table, the same table where he had once sat with his father and brother and sisters. She saw the little boy Rocky standing on his chair as she shouted at him to sit down, saw him beating his chest like a gorilla to make his brother laugh, saw that same pelt of black hair attached to a smaller body, a little pillar of potential. She looked and saw the boy he had been, the boy he never would be again. The smell of the burnt-out candle rose like a wail. "The hard part isn't living forever," Rachel said. "It's making life worth living."

Rocky regarded her with narrowed eyes. Rachel remembered the story her father had once altered about Abraham and Isaac, the parent who hurt a child just to prove a point. She looked at Rocky again, trying to induce him to forgive her. But he stood up abruptly, announcing the insult by loudly collecting dishes. "I'm going to go see what the kids are up to," he said. He deposited the dishes on the kitchen counter and went downstairs.

"What's going on with Dad these days? I'm afraid to ask." Hannah's voice was a hushed whisper. "Is Judy still destroying his life?"

Rachel shrugged. Her relief at the shift in subject was immeasurable. "There wasn't much left to destroy."

"I'm so sorry he's here," Hannah murmured.

"Don't be sorry," Rachel told her. "I'm a lifelong expert in dealing with people like him."

An earsplitting screech echoed from the room directly above their heads: "WATCH ME JUMP!"

Hannah and Daniel leapt to their feet. An instant later, everyone saw the boy fly past the window from the floor above and crash on top of the bushes outside, with a nauseating crunch.

Rachel rushed to the window and threw it open. Ezra was lying on top of the bushes, arms and legs splayed, dark curls blasted, his forehead bleeding. His parents immediately began pulling him through the window, Hannah screaming at him as they inspected his cuts and felt his limbs for broken bones. Rachel scanned his body in a panic until she saw how minor his scrapes were, how quickly he jerked his head up. She marveled at how children bounced. The boy smiled.

"Ezra, you IDIOT!" Hannah shouted. "You could have DIED!"

But Ezra was already standing, and laughing. "I'm the Amazing Jumping Man! The Amazing Jumping Man!"

"You IDIOT!"

Rachel didn't laugh until she went to get the first aid kit. Then in the hallway, she laughed until she cried. And told herself once more: *Stay here.*

CHAPTER 7

AN OLD FLAME

. . .

One week after they first met again, Elazar texted Rachel.

Meet me at sunset, he wrote, *here*. Following that was a strange series of numbers.

Where's "here"? she replied. The characters on the screen frustrated her, and so did something else. She thought of saying no, but already her body warmed, frustration pulsing through her skin.

Use GPS, he told her.

When she arrived where the numbers told her to go, she was in an industrial wasteland near the Hudson River. She drove in circles around abandoned warehouses, certain she had made a mistake. The navigation kept taking her back to the same spot: an empty lot next to a strangely unfinished highway underpass. Its walls were covered with rusted scaffolding, and it seemed to lead to nothing but darkness—or, when she looked a bit more closely, toward a dark wall about a hundred feet in. She drove by it three times before she saw a man step out of its shadows, in a coat and a dark hat. He waved until she pulled the car up beside him. To her surprise he went to the passenger side and climbed in.

It was strange to see him there, seated in her car. In two thousand years, this was something new: they had never been in a car together before. For a moment she imagined him seated beside her in so many other places—in third-class train compartments, in the backs of carriages, in open-air wagons, in the hulls of ships—and also all the times some other man had sat beside her in a car, staring with her through the windshield at the future. His wiry body shimmered on the plasticized seat, his old dark coat hiding a gleaming rip in the universe. She stared, awestruck. Elazar didn't notice. His mind was elsewhere, or elsewhen.

"Go straight ahead," he told her, indicating the underpass in front of them.

In front of the car was hardly a road; the surface was covered with gravel and mud, scattered with occasional debris. "Really?"

"Just go in," he instructed.

She pulled the car forward between the two large scaffold-covered walls supporting the highway overhead. They were barely within the underpass when he told her to stop. "Leave it here," he said.

She laughed. "If I leave it here, it won't be here when I come back."

"It will be."

She shut down the car, skeptical, and he began to get out. She followed him. The underpass was dark but warm, smelling only of burnt rubber. The traffic overhead sounded like waves.

"Don't you have an apartment?" she asked him.

"I have a feeling you aren't about to invite me over for dinner," Elazar said carefully, "and I'm not going to ask you why. Please, do me the same honor."

She was silent. He walked behind the car and began pulling on a railing in the side wall between two columns of scaffolding. To her astonishment, a large barred gate followed him, sliding out of the wall and closing off the passageway with the car within it. He secured it closed behind them with some sort of key.

"I told you, your car is safe," he said. He removed a flashlight from his coat pocket. "Follow me." They walked a short distance on the gravel until they reached a high cinderblock wall with a small metal door in it. Again he took out a key, working the lock.

"How do you have these keys?" she asked.

"I know people," he told her, "without them knowing me."

She knew better than to ask more questions. A moment later he took her hand and brought her through the door.

Behind it was a large deep tunnel, about sixty feet wide, its unfinished walls and ceiling lined with pipes, its floor moist earth. Hand in hand they walked its stunted length. It stretched before them about three hundred feet, and then stopped abruptly at a dirt wall.

"A few years ago some government agency tried to dig a new train tunnel under the river to the city," Elazar said, sliding English words between his own. "They started digging, but then someone didn't want to pay, so they stopped digging. Supposedly they're going to start digging again, but it will probably take years before everyone approves." He paused, and turned to her. "Obviously it was much easier to build these things with kings and slaves."

She looked around at the dark soulless space, at the pipes and steel panels and cinderblocks, and marveled. Everything about it was hideous, unnatural and untouched. Her body hummed with electric power.

"It was the best I could do," he apologized. His face opened, an expression of pure kindness. "It's so hard to find a place where a person can feel at home."

"Elazar," she said, and seized him.

She stripped away his coat, his shirt, his belt, casting off layer after layer of strange chemical fibers until she discovered him, the same tense warm breathing body as ever, and devoured him, filling herself with her only hope in the world of not being alone.

"SO WHERE ARE YOU going next?" he asked her one evening.

They had brought blankets and a hurricane lamp, camping out

like children as they met in the aborted tunnel each week. The lack of human evidence in that industrial box—no chisel marks, no inscriptions, no fingerprints, no mistakes except the enormous mistake of the tunnel itself—was strangely comforting to both of them. Even after they put their clothes on, they still liked to linger there, lying together on the floor of their dark hole in the earth.

"Elazar, please. Don't make me think about it."

"You need to start thinking about it. I highly recommend Jerusalem."

"Not so appealing right now," she muttered. But her body filled with a thick and heavy longing. Her hands withered at her sides.

"Come home, Rachel. You won't regret it. Don't wait until you have to."

"No one has to, Elazar. This place really is different from everywhere else," she said. It was something her husbands and children had had drilled into their heads for the past hundred years as an article of faith: America, the eternal exception to everything. It reminded her of how she had once been taught about the center of the universe, the Temple, eternal home of an eternal God.

Elazar looked at her sadly, as though she were a teenager about to do something stupid. "That sounds nice," he said. "I saw the idiots outside your store."

She grimaced. The tiny group of protestors had returned, with remarkable regularity and imperviousness to logic. Some of the younger grandchildren occasionally argued with them, demanding to know why they were there, redirecting them to the Bukharian guy, making daily calls to the police—all to no avail. For the most part the family ignored them, following Rachel's lead. After thousands of years it amazed her that she still didn't know the right thing to do. "Exactly," she said, "idiots. We don't make decisions based on idiots." But she had to force out the words. She could hardly think of a time when it hadn't started this way, with people yelling outside her store.

"Incorrect. We *always* make decisions based on idiots," Elazar said, switching in and out of English. "Idiots are the prime factors in our decision-making process. I should have paid a lot more attention to idiots the last time around."

"There are only seven idiots," she muttered. It was as if she were apologizing. "You haven't been living here, so you don't know. It's not a problem."

"Right now it isn't," Elazar agreed. "You definitely have at least another century or two here until it is. That's a nice long time for some people. Just not for you."

"Elazar, you are the most pessimistic person I've ever met," she announced.

"I disagree. I'm a very optimistic person. One day the Messiah will come, and then my father will come back from the dead, and he and I will go back to slaughtering goats. I believe with perfect faith that I'll live to see that day. See how optimistic I am?"

"There's no shortage of idiots where you are," Rachel said. "In any case, you must have a wife there, right? You're never long without a wife. And children too. I know you, Elazar. You're not a person who can be alone."

Elazar frowned. "In general you are correct. But at the moment none of those things apply. I recently died in Gaza."

The tunnel dripped idly, the air heavy and damp. She had so many questions for him, but she already knew that she did not want his answers. There was only one thing she needed to know, and she could ignore it no longer. She entered the subject sideways, using hidden keys.

"And now you're doing—what is it? Making money out of computer code? How did you even learn computer code?"

A stupid question, of course. Everything in the world was learnable—languages, professions, technologies, skills that didn't yet exist. The only reason that curious and intelligent people didn't master it all was a simple lack of time. But Elazar's answer still surprised her.

"Programming is the most familiar thing I've ever done," he said. "Everything is about step-by-step instructions, with conditionals built in and no room for error." He switched languages again, breaking into her father's verse-chant: "For one who is exposed to a dead body, locate a red heifer without blemish, in which there is no defect and on which no yoke has been laid. If the heifer has been blemished or yoked, it may not be used. If the heifer is unblemished and unyoked, slaughter it in the priest's presence. Sprinkle its blood seven times toward the front of the sanctum . . ." He broke off the chant. "Honestly, coding is the same thing. Just with less blood."

The mention of blood sent a chill through her skin. The thought she had been avoiding now bored its way into her mind. She sat up and faced him. "What are you doing with Rocky?" she asked.

"Just helping a friend."

She glanced around the empty industrial tunnel and heard Rocky's voice in her head, with a strange metallic clarity: *A photo of me holding my photo ID.* She stared at Elazar. "You want to steal his identity."

Elazar sat up beside her. His eyebrows rose along with him. "Stealing identities really isn't something you can do with this system, unfortunately," he said. "The whole beauty of it is that everyone is anonymous."

Rachel looked around at the hideous tunnel and felt an old fear. She kept talking, to hide it. "He told me he got into it because his computer was ransomed three months ago. He assumed it was someone hired by his ex-wife. I'm thinking it wasn't."

Elazar sighed. "You really need to learn to let your children grow up, Rachel. Let them make their own mistakes. Like you did in Hamburg."

"I'm serious, Elazar." The anger rose, hot and shimmering and horribly familiar.

"How many children did you have that time? Twelve, right? Each one parked in a different city of the Hanseatic League, with a different branch of the business, your own little empire. Except for that one son who wanted to do things his own way. As I recall, he nearly ran the whole enterprise into the ground."

"Fuck off, Elazar." English was one of her favorite languages—the least poetic, the one where insults required no imagination at all.

Elazar seemed not to be listening. "Do you remember when he got a new influx of capital, the investor who came in at just the right moment and made a deal with him in Rotterdam, to save all of you from bankruptcy? A gift from on high, your husband called it, even if the incompetent son took the credit."

Rachel ignored him. "You're going to kill him and make it look natural, like a heart attack or a suicide, and then help yourself to his social security number. Or not even that. Maybe you'd kill him outright and then just sit through a prison sentence."

Now he was listening. "I want to point out that a few minutes ago, you called me a pessimist. Someone who expects the worst."

"Yes, I did. Because you are."

"But you're the one who now thinks that I'm about to murder your son."

"Is that so impossible? Is that something you've never done before?"

He stared at her, with palpable pain. She looked at him, then looked around the tunnel, their tunnel, their filthy, abandoned tunnel, their tunnel that led nowhere. Rage animated her, as it always had.

"Why are you here, Elazar? It isn't only because of me. You know I'm not going to stay with you."

Elazar cringed as though she had struck him. The color left his face. When he spoke, his voice was low and small, sorrow distilled into sound.

"Maybe it's still worth it to me, even if it doesn't last forever," he said. "Maybe you're still worth it to me. Maybe you're the only thing worth it to me."

His voice stirred something within her, something she had forgotten was there. But she steeled herself. "I know you, Elazar. That can't be all. You want something more."

Now he lifted his face to hers, stricken. "You think I would kill your *child*? Why in the world would I want to do that? Rachel, what are you doing to me?"

"You've killed all of my children," she seethed.

"I did the opposite," he said. "The only reason I'm here is because I wanted to help your child. That's all I've ever wanted, from the very beginning. I'm not a monster, Rachel. I'm just a man who understands you better than anyone else in the world. Perhaps even including God."

IT WAS AFTER ANTIOCH, about three hundred years in, that she discovered the horrible truth about herself and Elazar. Three hundred years in—which included five cities, six husbands, seventeen children, and five of her own deaths. The Romans, who had flayed her sixth and seventh sons alive for teaching Torah, had recently been replaced by people she thought of as new Romans, people who used the same roads and tax systems and plumbing and only differed in their execution methods. They had protested outside her ink and parchment shop in Antioch and finally torched the synagogue, along with her and many others, including her husband and children. She had woken up on the beach outside of Cilicia shortly before dawn, still wearing her old clothes, her face and skin as soft as a newborn baby's. In a rare coincidence, Elazar, his face also new, was lying beside her. She had never been happier to see him.

"Elazar," she whispered.

He hadn't woken yet, his mind still working its way from one life to another. He lay on his back in the sand under the dim light of a slowly brightening sky, still dressed in a filthy robe, surf rolling beyond his bare pale feet. His beard was grown in the way it was when they first met, centuries ago, a sparse boy's beard that barely covered his soft cheeks. She touched his face, surprised, again, to find herself elated, a thrum of beauty running through her renewed body, in rhythm with the rush of the ocean behind her, the steady eternal power of water wearing away land. The tide was coming in.

"Elazar."

He stirred, then awoke and bolted upright, jolted out of a nightmare. He let out a frightened, agonizing moan, his mind still inside the flames.

"Elazar, it's over," she said softly.

"Over," he whimpered, like a little boy, without registering her presence. She watched as his eyes focused on the waves, then on the shore, dragging his fingertips across the soft damp sand. He carefully raised a hand before his eyes and moved his fingers one by one until his jaw went slack with disappointment. He shook his hands violently in the air, willing his body away. Then he saw her.

"Rachel!"

He grabbed her, clutching her like a drowning man, kissing her as if only her mouth could quench his burnt body's thirst. She burned with thirst too, and kissed and kissed him until she collapsed on his shoulder, too worn to move or think. They listened to the waves until Elazar spoke.

"Each time I hope," he said, still holding her. "Every time I burn, I get through the pain by thinking that maybe this time will be different. Just now I opened my eyes and saw the sky and the sea, and I thought, here I am, finally, freed beyond the borders of this world. I don't know how many times I'll burn before I give up that hope. But you're more practical than I ever was. You probably don't even think of it anymore."

"I do," Rachel said quietly. "Sometimes I walk around for days still hoping. I wake up and wander through whatever desert or valley I've woken in and I tell myself, This is a test, I'm about to reach the gate of judgment, I just need to find the gate. I just need to walk a bit farther and I'll find the entrance to the next world, and someone will let me in." She inhaled salted air, her throat still burning. "And then I walk and walk and walk until the sun sets and rises again, and all that time I pretend that the earth beneath my feet isn't real. I only give up when the thirst and hunger take me. I suppose that's why we still feel them, the hunger and the thirst and the pain. To remind us."

He stroked her thick new hair and sighed, his breath soaked with sorrow. The weight of his hand on her hair comforted her more than she knew possible.

"What will you do now?" he asked. He avoided her eyes.

She, too, looked away. "Go back to Antioch, I think," she said. "My mother-in-law might still be there. And my husband's brother. He was on his way back from Damascus, so he's definitely alive. When they see I've survived, he'll marry me. In fact, I owe it to my husband, may his memory be a blessing." But already she knew she wouldn't go back.

Elazar stared at her. To her astonishment, his face was wide with pain. "Go back to Antioch?" he cried, his voice high with disbelief. "Are you insane? There's nothing left in Antioch now. It will take fifty years to rebuild, and by then everyone but us will be dead again. You know it and so do I."

"Then I'll go to Sura in Babylonia. My husband had another brother at the academy there." She spoke as though mumbling to herself, as she usually did on those days when she awakened alone—working through options, figuring out what was left, what would hurt the least.

"Rachel, Rachel, Rachel, Rachel—"

His voice rose and fell with the waves. In each repetition she imagined hearing a different man saying her name, a different husband or son. But now she could only hear that voice from the tunnel, the one that could see her light, the one that told her, long ago, that she was almost there.

"Why are you still fighting me, Rachel? Why do you keep marrying everyone but me?"

She shook her head, looking down at the sand. "Don't make me explain it, Elazar."

Elazar snorted. The noise took her by surprise, a catch in her throat. "That can't be why. I know he meant nothing to you."

"He was my husband."

"According to the scrolls."

The words stung. Suddenly she was a girl in her father's house again, running out the door with her father's documents, hair flying in the wind, about to be caught and bound. She steeled herself. "It doesn't matter whether he meant anything to me or not," she said. "He was an innocent person, and you weren't. I can't trust you, Elazar."

He took her hand in his. She let him, feeling the grit of sand beneath her legs with her soft new skin. How beautiful it was, not to be alone!

"I sinned, Rachel. I know it. I confess it. But now I've wandered for so long, and if I ever sinned, it was only for you. Rachel, it's been so many years. Can't you forgive me?"

She looked down at his fingers, then up at his face—the same face, always, as the rest of the world shifted and changed and burned and disappeared.

"Marry me, Rachel. I've waited for you for three hundred years. You're the only thing in the world that matters to me."

She said yes.

To her surprise Elazar wanted an actual wedding. The community in Cilicia was happy to provide for the two orphaned refugees, especially a young virgin marrying a descendant of the priests; there had been an epidemic in the city, and such a wedding could only bring good fortune to all who rejoiced in it. At Rachel's many weddings she had often missed her parents, even though the only wedding of hers that her parents had attended, her marriage to Zakkai, was the most miserable of all. At the other weddings, she always looked around at her young groom's young parents, his brothers and sisters and nieces and nephews and everyone else as she stood hennaed and veiled and battered on all sides by a relentless phalanx of other people's love, and each time, smothered in light and music, she endured a sudden and debilitating sorrow—aware, as she rarely was on ordinary days, of the bottomless void into which she had plunged, forever a girl falling through darkness, alone. But that night in Cilicia, she looked silently at Elazar's fresh and solemn face amid hundreds of oil lamps carried by strangers, and an unfamiliar wedding feeling rose up within her: pure, incandescent joy. Like a bride—was she really a bride?—she stood in awe of her new husband's radiance, watched the dancing strangers swirling around her through the night, and saw a boundless future.

After that, for years, every day and every night was luminous. They lived in tiny rooms and large villas, plush caravans and filthy hovels, above or behind one shop or another, poverty and wealth and ambition and sloth as irrelevant to them as they had been for centuries—but now every space they shared was full of light. For the first time ever they made love without hiding, stripping each other with a weird and intoxicating freedom. They walked through their rooms or alcoves naked, grabbing each other any time, lounging together for hours, for days. They laughed out loud about the children they would have together, the first since Yochanan, bracing themselves ecstatically for their liberty to crash down on their heads with the very first pregnancy and birth.

But then the babies did not come.

It made no sense. Her body worked as always; his did too. She went to the monthly women's baths in whatever town or city they chose to live in—for because of Yochanan, there were elaborate edifices of religious rituals and institutions and customs and laws that were nearly identical in every town or city they chose to live in, including women's baths and children's schools and prayer-houses and study-houses where people asked questions about the words her father copied, and homes full of people who said the same blessings and knew the same stories, each town or city an astonishing miniature portable Jerusalem, all thanks to Yochanan. She immersed herself naked each month on the appointed night in each town or city, each month hoping not to return, and each month returning again. After half a year the women who managed the baths would ambush her with advice, amulets, potions, portents. The other women in the town would follow, pulling her aside from her loom or her market stall to hand her magic herbs and whisper spells and prayers in her ears. A year or two of this was the limit of what she could endure. Then she and Elazar would move on, find another town or city or country, begin once more, try again. Elazar kept telling her to wait, and she kept waiting. Who minded waiting, he insisted, when they were so happy? Except that now she cried, and did not eat.

"Why are you crying? Why don't you eat?" he asked as he held her, stripped her bare, ran his lips along her shoulders, cocooned her in his arms. "Aren't I worth more to you than ten sons? You've already had ten sons!"

She kissed him back, fighting tears. She ate, though there seemed no reason to bother—unless this were some kind of test. Perhaps she needed to try harder, to live more, to eat and dance and run and sing, or simply to love him more fully. And so she tried. Because wasn't there always a chance that things would change?

After seventy years they could deny it no longer. They had discovered the final price of the vow.

By then they were living in Pumbedita in Babylonia, and Elazar was teaching at the academy, despite Rachel's protests that they ought never to take on tasks where people might remember them. It had happened almost by accident. When they first arrived, selling dry goods and treats in the marketplace, a group of scholars stopped by their stall for a snack, debating the day's texts as they munched on roasted nuts.

"When you ask why the Temple was destroyed, you have to admit that it was because the people neglected to observe the Sabbath," said one of the scholars to the others, bits of nuts lodged in his beard.

"No, the Temple was destroyed because the people neglected to teach their children Torah," countered another.

"No, the Temple was destroyed because of causeless hatred, infighting among the people," said a third.

Elazar cleared his throat. "Actually, the Temple was destroyed because of the enemy's superior weaponry."

Rachel kicked him under the counter. The three scholars stared at him, derision in their eyes.

"What would you know?" the first scholar sneered. "You're selling dry goods."

"Yes, dry goods," Elazar said. He looked around the stall and removed a single twig from a bundle of dry-leafed herbs. "When most fragrant plants burn, the incense clouds dissipate low in the air, which is good if you only want people to smell it," he said. The scholars exchanged glances, silently agreeing to indulge a fool. "But what if it isn't for people? What if you need the fragrance to ascend straight up, to offer its beauty on high?" Elazar touched the tip of the plant to the fire under the stall's cooking pot, and then held it upright before them. Their eyes followed the thin dark plume of smoke as it ascended higher than they could see, inscribing the sky like ink on parchment. "This is ma'aleh ashan, the only plant that can produce this effect for an incense offering," Elazar told the gaping men. "I'd sell it to you, but what's the point? It's been four hundred years since anyone needed any." He snuffed out the flame, dropped the plant in the dust, and returned to adding up receipts.

Rachel kicked him again, to no avail. He began teaching at the academy the following day. Soon she too was teaching—hosting students in their home, debating with them over meals, reminded daily of her father, and of Zakkai. But then more years passed, many students came and went, and nothing changed.

One hot summer night with a fat full moon, the two of them lay outside, escaping the heat on a raised stone path above the muddy bank of the Euphrates. The little oil lamp at her side was hardly necessary in the brilliant light of paired moons, one suspended in the sky and one reflected in the ink-dark river. She had told him, during the fast day earlier that week and during the days that followed, that she was going to leave. Without him.

"Please don't," he said to the sky. He turned to her, their faces silvered, inhuman. "I know you want children. All women want children. But the world is full of children who need parents. The students adore you. You want younger ones? Take in orphans. Or open a school for girls. Some people might disapprove, but—"

"It isn't because of the children," she said. Or lack of children, she thought, though each child they didn't have stood perfectly vivid in her mind, alive and breathing, as clear and imaginary as a reflected moon. But then she looked at Elazar and knew, more profoundly and painfully than she had ever known anything, that that wasn't the reason.

"Of course it is," he muttered. She could hear the edge in his voice. The evening breeze had ceased. The night air hung immobile, stagnant and oppressive even by the water; the Babylonian river smelled of urine and sweat. She untied the linen scarf on her head, letting her long braid fall like a rope on her shoulder.

"No, Elazar," she said simply. She meant it. "The problem isn't the children. The children we don't have are a just a sign of something else. The problem is us."

Elazar's eyes grew wide. He spoke quickly, hoping to hide his fear. "You won't be happy with someone else, at least not for long. You know that, Rachel. With anyone else your life is just a lie. But with me—"

"With you nothing grows."

"We grow. Our—our love grows."

Already she could feel the fire within her, spreading. "No, we don't, Elazar. That's the problem. We don't grow. We're like an old book, full of stories and also full of errors, and no one can completely understand us, even though many people try. But the problem is that we don't change. Only the people around us change."

He turned toward her, sitting up on the stone slab. As she sat up to face him, she suddenly saw his mouth shift, contorted, anger flaming through his eyes. "But Rachel, can't you see it? This is a blessing!"

She stared at him. "A blessing?"

"Yes, a blessing! The only blessing you and I have ever had!" His face blazed. "Think of everything you've suffered, Rachel. Think of the worst, the absolute worst moments of the past four hundred years. You know what each and every one of them is: when one of your children dies."

Rachel felt her skin tingling, the first pricks of pain before the fullness of the burn. She twisted the end of her braid in her hand.

"Just think of the most recent ones. That beautiful brilliant girl in Antioch, the one who had just been betrothed—what was her name? Hannah, named after your mother, right? And the oldest boy, Azaria, named after your father—the one with the baby twins? Think of every day you spent with them, every laugh, every kiss, every meal you made them, every time they were ill and you stayed up with them through the night, every time they recited back your father's verses—and for what?"

"Stop it, Elazar."

"Those recent ones were worse than usual, because they died young. But were they really worse? Maybe the ones before them were worse! Maybe the Hannah before that one, the one who lived to be older than your mother, the one you taught to read, the one who didn't want to learn? Or the Azaria before that, the one you barely had to teach because he was so obsessive about every last letter on his own, the one who became the head of the academy, with three generations of students! Oh, your father would have loved him. How proud the old master scribe would have been of Azaria number four! And how proud you were yourself! But you buried him too, even if he didn't know it."

"Elazar, stop."

"I don't even care how old the child is when it happens. He could be a day-old baby, he could be a hundred and twenty years old, but no matter what, that child is going to die, and you're going to endure it. And it happens every time, Rachel. Every time."

"Elazar, stop."

"*Why should I stop, Rachel?* Why should I stop when our lives don't? You think it hasn't happened to me too? You think I don't care about each and every one of those children and wives?"

Rachel winced, a physical revulsion. "I didn't think you did," she said.

"I try to protect myself by caring less. But I've held every baby. I've kissed every girl's hair. I've taught the alphabet to every boy. I've lain with all their mothers—and not just lain with them, but lived with them, Rachel. I watched them cry and laugh and age and wither. I saw every child grow up; I saw the lucky ones grow old. And I watched every single one of them die."

To her astonishment his eyes were glassed with tears. He paused, ashamed.

"It will never stop happening, Rachel. Every single child you ever have, whether it's next spring or ten thousand years from now—with every single child, you are going to watch that child die. And your husbands and lovers too. All of them. Think of all the unbearable pain still ahead of you! The burnings don't even compare." He paused again, regaining his breath. "But look how we've been blessed! Now we have a way out! God has blessed us, Rachel! Stay with me, Rachel, and never suffer through that! Never again! It's a blessing, Rachel! Can't you see that? Choose life, Rachel, and stay with me!"

He reached for her, his lips parted. In the reflection of his eyes she saw a dark and bottomless void.

She rose to her feet, holding the oil lamp aloft in one hand. In her other hand she held her long dark braid.

"I will miss you, Elazar," she said. Then she dipped the end of her braid into the flame.

"RACHEL!"

Before he could scramble to his feet she had already taken flight.

The flames spread as she ran with the river at her back, her hair and clothes and skin igniting until she became a pillar of fire flying through the night. She usually screamed, usually heard herself scream, but this time she used the breath she still had to keep running—running and running without stopping, because there was no stopping, nothing ever stopped, nothing ever ended but that meant that she could believe with perfect faith that there was always something more to come, something waiting for her, some reason for living. She was a pillar of fire rising up to the sky. She heard screams and thought they were her own, but her throat was scorched and the screams were Elazar's, Elazar screaming behind her as he gained on her, reaching for her, pulling her down from the sky and throwing himself on top of her, plunging her back down onto the dark soft earth. By then she was already gone.

When she awoke, the moon was still full. But she was in a forest full of trees of a kind she had never seen before—tall thick trees with leaves that changed colors and shed like children's teeth, sloughed off like old fingernails or callused skin, in a place she later learned was Europe.

Two more centuries passed before he found her again. But he came back to her, and she to him. Because she always did.

CHAPTER

8

ABUNDANCE

. . .

@highpriest

#EternalLife =extremely overrated. You do realize that for all that time, you have to live with yourself. Is this something you really want?

@DrTitus

Yes, #EternalLife is devastating. FOR IDIOTS. But what about scientists who would have more time to improve the world? Big picture, please!

@highpriest

.@DrTitus Improve the world? For whom? Our infinite children? Here's your big picture: they do NOT want us around for #EternalLife

@DrTitus

.@highpriest Maybe yours don't. But I hear time heals all wounds...Have you tried therapy? I know it's time-consuming, but hey: #EternalLife

@highpriest

.@DrTitus After 2000 years she still doesn't love me like I love her. In a normal lifespan I might not have noticed. #EternalLife's a bitch

@DrTitus

.@highpriest Give her time to come around. She will...eventually! ☻

@poncedeleon

.@highpriest Um, maybe it's time to move on? 2000 yrs seems like long enough to get over your ex. We're talking about the human future here

@highpriest

.@poncedeleon I waited for her for 300 years once. It worked out then. But with #EternalLife, there's no happily ever after. You can't win.

@poncedeleon

.@highpriest Your problem is your attitude. Life isn't about winning. It's about the adventure. I say bring it on! #EternalLife

@highpriest

.@poncedeleon Yes, it's about the adventure! 17 expulsions, 5 beheadings, 12 of my kids gassed to death. Bring it on...and on... #EternalLife

@poncedeleon

.@highpriest Plenty of time to find the silver lining, though, right? #EternalLife

@highpriest

.@poncedeleon Silver lining...silver lining...OK, here's one. Once a Grand Inquisitor tried to flay me to death. Epic fail!

@DrTitus

.@highpriest Everything happens for a reason. What doesn't kill u makes u stronger. Build character! God has a plan for you! #EternalLife

@highpriest

.@DrTitus God definitely has a plan for me. That's exactly my problem. #EternalLife

"Is Rocky home?"

The voice startled Rachel. She had sat down on the staircase in her house's front hall with her head dipped toward her phone, engrossed in what appeared to be an endless loop of uncomfortable truths in 140 characters or less. She was so immersed that just looking up felt like being yanked into another life. A woman she had never seen before was standing in front of her, pulling her front door closed. Rachel wondered if she might be dreaming.

"I rang the bell a few times, but no one answered. I was going to leave, but I saw you through the window, sitting right here, and I thought, maybe I can try the door. It was open." The woman spoke with an accent that Rachel could not immediately place.

Rachel stood up quickly and stuffed her phone into her pocket, still bewildered. She felt as though she were the one who had just entered a strange house. She noticed that the woman did not apologize. Rachel did.

"I'm sorry, I suppose I'm so old that I'm going deaf," she said.

She was relieved when the stranger laughed. The old-lady card always worked with young people. But this woman, Rachel now noticed, was hardly young. She wore a leather jacket and a colorful scarf, and as she unwound the scarf Rachel saw that her face looked slightly worn around the mouth and eyes, as though she were in her late forties or so, Rachel guessed. The woman was short, almost as short as Rachel, with thick black wavy hair that showed the slightest shadows of gray roots. Her skin was a dusky color, similar to Rachel's. *My general racism regarding tan people*, Rachel heard Rocky say in her head. But what was most remarkable about the woman was her smile. Her teeth were far from perfect, but they were large and white, and she smiled with a sincerity that Rachel couldn't remember seeing in anyone over thirty, at least not since her most recent husband's death. The house's cold front hall seemed warmed by the woman's presence. In the space of seconds, Rachel forgot that this stranger had just barged into her home.

"I'm looking for Rocky. I mean Rachmiel," the woman corrected herself, pronouncing the guttural exactly. The accent was Israeli, Rachel realized. But what was this about *Rachmiel*? She hadn't heard a stranger say his real name aloud in years, not since that last bail hearing. Catastrophic scenarios ran through her mind, as they always did when Rocky was involved. Was this woman with the IRS? "Is he home?" the woman asked again.

"No, he's in court," Rachel said.

Immediately she knew that this was a mistake, a typical mother mistake. Why did thousands of years of being a mother do absolutely nothing to help her avoid these mistakes? She thought of adding to

Elazar's online feed: *#EternalLife: the more you live, the less you learn.* "I mean, I'm not sure where he is," she said.

The woman laughed again. "I know he's in court. He should be back soon. May I come in?"

Rachel was still bewildered. IRS agents probably don't laugh much, she reassured herself. But how did the woman know about the court date? And hadn't she initially called him Rocky? Rachel wondered how to answer, but she soon saw that her answer was irrelevant. The woman took off her coat and hung it in the closet herself.

"I'm sorry, what did you say your name was?" Rachel asked.

With her coat off, the woman was thinner than Rachel had previously noticed. The woman laughed for the third time. She was like a living laugh, with a body attached to it. "I never said my name. Meirav. Very nice to meet you." She stuck out a hand, a gesture that seemed theatrical, as though she felt such gestures were absurd, or as if she were playing a part. Rachel took the hand, which was warm and strong in hers.

"My name is Rachel," she said carefully, and hesitated before adding: "I'm Rocky's mother."

The woman smiled. "Oh yes," she said. "He mentioned that his mother had moved in with him."

Rachel pretended to cough, to avoid choking.

"You look so young, you could be his sister," the woman said cheerfully as Rachel gagged. Then she added, "Do you need a glass of water?"

Rachel swallowed. "No thank you," she said, feigning lightness. Maybe this woman wasn't from the IRS, Rachel thought. Maybe she was FBI. In either case, Rachel told herself, better to cooperate. "I'm fine," Rachel announced. "Please, come sit down." The invitation was irrelevant. The woman had already strolled into Rachel's living room, plopping into what had been Rachel's husband's chair. What was her name again? Meirav, Rachel reminded herself. It was an old name, and an even older word, old enough for Rachel to remember it from her father's scrolls. *Abundance*. Would an Israeli work for the FBI? "Can I get you anything?" Rachel asked. Meirav shook her head, but Rachel understood that this too was irrelevant. Surely if Meirav had wanted anything, she would have helped herself.

"The court is really backed up today. I almost didn't get out myself this morning," Meirav said, twirling a finger in her hair.

"You were there?" Rachel asked.

Meirav smiled. "Sure. Where do you think we met?"

Rachel stared at her. Everything about her seemed unreal. "You work at the court?"

Meirav laughed out loud. "I wish! No, I'm just being punished for a bad marriage, like everybody else." She sat completely relaxed in Rachel's husband's chair, slouched on an armrest like one of Rachel's children. Was this some kind of cover story? "It's actually a very good place to meet people. It's like a singles bar over there. Everyone is sitting forever, just looking at each other. In the waiting room where we are, they don't even let you use your phone. It's like an existentialist play."

This time Rachel smiled. If Meirav was an FBI agent, she was at least a pleasant one. "Which is it, a singles bar or an existentialist play?"

"They really aren't so different," Meirav said. Her smile felt familiar, as if Rachel had known her for years. Rachel had to remind herself that this woman had just broken into her house. "Your son is my favorite character in this existentialist play," she said. "He's made it all bearable. Rocky is just that kind of person, isn't he? The kind of person who lightens everyone's burdens. Everyone ought to know at least one person like that. Of course, I don't have to tell you. You know better than anyone."

Rachel wondered briefly if the woman had the wrong house. Or was she just undercover, and doing a lousy job? *The kind of person who lightens everyone's burdens*? "So how is your case coming along?" Rachel asked, as a test.

Meirav let out a snort, a dismissive noise that made Rachel suddenly like her, though she could not fathom why. "It's just some silly things to work out with my ex-husband. It isn't worth explaining." Rachel suspected that it was worth explaining, but didn't ask. She was still enjoying Meirav's dismissive snort, which returned, twice. "We're already divorced in Israel. It's complicated."

Rachel was confused. "Do you—do you live in Israel, or here?"

"Both. I've mostly been here for the past year or so. My mother was born in America, so it isn't hard for me to move back and forth. Maybe I'll go back sometime soon. Or maybe not. I'm not a person who likes to plan too much," she said. "Life's about the adventure, isn't it?"

"Sure," Rachel muttered, and thought of the feed on her phone. *Bring it on*. She tried to change the subject, to test how deep the story went. "Do your parents still live there?"

"My crazy mother, yes. My father died thirty years ago. Actually more than thirty years ago now. In the Lebanon War."

"I'm sorry," Rachel murmured. But she was doing math in her head; she was terrible with dates, but something didn't add up. If it was a cover story, it was, as Rocky would say, piss-poor. "You said—in the Lebanon War? Your father? But aren't you—"

Meirav laughed again. Even death is funny to this woman, Rachel marveled. "You don't need to guess my age," Meirav said. "I'm fifty-two. And you're right, it's strange, because he was the same age I am now. He was in his very last year in the reserves, which went past fifty for men back then. He used to joke about it. Like, 'Don't worry, Meirav, I still have one more year, I can still get killed, and then you can go to university for free!' Because in Israel they have all these government benefits for war orphans."

This seemed like a higher level of improbable detail than a fake story would include, Rachel reflected. She felt vaguely reassured. "Of course, I didn't appreciate what it really meant until I had my own children," Meirav was saying. "Children are a gift from God, right? Why? Because they're so wonderful? Honestly, they aren't so wonderful. They're a gift because they give us permission to fail. Because then we can at least imagine we've done something for the future, and we can die without thinking about what we haven't done."

Rachel pondered this, but Meirav had already lost interest. She stood up suddenly and began strolling around the room. She was the kind of person who did not know how to sit still, Rachel noticed. Like Rocky. Rachel rose and followed her, watching her as she inspected the various family photos on the walls and shelves. Suddenly Meirav laughed out loud again.

"This isn't Rocky's house," she said.

Rachel hesitated, trying not to make another mistake. "You've come to the right place," she said carefully.

Meirav was still laughing. "I know he lives here. But this is your house. You didn't move in with him. He moved in with you."

Rachel opened her mouth to protest, but Meirav waved her off. "No man would have this many pictures of children and grandchildren on the walls. Also, what's this? Your wedding photo? No, not his house. But is this his father? Rocky looks more like you, except he's so pale."

Rachel glanced at her dead husband, who had given up hope in Rocky long ago. "And he wouldn't have childhood photos of himself, either," Meirav said. She pointed at a portrait of Rocky at age ten with his brother and sisters, his wiry hair slicked back with some hair cream product that was no longer sold. Every time Rachel saw the photograph, she could still feel the hair cream on her hands, running her fingers through ten-year-old Rocky's hair, hair that was as unmanageable as he was. The interval from then until now was more than meaningless; it didn't exist. Years upon years lay before her in every moment. *It goes by so fast*, she heard every parent "her age" say in her mind. If only.

Meirav smiled and turned to Rachel. "It's sweet, isn't it?" she asked.

"What's sweet?"

"That he told me it was his house. He wanted to impress me. Don't you love that?"

I don't love lying, Rachel was about to say, until she realized that was a lie. Lying was what made her life possible. Instead she said, "Rocky has always been an inventive person."

Meirav grinned. "So am I," she said.

As Rachel tried to guess what that might mean, she heard Rocky slam the back door. He typically stopped at the refrigerator, already groaning about whatever had just happened wherever he had just been, but he must have seen Meirav's car outside. Clearly he was expecting her, because he was in the living room in seconds.

"Well, hello," he said, his voice deeper than Rachel had ever heard it. Rachel grinned. Suddenly he was a teenager again, except that he was a grandfather. The distinction between teenager and adult seemed trivial to Rachel. In fact she recalled many centuries when that particular distinction didn't exist at all. It *was* trivial, she thought, along with the distinction between birth and death. Everything and everyone blew through the world, leaves carried on wind. Did everything matter, or was everything an outrageous waste of time?

"Sorry I'm late. Mom, this is—"

"We've met." Meirav smiled. "Your mother is lovely, and she has a lovely home."

Rocky purpled, then glared at Rachel. But Meirav was laughing. "Come, let's go. I'm starving," she said.

Was Meirav who she said she was? Or was she some sort of

agent, human or divine? Either way, Rocky smiled. Rachel watched as they left together. She waved goodbye and then turned back to her phone.

@highpriest

#EternalLife: I will love her until the end of time. Every man on earth will tell her that, but I am the only one who will ever mean it.

Oh, Elazar.

CHAPTER

9

EXCEPTIONS

. . .

"How old are you, Gram?" Hannah asked as rain poured down outside.

The children would be eating soon in Rachel's kitchen, and then Daniel would pick them up after Hannah left for a conference. Rachel's house had become a tavern again, just as it had been long ago, somewhere else. Rachel didn't mind. In fact, she preferred being with children when their parents weren't present: grandchildren and grandparents got along so well, Rachel knew, because they had a common enemy. But Hannah was the exception to agreeable grandchildren, and Hannah was insistent. Rachel immediately felt uneasy, and continued chopping carrots with an unexpected vengeance. She ignored the question until Hannah asked again.

"How old are you, Gram?"

"Forever twenty-one, right?" Rachel said with a forced grin. "I'm assuming this is a joke."

Hannah finished setting the table and sat down in what was once her father's seat, her narrow body taut against the table's edge. "Seriously, Gram. When's your birthday?"

"You know I don't let anyone celebrate my birthday," Rachel said. "So you better not be planning anything for me."

"Your passport says you were born on July 4, 1934. Happy birthday Gramerica! The fireworks are a party just for you."

Rachel glanced at Hannah mid-chop, still holding her knife. "What are you doing with my passport?"

Hannah laughed. "Gram, you're the world's most paranoid person."

"There's a lot of competition for that," Rachel muttered.

"I'm not doing anything with your passport. I just remember seeing it once."

"Well, there's your answer then. Thank you, federal government, for clearing up the mystery of my birth. Though I'm not sure why you're asking me, if you already know."

"I'm asking you because you have the genetic deterioration of a teenager."

Rachel stopped breathing. She looked at her own hands as she put the knife down on the counter. What Hannah had just said could mean almost anything, she told herself. *Stupid girl!* her mother shouted in her head. She breathed again, slowly, and asked, "The genetic what?"

"You have the genetic deterioration of a teenager, Gram."

Rachel turned toward Hannah as slowly as she could. With intense effort, she made her voice light, carefree. "What in the world does that mean?" she asked. "And how would you know anything about my genetic anything?"

Hannah colored. "Dad helped me out," she said quietly.

"What are you talking about? Helped you out with what?"

"With taking a sample."

Rachel shuddered. "A sample of what?"

"DNA," Hannah said.

"Excuse me?"

"You didn't want to give me any, so we—we took it."

Fire seared through Rachel's veins. "You *took* it? How is that even possible? What did you do, come into my room at night and suck my blood?"

Hannah shrugged, though Rachel could see that the nonchalance was a ploy. "I just had Dad take some hair out of your hairbrush. He found some nail clippings too. Bathrooms are a veritable fountain of DNA."

Rachel's skin crawled. "So you stole little dead pieces of me, and now you magically know everything about my genes." As she spoke, an unfamiliar wisp of wonder crossed her mind: are those pieces of me really dead?

"Well, I don't know everything, because nobody knows everything. But did you know you're ninety-eight percent Middle Eastern?"

What's the other two percent? Rachel wondered, and thought of Elazar's green eyes.

"Anyway, that's not what's extraordinary about you."

The tide of Rachel's panic rose, blood rushing through her body the way it did before she burned. She brandished sarcasm as armor. "Thanks," she sneered. "I like to think I'm extraordinary because of things I've achieved in my life, rather than because of what you discovered in my fingernails. But I never achieved anything that extraordinary, so I guess we just have to go with the nail clippings."

Hannah wasn't listening. "I mean, the Middle Eastern thing actually is pretty remarkable, because ninety-eight percent of anything just isn't a number you see when it comes to genetic ancestry. Plus, Dad seems to think your parents came from some dump in Poland."

"That's a rather rude way to put it."

"That was how Dad described it, not me. Supposedly it was how you described it to him."

In fact, it was how Hirshl described it, Rachel remembered, two husbands before Rocky's father. *Rucheleh, let's get out of this dump*. Elazar was right, Hirshl was a fool; of all the people to marry, why had she married him? Then again, getting out of Poland was the only good idea Hirshl had ever had. If only Elazar had thought of it. "I doubt I ever said that," Rachel replied. "In all likelihood it was a dump, by your standards. But I wouldn't know. I've never been there."

This was a dodge, and an ineffective one at that. Hannah wasn't having it. "What's extraordinary about you is your deterioration," Hannah announced. "I mean, your lack of deterioration. According to your genes, you're about eighteen years old. What do you think of that, Gram?"

Rachel's throat ran dry, as though she were a well in a drought. She turned on the faucet to rinse off the knife and thought of the drought in the year before she met Elazar, the dusty ground pitted at last with late rain. She thought of skins filled with water, sheepskin against bare wet skin, water in an ancient tunnel rushing against her feet, liquid heat between her legs, a thirsty baby's tiny mouth latching to her breast. She thought of Yochanan.

"What do you think of that?" Hannah asked again.

"I think you've got your test tubes mixed up," Rachel said.

Hannah smirked. "I thought so too. I even wondered if Dad had some new teenage girlfriend who messed up your bathroom. That's why I came back with him myself and took more samples. We did it three times. We analyzed them all. This is you, Gram." She drew in her breath, gathering words. "And it's—there's just no other way to describe it: it's a medical miracle. You're a medical miracle, Gram."

Rachel scrambled mentally, keeping her face still. Then she shrugged just as Hannah had shrugged, neither one meaning it. "Well, then I guess I'm a medical miracle," she said. "What can I say, everyone is special in their own special way."

Hannah narrowed her eyes, and resembled her father. "Special in their own special—what the hell is that?"

"I think it was something your son told me about twenty minutes ago, before he went downstairs. He told me he learned today in kindergarten that everyone is special in their own special way." Rachel spoke quickly, like a demented person, running on a tightrope across an abyss. "When I was a child, we didn't have those kinds of educational opportunities where we could learn how special we were. So instead of learning that in kindergarten, I get to learn it from you. Now, thanks to you, I know that I'm especially special. With especially special nail clippings."

Hannah stared at her. "Holy crap, Gram. Are you making fun of me?"

"I'm making fun of the idea that you can learn anything worthwhile about who I am by raiding my bathroom. While you were in there, did you find my lithium prescription?"

"You're on lithium?"

"Clearly you're doing a lousy job of looking. I hear bathrooms are a veritable fountain of detritus from other people's lives. Look harder and you'll find all your father's meds too. The man could run a dispensary for Adderall."

Hannah pressed her hands down on the table in front of her, like a defendant in court. "Okay, Gram, I get it. You're mad at me. I'm sorry," she said. Each phrase was a stingy concession. "But I can't ignore this. I mean, I know you're not miraculously eighteen years old. But whatever's really going on with you, it's—it's something that could change everything we thought we knew about biology. I'm going to have to bring you in for more testing. The lab has to—"

Rachel slammed the knife down on the cutting board, making Hannah jump. "Stop it, Hannah!"

Hannah paled, and Rachel felt instantly sorry, the way she always did when a child showed fear. But she kept her voice firm, and turned toward her grandchild, her favorite grandchild, the one she loved.

"Hannah, I'm an old, old woman, and it has taken me a long time to learn what I know," Rachel said. "And I know that no matter what Google thinks, I do not have a lot of time left in this family. And I do not have time for this shit."

Hannah nodded, chastened—or more likely, she simply decided she was better off biding her time. She rose and went downstairs to get her children. And Rachel turned back toward the sink, chopping away at the cutting board like a slave chipping through a mountain for years upon years, so that no one would see her crying.

As soon as Daniel took the children home, Rachel rushed to the tunnel, in a panic that felt more than familiar. Elazar was waiting for her when she arrived, holding open the door as she sprang from the car, barely remembering to pull the gate closed behind her. It wounded her that he was right. *You need me. You just don't know it yet.* When the door closed behind her, words ran out of her in torrents.

"My God, my God, my God, Elazar!" she gasped, after she had explained it as best she could. She wondered briefly if Elazar understood, then knew that was foolish. Elazar always understood. "Elazar, what are the odds that *my granddaughter* is the one doing this research? My granddaughter, of all the people in the entire world?"

"The odds of that are exactly one hundred percent," Elazar said. He took her hands in his, pulling her down to the dirty floor. The damp air between them comforted her. "Eventually everything will happen to us. You know that, Rachel. Your job is to never be surprised."

Rachel felt her breathing slow as his hands warmed hers. She said, "No, my job is to keep her from dying."

"Good luck with that," Elazar smirked.

"I don't mean from dying someday. I mean—I mean from knowing. You know exactly what I mean, Elazar."

Elazar knew.

A century and a half earlier, as they lay naked together one evening in fading lamplight, newly and briefly together once more, she had told him about the first Hannah—the angry Hannah, the Hannah she had killed. He had stared at her, horrified. Long and terrible moments passed before he could speak.

I killed three of my sons, he finally said that night. *The same way.*

She had looked at him, washed with pain.

The first time was in Byzantium, he said. *I needed to show him. You know what that's like, needing to show them. I had held back so many times. But that night I tried to show him, just like you did, with fire. And he—he—*

She stopped him. *You don't have to tell me*, she said. *It was an accident, Elazar.*

I thought that, too, Elazar said. *I told myself that for hundreds of years. But then it happened again recently. Only eighty years ago. With a pistol.*

A pistol? She had tried a gun once herself, one night when a drunk army officer had passed out in her tavern near Krakow. She took his revolver out to the empty alley behind the tavern, checked the loaded bullets, and put the barrel in her mouth, pointing up toward her brain. She felt like one of her own little boys, shouting "Bang." The sound was deafening, and there was a great deal of blood. But by the time the neighbors came out to see what had happened, she was already back inside, her bloody shirt and headscarf changed, and the gun back in the drunk man's holster.

A pistol would do nothing to you, Rachel pointed out. *You might not even wake up somewhere else.*

Exactly. But it would prove something to him, Elazar said. His voice had dropped. *Or at least that's what I thought. I told him beforehand. Of course he didn't believe me. I made him promise to watch while I proved it. But he—it was as if he couldn't. He wrestled the gun out of my hands, and when I tried to take it back from him, he fell, and the latch was loose, and—*

Elazar swallowed, blinking. *It was an accident, I told myself over and over that it was an accident*, he continued. *But then I couldn't stop thinking about what happened in Byzantium. And in Spain, in Cordoba. Especially in Cordoba*, he said. *In Cordoba it happened differently, but the ending was the same.*

Rachel's skin crawled. *What happened?* she made herself ask.

I decided to come back, he said. *Just one time. Just once.*

Rachel thought of all the times she had considered coming back—to burn and return, not merely to see what had become of those she had left behind, but to reveal herself to them, to prove it. But there had always been a reason to leave, some terrible reason to give her children the freedom of her death. And all that returning would have given her, in the end, was the opportunity to see more of her children die. The deepest truth was that she had never wanted to come back. But she wasn't Elazar.

I had a reason, he said, as if expecting her to object. Rachel didn't object.

I had been burned at the stake there by the Inquisition, he began. *It was a public event, in front of a crowd. It's amazing how much crowds enjoy that sort of thing.*

Rachel nodded. She knew.

They had my son right beside me, and they would have burned him too, except that he agreed to pray to their god, or whatever it was they wanted then. He was smart, a scribe, like your father, Elazar said. *He had consulted with scholars about it, about whether it was better to be martyred or to simply pretend. He had the idea that he could fake it.*

He sounds like you, Rachel said with a smile.

But he saw that I had chosen to burn instead of convert, Elazar said. *I could see in his face how betrayed he felt. I thought, he's going to live his life thinking I'm angry at him, or that he disappointed me. I just wanted to spare him that.*

I woke up in another part of the country; it took me weeks to come home. I went to his house where he was living with his family. It was nighttime.

I woke him up, and he was stunned. He kept screaming, "Papa, papa!" like he was a child. I wanted to explain everything to him, but he was hardly awake more than a moment when four soldiers and an Inquisitor burst into the room. It was a walled city, I had entered just before the gates closed at dusk, and someone had recognized me at the gate and followed me. They said it was witchcraft, that I was a devil, they arrested all of us—me, my son, his whole family—and they burned us all alive, though this time it was a private burning, just before the soldiers and the priest. Then I had nothing, there was nothing left to lose. I don't know what you would have done then.

The same thing we always do, Rachel said softly.

That time I couldn't, Elazar said. *I had to go back and kill those soldiers and that priest.*

Rachel heard the anger in Elazar's voice, the familiar anger, the fire within him that was so much more powerful than hers. In centuries she had never dreamed of killing.

I came back to the city again, this time just looking for those five men. But when I finally arrived, I learned that the priest and the soldiers' company had left on a campaign against the Moors, a battle the Moors won. They never came back. And then in the city there was a plague, bodies piled in the streets. Rachel, are you listening?

Rachel was listening, present, witnessing.

All of these things by themselves, they mean nothing, right? Elazar tried. His voice caught, and she heard the boy within him. *Accidents, those times with the fire and the gun. And in Cordoba it wasn't even my fault, was it? All three of them, those three sons, their deaths were just coincidental disasters. It's just my restlessness that makes each son remind me of the others. When you live like we do, everything seems connected to everything else, everything reminds you of something.*

And everyone reminds you of someone, Rachel thought.

I've told myself that it all meant nothing, for hundreds of years. Just three dead sons out of so many others, three coincidences, three moments of meaningless misfortune, Elazar said. *But I didn't know it had also happened to you.*

Suddenly the full veil of horror lifted as Rachel understood.

They can't see it, she whispered. She swallowed wonder. *We can tell them all we want, but they can't see it. It's like the verse my father copied: No man shall see me and live.*

Elazar snorted, a shadow of the noise she remembered hearing from him long ago. *You're not God*, he said.

But I'm not human either, she told him. *Not anymore. And neither are you.*

Now Elazar looked at her, his eyes in the industrial tunnel hardened into steel. His voice was cold.

"You need to leave them," Elazar said. "Immediately. Don't say goodbye."

CHAPTER

10

DO UNTO OTHERS

. . .

What does a mother think of when she thinks of her first child—especially a child who has grown up, even grown old? For a first child is more than just a child. Other children get to be blessings, gifts, burdens, even, occasionally, people. But a first child is something else: a witness, an opportunity and, above all, a test.

Does she imagine that child as he once was, a small soft animal sucking at her breast, or red-faced and screaming and spewing hot tears, or curled up in his cradle like a baby bird enfolded in an egg? Does she imagine him as a boy, hunched over a scroll with a finger resting on a letter, his dark curly hair hanging over his eyes like a curtain between him and the world? Does she imagine him taller, head cocked back, smirking as he challenges the grownups with his new deep voice? Does she imagine him bald, with sagging jowls, surrounded by his devoted students, his voice rough and worn as he teaches, heavy eyebrows above eyes that still burn with an inner fire? Are each of those people hidden inside the old man whose body lies in a coffin, each previous person contained within the one that succeeded it like nesting sarcophagi, so that she might open each lid and find each person's predecessor, the person who died before he did? Does she have the imagination to think of him beyond the body that contained him, to think of some essence of the person that exists beyond the baby, the boy, the man, the corpse?

Or does she not think of him at all, but of herself, and wonder whether she passed the test?

WITNESSING YOCHANAN'S RECOVERY was like watching time flow backward, dry bones restored to life. First the little boy's breathing calmed; then he swallowed water, then goat's milk, then a bit of porridge, then bread. In days the sores on his skin healed; then his color returned. In a week Rachel held his hands as he shakily rose to his feet, and Rachel felt the power flowing from her body into his. Within a month Yochanan was singing his grandfather's verses again as he ran away from her, forcing her to chase him through the streets as he screeched nonsensically: "I place before you the blessing and THE CURSE, THE CURSE, THE CURSE!" She cursed him, laughed at him, immersed herself in the ritual bath of cold rainwater, her naked skin shocked and shivering and alive as her shorn head broke through the water's surface. Rivers of living water ran down her back. Zakkai went to the Temple and bowed before God, offering sacrifice after sacrifice of thanksgiving. Rachel went to the Temple and delivered a blank scroll for the high priest's son. At sunset she raced to the tunnel, her bare feet dancing through rushing water as she climbed further into the mountain. She imagined throwing herself into his arms, joy overflowing. But when Elazar arrived, she held her breath.

She had forgotten about his shaven head. He came around the tunnel's corner with his beard still sparse, his head covered with a weak shadow of dark down. In the dim light of his lamp, she saw his bare skull and touched her fingers to the thin skin of her own shorn scalp. A dense silence hung suspended between them, the pulse of the world interrupted. Rachel looked at Elazar and saw not her lover but a living corpse.

"He—he survived," Rachel whispered, when she finally spoke. "Yochanan is alive. God answered our prayers."

Elazar looked at her, unsmiling. "Not prayers," he said. "Vows."

Was there a difference? She thought of the smell of her own burning hair. "Did you—did you vow?" she asked.

Now Elazar smiled. His smile should have restored her joy, but his face in his shaven head seemed drained of its old exuberance. "Yes. I gave up my own death. Or some nonsense like that."

"It isn't nonsense. Yochanan recovered!" Wasn't that all that mattered?

Elazar sighed, a heavy sigh, like an old man's. "Yes, I know. And now I have an eternal bond with God." The light from Elazar's lamp shifted. Rachel glanced down and saw that his hands were trembling. His eyes in his deadened face met hers. "I don't want an eternal bond with God. I want an eternal bond with you."

She took his open hand in hers, and tried to recover the happiness she had brought in with her. "You have one. You saved our child," she said. Why didn't it seem like enough? "He'll outlive us one day," she added. The vow she had made didn't cross her mind; it was like the ground a hundred cubits above them, unreal and irrelevant. She looked at Elazar and imagined: she could bring Yochanan to the tunnel and the three of them could flee to the countryside together; they could raise Yochanan there and even have more children; they could embrace this blessing that they had been given; they could—

"I'm getting married, Rachel."

She leaned back against the tunnel's wall. This shouldn't have hurt; as Yochanan recovered, she had promised herself that she ought to feel nothing but gratitude, to be immune from any pain but death. Elazar kept talking. "My father told me about it that day, right after you made your vow and right before I made mine. She's the daughter of his deputy. I turned down every girl he proposed for the past two years, but this time he knew I couldn't refuse him. He wouldn't have given me the vow." He paused, and swallowed damp air. "I thought it was worth it."

Rachel did not cry. How could she cry, when her son was alive? "It was," she agreed.

"I know we can't meet here again," Elazar said.

Rachel opened her mouth to argue, but could think of nothing to say. She thought of her fantasy of flight and knew how impossible it was. The two of them only made sense here, in a vein within the earth.

Then Elazar grinned. "But if what we vowed is really true, then anything can happen," he said. "Your marriage won't last forever, and mine won't either, but maybe we will."

Rachel laughed, to hide her fear. In the days since the vow she hadn't thought about what it meant. She had thought only of Yochanan, of Yochanan eating and walking and singing, of Yochanan living. But there was an eagerness in Elazar's gaunt face that frightened her. And now he was waiting for her answer.

"Please don't do this to me, Elazar," she said. Her voice shivered along with the water at her feet. "You might think it's nice to hope and dream, but it isn't. You're only hurting both of us. You haven't been married yet, so you don't know." She thought of Zakkai, of his earnestness, his innocence, of how he waited for her at home, of how he held Yochanan on his knees, of how, when he peeled off her robes and touched her in the dark, her body convulsed with a humiliating, sickening pity. "Marriages do last forever," she said, and stared down at the water running between her feet. "You know and I know my husband will never divorce me. Even if he did, priests can't marry divorced women. And how would you ever divorce your wife, with your fathers both priests, unless you had a reason? You would have to wait until your fathers died." She looked back at him, at the ruin he had become. “Please, Elazar. Don’t make impossible promises. You’ve given me my life’s greatest blessing. You saved Yochanan. It’s enough.” But it wasn’t enough.

“I thought of a way to save our child, and it worked,” Elazar continued. His voice was louder now. “That means I can think of a way to save us too. It may take me a long time, but I will, as soon as I can.”

Rachel managed to hold back her body, to release his warm thin hand. “Thank you for Yochanan,” she said simply. And then she turned around.

She was relieved when Elazar did not follow her. But as she turned the corner into the darkness, she heard his voice again. “I’ll come back for you,” he called behind her. “Wait for me.”

She did not wait for him. Instead she returned to the city, to her parents, to her husband, to her child, to scrolls and parchments and ink. She taught herself, slowly, day by day, to live with incompleteness and ambivalence, to face each incomplete and ambivalent day not with certainty but with wisdom. And she taught her son to become a sage.

WHEN YOCHANAN WAS SEVEN YEARS OLD, while Zakkai sat recording the judgments of the High Court, in the heat of the day, Rachel sat with the boy on the roof of their house and taught him what it means to read.

“You’re very good at reading,” she told him. She was carding wool, and her little boy had an open scroll in his lap. He had his grandfather’s dark eyes, but they were half closed now; his body drooped over the scroll. “I know you’ve been reading for years.”

“Reading is boring,” Yochanan informed her. The roof was hot, and the boy was impatient. Already he was tugging on a lock of his dark hair, and edging away from her. “There’s no reason to read, because I memorized all the words already.”

"I know," Rachel said. "But today I want to see if you can read the words between the words."

She had thought he would be curious, and was hurt when he laughed. He pointed at the scroll on his knees. "You mean the empty spaces?"

She drew in her breath, fighting disappointment. "There are thousands of words between the words," she said. "And even if all the skies were parchment and all the seas ink, no scribe could ever record them."

"That's stupid," seven-year-old Yochanan announced. "I can already read all the words. I don't even have to look at them." He launched into his grandfather's chant: "For in six days God made the heavens and the earth, the sea and all it contains, and . . ." He was a boy who loved rituals, who loved answers, who loved being right. He would have made an excellent priest.

Rachel put down the wool, and rested her hand on his. The boy stopped. "Tell me again, Yochanan," she said. "How long did it take God to create the world?"

"Six days," Yochanan said, and then returned to the chant, from a different verse this time: "Six days shall you labor and do all your work, and on the seventh day—"

She cut him off. "And when was the sun created?"

He answered her, still in the chant: "And there was evening and there was morning, the fourth day." He beamed at her.

"So how long were the first three days?" Rachel asked.

Yochanan hesitated. He narrowed his eyes, and she could see him searching for the answer. He still thought there was an answer. "Three days long," he said in his high little boy's voice.

"But if there was no sun, then how long was each day?"

He snorted. The noise caught in her ear, a tiny rip in the curtain separating reality from dream. "The same as a day with a sun, except with no sun."

"Maybe," she said, "or maybe not. Maybe it was an hour. Or maybe it was seven hundred thousand years."

Yochanan turned toward her. Usually an invisible wall stood between them, a little boy's pride that broke down only when he was sad or frightened or needed his mother. But now his dark eyes were wide and his mouth hung open, as though he himself had disappeared, replaced by a thought. She had not seen that look of wonder on a boy's face since she first met Elazar in the tunnel, when he said to her, *I didn't think you'd come.*

"Why would it say that it was the fourth day, if it wasn't the fourth day?" Yochanan asked. It was not an objection; it was a question. "What's the reason for writing 'the fourth day'? If it were a mistake, Grandpa would correct it. He corrected lots of things, but not this."

Rachel said nothing, and combed through the wool.

Yochanan was thinking now: not waiting for answer, not trying to be right, but thinking. "Maybe it says that for people, because people have days, even if God doesn't?" he asked.

"Maybe," Rachel said, and picked out the burrs in the wool.

"Or maybe it's like a secret message? Simeon once told me about a Greek messenger who had words tattooed on his head so that the words would be hidden under his hair after it grew back, and when he got to where he was going, the officers shaved off his hair to read the secret message."

Rachel remembered that Yochanan was seven years old. "Maybe," she said.

But Yochanan no longer needed her approval. He was thinking. "Actually, everything in the story is kind of like a secret message," he said, "because God has to tell everything to people, in people's words, but people aren't as smart as God, so everything is like a stupid version of the real story."

Rachel had not considered this. She looked at her little boy with sudden and frightening understanding: her entire life, every person's entire life, was a stupid version of the real story, a tiny glimpse of a tiny sliver of the briefest of moments, a few days out of eternity. But the boy was turning away from her. "Mama, can you please leave me alone now?" he asked. "I want to read."

She left him, as she always would.

The next day Rachel stood at her ink and parchment stall while Yochanan ran through the city, delivering her father's scrolls. On market days Yochanan would meet her at the stall at sunset. He liked to sneak up on her, creeping up behind her as she was packing up her cart and pouncing on her with his fanged seven-year-old grin. Each time she pretended to be surprised. When she felt a weak tug on the back of her skirt that evening, she spun around with eyebrows raised, ready to shriek. And then she shrieked. Before her stood her little boy, his forehead covered in blood.

My baby! she screamed, soundlessly, sucking in a sob. Already she knew how essential it was for him not to see her cry. Instead she poured water from a skin onto a rag from her cart and wiped it on her little boy's brow. His curls were matted in the blood, but it wasn't flowing anymore, she saw. A large lump crowned his forehead, the skin raw. "You fell," she told him. Told, didn't ask. "You fell, but you're all right."

"I was reading the story for the new year, the one about Abraham tying up Isaac," he said. He was babbling, incoherent. "I brought it from home to read. I was reading it while I was walking, just reading it while I was walking, walking," he stammered.

"Don't read while you're walking," she told him, still wiping his face.

"I didn't see them. I really didn't see them."

"Who?"

"The soldiers. I walked right into them. I didn't see them. They wanted the message I was delivering."

"I hope you gave it to them," she said warily. What was it, she wondered?

"I did, but then they also took the story I was reading. That wasn't fair, so I tried to take it back." His lips crimped. Rachel sickened as she suddenly understood. He had been holding his jaw steady, but now his voice broke, his little boy mouth quivering. "I lost it. I lost the story. I'm sorry, I'm sorry, I'm sorry—"

"I care about you, not the story," she said softly.

"But I care about the story," he wailed. She put him on top of her cart, still wailing, and wheeled him home.

That night she sat with Yochanan on the bench where he slept, rubbing a salve into the raw skin on his forehead. It was dark in the house, and Yochanan was almost sleeping, a suspended state that reminded Rachel of five years earlier, of holding him as he hung, barely breathing, between life and death. He was drifting now, unconscious and beautiful. "I lost the story," he groaned, and rolled away from his mother.

"You are the story," she whispered, and kissed him goodnight.

RACHEL'S MARRIAGE WAS DIVIDED in two: life with Zakkai, and life without him. For two weeks of every month—for that was the law, according to the scrolls her father copied—she was free, unmolested, untouched by any male besides her little boy. At the end of those two weeks she would visit the ritual bath with absolute earnestness. She immersed herself naked in the cool water of the stone cistern each month and imagined an unquestioned love for her husband; each time she burst through the water's surface, she willed that serene stasis to emerge along with her. But by the time she put her robe back on she was already dreading the thick heat of their tiny curtained chamber, the hot sheepskin under her bared backside, the suffocating smell of Zakkai's breath on her face, the weight of Zakkai's hairy body pressed against hers, as though he thought he could crush her into believing in him. Her deep desire to be crushed into believing in him never made her loathe him any less.

Zakkai never noticed that anything was wrong, and this great mercy was the solid slab of fiction on which their marriage stood. Rachel had hoped at first that things might change between them, that something might grow, and she was right. The thing that grew was her revulsion. To her astonishment, and against all reason, honest and blameless Zakkai—Zakkai who asked for her opinions about writing and the law, Zakkai who sang her praises to everyone he met—became more repulsive to her with each night she lay beneath him. During the first years she sometimes tried to fantasize that Zakkai was Elazar. But so much was so different—the hot air in place of cool water, the crush of lying on the floor instead of standing face-to-face, the forced silence of her parents' and child's presence behind the curtains, and something more than that, something that no amount of Zakkai's kindness or generosity could replace—that this proved to be beyond her imaginative powers. Instead, she imagined that she herself was a different woman, one of the household slaves.

One evening as Rachel returned from the baths, slowly unwinding the scarf that covered her wet hair, her mother sat in the house crushing herbs by lamplight. "It fades," her mother said, without looking up.

"What?" Rachel asked.

"What you feel, what you want, what you can't have," her mother said, accenting each phrase with mortar against pestle. "It fades. You get older, you have more children, and you forget you ever felt it. Give it time, and it will fade for you too."

Rachel stared at her mother, who still did not raise her head, and marveled at the hidden life of every old woman. Rachel's wet hair dripped on her shoulders, soaking the back of her robe as she went, renewed, to Zakkai. For a time she lived with the dim hope her mother gave her, and waited for the memory of Elazar to dissipate like a smell. But to Rachel's surprise, her mother was wrong. It never faded, even after a dozen years. Rachel's marriage was an act of endurance that almost resembled faith, and Rachel was rewarded—or cursed, according to Zakkai—by never becoming pregnant. As the years passed, Zakkai's yearning for more children transformed into an obsession with Yochanan. Zakkai loved Yochanan, admonished him, encouraged him, pressured him, would do anything for him. The feeling was hardly mutual, but Zakkai didn't care. He was a father, and a father thinks only of the future.

By the time Yochanan was ten years old, the old master scribe Azaria was dead, collapsed on his writing table with blood leaking from his nose onto parchment. His death instantly transformed Zakkai into head of the household and master scribe, recording not only holy books and court documents, but also the arguments and discussions of the sages. Zakkai could hardly have done the job if it weren't for Yochanan. For Yochanan, in a very short time, had developed a specific gift, one that brought Rachel into a state of awe. By the age of ten he was a tanna, or in other words, a living book.

Every scribe memorized long texts; that was as commonplace in Jerusalem as a sacrificial goat. But a tanna memorized *conversations*, sitting beside the scholars in the academy and recording in his mind every word spoken, every nuance of the unspooling, contentious, unending oral law, which of course was also given by God at Sinai, even if only these conversations between scholars revealed it. The tanna's job was to remember it all, and to report back what the scholars needed from yesterday's discussion, last month's discussion, last year's discussion. A tanna, until now, had always been a grown man. But Yochanan already sat in the academy, committing to memory every spoken word, and the academy needed him. Zakkai could not believe his good fortune. His only son was a miracle, a vindication of his own small life. Until Yochanan began coming up with ideas of his own.

One night when Yochanan was twelve years old, Zakkai lay at Rachel's side and turned toward her, brushing her hair away from her face. Moments earlier she had barely tolerated his body against hers, but now the gentle touch of his hand across her hair made her feel a strange affection, an emotion she wished she could exaggerate into something more. In a voice quieter than she had ever heard him use, he asked her, "Do you ever think about Yochanan's future?"

"It's the only thing I think about," she said. She tried to decode what Zakkai meant. Yochanan already had a trade, and it was hardly time to find him a bride. Was there something else she was supposed to be doing for her child, other than preparing him for some distant life without her?

"We can't allow him to live like this," Zakkai said.

This puzzled Rachel. She propped herself on an elbow and faced him. "Allow him to live like what?"

"Like a slave," Zakkai answered. He lay back on the floor, and contemplated the ceiling in the dark.

"What are you talking about?" Rachel asked. She recalled Zakkai's first entrance into the house, his seven-year contract to repay his brother's debts, his straw mat in the wine cellar among the slaves, seven-year slaves like him, while she slept upstairs, the daughter of his master. "Yochanan is a free person."

"Yochanan isn't a free person, and neither are you or I," Zakkai said.

Rachel recalled the recent arguments she had heard in the house among the scribes and sages. She felt the words that were coming next before they arrived, like a breeze before a storm.

"Ours is the only province in the entire empire that refused to worship Caesar," Zakkai began. "The sages all think it's some great victory. But look how we've paid! The Roman procurator helps himself to the Temple treasury like it's his personal account. When crowds gather to protest, the Romans put their soldiers in civilian clothes and then surprise everyone by clubbing people to death. The priests are in the Romans' pockets, the High Court has no power over anything but domestic disputes, and our own laws are subordinate to the Romans' whims. I was a slave, Rachel. I know what it's like. This is only different if we pretend it is."

Rachel stifled a grimace. So why not pretend, she thought, like every girl or woman, or really, like nearly everyone in one way or another—every person who ever lived a daily life formed from other people's whims? Wasn't that simply what being alive demanded? But Rachel said nothing.

"I just don't see the point of any of it," Zakkai said. He stared again at the soot-covered ceiling. "What's the purpose of being a sage when wisdom has a limit, when you can only say what's true until you offend some Roman guard? I feel like I'm living my life as though I had all of eternity, as though one day the kingdom will be restored and everything will matter again, but until then I'm just waiting," he said. "Lately I can't stop thinking about it. And I just keep thinking that while I'm waiting for something to change, what I'm really doing is stealing Yochanan's future."

Rachel sat up and struck a flint, lighting the lamp beside their bed. Now she could see Zakkai's glistening face, his curly hair stuck with sweat to his beading forehead. His body had thickened since their marriage, but his face was still as narrow as a boy's. "There's no need to worry about Yochanan," she told him. "He already knows how to get along with everyone, how to tolerate everything. He'll do better than either of us."

"That's exactly what I'm worried about," Zakkai said. "I'm worried he'll become like me, pathetically grateful for living less than half a life." Suddenly he sat up and took her hands. Usually she resented his touch, but his hands were warm and agitated, trembling in a way that made her feel all of his sweet and sickly innocence. "Rachel, may

I tell you something?" he asked. "I shouldn't tell anyone, especially not a woman. But I have to tell someone or I'll go mad."

He really was like a boy, Rachel thought. "What is it?" she asked.

"There's a priest on the High Court who's also a sage, one of the high priest's deputies," he told her. His words were low and quick, as though he were trying on a new voice. "He passed me a message today while I was recording the proceedings, telling me to meet him afterward, privately. When I did, he told me he and some other people—important people, Rachel, people on the High Court!—are making plans. They want me to join them."

"What plans?"

Zakkai did not answer. Instead he lay down on his back again, his dark eyes shining in the lamplight. Rachel looked at Zakkai's body, stretched out on the sheepskin bedding she once shared with her sisters, sweaty and hairy and trembling. He was smiling more brightly than she had ever seen him smile, with an excitement he had never shown before. He turned toward her, and still did not answer. "For the first time in my life I feel like there's a reason I'm alive," he finally said. "And that there's a reason I'm Yochanan's father."

Rachel stared at him. Suddenly the full abundance of Zakkai's innocence reared up before her, and she saw what was concealed beneath it: an extravagant stupidity. "I thought you said you were worried about Yochanan's future," Rachel said delicately. "Why would you—"

"That's exactly why," Zakkai interrupted. His eyes were radiant. He sat up again, once more taking her hands. "There's a sage I want you to meet, one that Yochanan already knows well. I wasn't sure what to do until I heard his latest teaching. Yesterday he taught us: 'If I am not for myself, who will be for me? And if I'm only for myself, what am I? And if not now, when?' "

"What's that supposed to mean?" Rachel muttered. She still could not get beyond what Zakkai had said, the colossal scale of his idiocy.

"It means what it means," Zakkai said happily, as if that explained everything. "If I were Yochanan, I would want my father to do whatever he could for me. In any case, I've invited the sage to dine with us tomorrow evening. So please prepare something good," he told her, still smiling.

As if she were a piece of furniture in his way, he leaned across her body and blew out the flame, then rolled on his side, content.

Rachel lay awake in the dark, afraid for Yochanan's future.

HILLEL THE ELDER WAS rumored to be almost a hundred and twenty years old, but that only made sense if you counted two new years, the one in the spring and the one in the fall. He was old, but full of energy. He appeared at their door with several disciples and without a cane, and to Rachel's surprise he made his way up the ladder to their rooftop for a moonlit meal like a limber young boy. He spoke with a Babylonian accent, which Rachel usually found pretentious. But what Rachel noticed most about him as they settled around the set table was an aura of patience, a quiet, humble awareness of other people's presence. He smiled not only at the men, but at her too. She watched in awe as he led the blessings, washing his hands in a basin at the table like a priest before passing around the bread and wine and barley stew, acknowledging each person with his cheerful face.

Zakkai stirred in his seat as the scholars began a tedious conversation about civil damages. Rachel could see that Zakkai was itching to speak, to stir the old man like a pot. At last, in a lull, he put in a word. "Our teacher told me recently about an amazing thing," he finally said to the group. "A pagan came to his house and asked him, 'Can you teach me the entire Torah while I'm standing balanced on one foot?' Most of us would have sent the man away, but—well, Master, tell everyone what you said to him."

"Really very little," Hillel said. He seemed embarrassed. "All I said was, 'What is hateful to you, do not do to your neighbor. That is the entire Torah. Now go out and learn.' "

Rachel found this dubious. Was that really the entire Torah? Or was it the Torah, stripped of all its majesty and power? What about the divine presence alive in a cloud, the burnt offerings to God, the chance to die without dying? She glanced at Zakkai, who was smiling, basking in the sage's presence. But Yochanan, she saw, was thinking. Her son's face had become longer in recent months, a shadow of a mustache forming on his upper lip. He squinted at the old sage with dark eyes full of doubt. She considered asking a question herself. But being a mother meant something other than voicing one's thoughts. Her task, she knew, was to bear witness.

"One of the wonderworkers in the city has taught the same thing," Zakkai volunteered. "He teaches what he calls the Golden Rule: Do unto others what you would have others do to you. Your Torah has traveled far, if even wonderworkers are quoting it."

Hillel smiled, though Rachel detected something insincere in his face—as though he didn't quite agree, but didn't wish to insult his host. He looked away, and took more bread.

But Yochanan, his twelve-year-old voice still high as a girl's, didn't care if he insulted his father, so long as it was for what he saw as a higher cause of truth. Yochanan loved doing things for a higher cause of truth—a habit Rachel found endlessly exasperating, not least because he had so clearly learned it from Zakkai. "Father, that's not the same teaching at all," he said.

Zakkai turned to Yochanan, grinning to hide his annoyance. "Of course it is. Weren't you listening?"

"All I do is listen," Yochanan murmured meekly. "It's my job."

Zakkai answered Yochanan, but turned his face to the sage. "One says 'Do unto others what you would have others do to you,' while our teacher here says 'Don't do unto others what you would not have others do to you.' The wording is different, yes; one is positive and the other negative. But they are identical. And it's an important teaching, so I'm glad it's become popular," Zakkai added, as though plastering over a dent in a stone wall.

But Yochanan wouldn't let it go. He never let anything go. "They're not the same, Father. You're a scribe. You should know. If they were the same, why would Master Hillel use different words to say it?"

Zakkai fumbled. In the time since Azaria's death, Rachel had noticed his lack of confidence, though he usually succeeded in hiding it in public. Now Rachel could feel her husband losing his mental footing, becoming, again, the bumpkin boy from Tekoa. "Two different sets of words can mean the same thing," Zakkai muttered.

"They are indeed very similar," Hillel offered gently, in his delicate accent.

"Not in this case," Yochanan insisted. "Not at all. Think of it this way. Imagine that a king of flesh and blood was a pagan, and prayed to idols."

"I don't need to imagine that," one of the scholars laughed. To Rachel's amazement, all eyes were now on her son.

"Now imagine that the king's son was ill, and one of the pagan priests told him to pray to an idol. So he prayed to the idol, and then his son was healed."

"A coincidence, if it was an idol," Zakkai said.

Rachel glanced at her healthy growing son, and felt her confidence in the world shaken. Suddenly she wondered: Could it have been a coincidence? What if Yochanan as a toddler had simply spontaneously healed? What if all of it—the Temple, the priesthood, the vows, all of it—was a fraud? She thought of what Elazar had said about the ritual for a woman accused of adultery, how the ceremony's power came only from what it meant to the people doing it. As she recalled her own vow, a new thought entered her mind: Did it even matter whether it had been real or not? Wasn't the vow's sole power derived simply from its existence—that it had brought her a sense of control over her son's future, that it had reassured her that there was hope, that it had given her a reason to see Elazar one last time? The world didn't need to be created in six actual days, and the Temple didn't need to actually heal the sick or bring the rains or reveal a wayward wife, so long as the metaphor had meaning. So what, she thought, if Yochanan's imaginary king of flesh and blood wanted to believe in an idol? What difference did it make, in the end? None at all. In the years since she had burned her own hair on the altar, her hair had grown back a bit more brittle; her sunburnt skin had developed tiny wrinkles around her eyes; her breasts, after the years of nursing, now drooped slightly; evidently her body was already edging toward the grave. She had vowed away her own death, whatever that might mean, but she wasn't going to live forever.

"But now the king believes in this idol even more," Yochanan continued. "And he says to the people of his country, 'Dear loyal subjects! I have discovered the wonders of Jupiter, Healer of All, thanks to the good deed of this priest. And now I wish to do unto others as I would have others do to me. My priest brought me to Jupiter, and now I will bring Jupiter's wonders to all of you! I now decree that everyone in my kingdom must bow before Jupiter.'"

Rachel stared at her son. The scholars were silent.

"'Do unto others' is cruel, even if it sounds like kindness. It's arrogant to think that others want exactly what you want."

Rachel glanced at Hillel, whose gentle face was silver in the moonlight. "Thank you for teaching us," he said to Yochanan. "That is why I told that man to go out and learn. It isn't obvious how to be a good person."

The scholars looked at Yochanan in awe. Zakkai, Rachel saw, was humiliated, and struggled to contain himself. Finally he couldn't. "But if you believe in yourself, how could you not do your utmost to share the best of yourself with others?" he asked. He looked at Hillel rather than at Yochanan. "Master, you taught us that you have to be for yourself, or no one else will be."

"Yes, but I also have another teaching: Don't believe in yourself until the day you die."

Zakkai looked down at his food, and Rachel felt a deep pity that almost resembled love.

"How could anyone know the day he's going to die?" Yochanan asked.

"Exactly," said Hillel, and smiled.

That night after the guests left, Zakkai left too, walking through the city in the night, steaming with anger and shame. But as Rachel finished clearing the table upstairs, she was surprised to hear the ladder creak. She glanced over the table to see her son's curly head emerging from the hole in the floor. "Yochanan?"

"Yes, Mother," he said. His voice seemed lower again, though perhaps that was Rachel's imagination. But when he emerged onto the roof, she stepped back. Tall and thin in a fresh evening robe, Yochanan stood before her in the dim moonlight. She saw for the first time how much he resembled Elazar.

"I cleaned out the ashes from the oven," he said.

"Really? Why?" Never before in her life had a man done a household chore for her; nor would it happen again for another two thousand years.

"Do I need a reason?" Yochanan said.

Rachel knew the reason: to make up for his father's humiliated absence, to show his mother that she wasn't alone. She also knew that her son did not know the reason, which meant he was still a child, dizzyingly still a child. She reeled as though peering over the edge of a cliff, and sat down on the parapet. He noticed, because he was still a child, and sat beside her.

"Cleaning out the ashes made me feel like a priest," he said.

"It doesn't make me feel that way," Rachel murmured. Over the years, as it became clear that Yochanan would be her only child, Rachel had found herself silently resenting the labor of daily living, the thousands of threads woven and water buckets carried and bowls of dough kneaded and animals skinned and floors swept and garments washed—all those tasks that other women her age performed with a pack of descendants accompanying them. To her, it all seemed more and more meaningless with every passing year. Yet here before her was her only child, oblivious.

"That's the first thing they do in the Temple each morning, clean out the ashes from the sacrifices of the day before," he continued. "Every single thing they do is an act of total devotion."

If that's true, then every parent who ever lived is a priest, Rachel thought, but did not say. Then Yochanan said something she would remember for many years.

"Maybe we wouldn't need a Temple," he said, "if more people knew how to be priests."

She looked at Yochanan and saw him as a tiny boy again, dying in her lap as she pleaded with God. There was so little that children knew.

"Thank you for cleaning it, Yochanan," she said.

For the sliver of a moment before Zakkai returned, she sat beside her half-grown son in silence, her son's still-small hand in hers, full of wonder and devotion.

AT TWELVE, BOYS START PULLING away from their parents. Rachel would notice it later with many, many others, but she first noticed it with Yochanan. Most of the time he was at the academy, from early in the morning until late at night. When he wasn't, he worked as a scribe, or alongside Rachel in the marketplace, selling parchments and ink. Even when they worked together, it was rare that they talked. One hot day when business was slow, she seated herself on the street beside Yochanan. They slurped water from a skin as they waited for customers. A Roman soldier stood across the street from them, a teenager barely older than Yochanan whose uniform showed too much hairy skin. Two little boys walked by and spat at his feet. Rachel thought he might kick them, but he only wiped his foot with the end of his spear and yawned. Boys were a conundrum, Rachel noticed, their minds clouded with incense, politics, sex, war—anything to drive off the boredom and fear at the root of their souls. She turned to her son and wondered what lay within him.

"Do you like working at the academy?" she asked.

She was surprised when he answered, "Yes, because it's hilarious."

"Hilarious? Why?"

"Like this," Yochanan replied with a grin. "One person will say something like, 'Don't trust the government, because they never help anyone unless it benefits themselves,' and then the next person will say, 'Pray for the welfare of the government, because if people didn't fear it, they would swallow one another alive.' Those two teachings are almost opposites. But I have to memorize both of them, because supposedly both of them are true. And not just true, either. These arguments are supposed to be the word of God, in our time, through the sages' mouths—and it's completely impossible for all of it to be true! The last time they had an argument like that, with two ideas that were total opposites, they told me, 'These words and those words are the words of the living God.' Which is impossible if you think about it. But almost everything is impossible if you think about it. See why it's funny?"

Rachel looked up at the Roman soldier, who was idly scraping his spear against an ancient inscription on the wall. She looked at the boy who should have been dead and told him, "I think so."

Yochanan was still grinning. "Maybe it isn't funny, exactly. It's something different from a joke. But I can't help smiling when I think about it. All of these sages are arguing about what God wants from us. But I think God actually wants us to live an impossible life. All the evidence points in that direction."

"Why would God want that?"

"I don't know. Maybe it makes him laugh," Yochanan said. "It makes *me* laugh. Once the sages in the academy had an argument about whether or not people should have been created at all. Guess how long they argued that one for."

"Three whole days," Rachel guessed, and hoped she was wrong.

Yochanan laughed out loud. "No. Three whole *years*! Or maybe it was two and a half. I was only there for the last six months. In the end they even voted on it."

"What did they decide?"

"That it would have been better if we had never been created. But since we're here, they decided we might as well try to improve our deeds. See what I mean? Sometimes I miss a line in an argument because I'm trying too hard not to laugh."

"Does Father also find this funny?" Rachel asked.

Yochanan scrunched his mouth into a hideous pout, then screeched, in Zakkai's voice, " 'What did you learn today, Yochanan? Recite!' 'What did you learn yesterday, Yochanan? Recite!' 'What will you learn tomorrow, Yochanan? Recite!' " The imitation was perfect, and wicked. Rachel was alarmed by how much it hurt to hear it.

"He gets angry when he sees me smiling," Yochanan continued in his own voice. "He thinks I'm not taking it seriously. Once when I couldn't stop myself from smiling, he even beat me afterward. But obviously I'm taking it seriously if I'm laughing about it!"

Rachel thought of the Zakkai she knew, the one her son had never met: the taunted country boy, the frightened slave standing at the curtain, the person burdened with something to prove. Where had she been, she wondered, when Zakkai beat her son?

"I don't think he likes the academy," Yochanan was saying. "He hasn't been there at all for the past two weeks."

Rachel was confused. "He's left the house with you every day."

Yochanan smirked. "Sure, he walks out the door with me, but then he tells me that he'll meet me later, and I don't see him again until the evening."

"Maybe he has business at the High Court," Rachel tried.

Yochanan pursed his lips. For a brief moment he resembled Elazar. Then he said, "Or maybe he doesn't."

Before she could ask what he meant, a customer approached: a clean-shaven Roman in official dress, asking in Greek for the price of a blank scroll. Yochanan served him with a broad smile, his head bowed before him. As Rachel watched her son, she couldn't decide: did her boy with his head bowed look like a young man who never did hateful things to his neighbors, or did he simply look like a slave?

"MOTHER, WE NEED TO do something about Father," Yochanan told her one early summer evening. It was a few days before the pilgrimage festival; the city teemed with people, and Zakkai wasn't home. He often wasn't home. His absence blew through the house like a fresh breeze, pure relief.

"What are you talking about?" Rachel asked.

Yochanan led her to the wide bench below the window where he slept and pulled back a corner of the folded sheepskin mat. Beneath it lay a dagger, its sharpened blade gleaming in the fading sunlight. "I found it in the wine cellar this time," Yochanan said.

"It must belong to one of the slaves," Rachel muttered, though she already knew it didn't. Then she asked, "What do you mean, this time?"

"This is the second one I've found. The first one was under his cloak a few days ago, hanging on the hook by the door. He has a strap sewn inside the cloak to hold it in place."

Rachel looked at her son, astonished. "What did you do with the first one?"

Yochanan pulled back the sheepskin a bit more and revealed the second blade.

"You can't keep them here," Rachel whispered. Since the riots during the pilgrimage festival two months earlier, the Romans had begun arresting people at the slightest sign of trouble; everyone was living in fear. "He could be crucified for this. *You* could be crucified for this."

"I know," Yochanan said. "But I don't know what to do with them. I tried burying them outside, but there were too many people around. I tried it at night, but even then there are night watchmen on patrol. And whenever I take one, he gets another, so what difference does it make." He didn't make it a question. Rachel was shaking.

"Where was he going this evening?" she asked.

"To deliver a message to the procurator's house."

Rachel didn't need to hear any more. She yanked the skins back over the blades and ran out of the house, pulling her son by the hand behind her.

THEY RAN THROUGH THE neighborhoods the way she had when she was a girl—through alleys and over garbage heaps, between columns and market stalls, up and down hills and stairs, around cisterns and past soldiers and beggars. The number of people in the streets had swollen for the pilgrimage; there were lines of people clogging every alley, and the garbage heaps had grown. The sun was still bright in the sky, blinding them as it gilded the stones while they ran together, riding thick waves of air blending smells of food and incense and dung. Her son's hand sweated in hers, melded to her as though they had once again become one body, running and running and running until they reached a mass of people in the street in front of the procurator's villa, a noisy crowd in front of a row of soldiers brandishing spears. Rachel pushed through the people with her son at her side, looking around desperately. It was Yochanan who said, at last, "Mother, there he is."

And there he was, stripped to the waist, his arms and legs shackled, surrounded by a phalanx of Roman guards. His face was radiant.

"Father!" Yochanan shouted.

Zakkai turned toward them and smiled.

"I'm happy now, Yochanan," he called. "It's the day of my death, and that means I can finally believe in myself."

His eyes glistened with a strange and terrifying power. As Rachel and Yochanan watched, he laughed out loud and lunged at one of the guards, biting the man's cheek until it bled.

The soldiers closed in. One turned his spear toward Zakkai; another shoved him to his knees. The crowd behind Rachel and Yochanan pushed at their backs.

In a haze of heat Yochanan rushed toward the soldiers. Rachel grabbed his arm and yanked him back, the way she had when he was a little boy running away from her. She turned her shocked son around and pushed him with all the force she had, shoving him through the tide of people until they both emerged again behind the crowd, fighting for breath.

"I need to go back to him," Yochanan gasped.

"No," said Rachel. "You are not going to die today." The crowd behind her was growing, throwing garbage at the soldiers, who responded with clubs and spears. She pushed Yochanan into an alcove in a wall and shielded him with her body. In seconds the riot became a stampede. Behind them waves of people roared and crashed until blood ran between the stones beneath their feet. And then there was nothing to do but carry Zakkai's body home.

For the next thirty days Rachel followed the orders of her twelve-year-old son. The sages had created elaborate rules for mourners, and Yochanan remembered them all. They removed their sandals, tore their robes, wore sackcloth, didn't bathe, smeared their faces with ash. For seven days they sat on the floor as visitors filed in and out, bringing food and platitudes; for thirty days they barely left the house. On the thirtieth day the sages assembled with them, reciting psalms and repeating arguments about reward and punishment that Rachel barely followed. At dawn on the thirty-first day, Rachel prepared to go back to the marketplace. She moved as though underwater, dressing herself with careful movements and slowly assembling the parchments on her cart beside the door before undoing the latch. When she opened the door, a man was standing on her threshold, dressed in white and staring at her with weary green eyes.

"Elazar," she whispered.

"Rachel!"

He looked different from how she had imagined him over the past ten years. His hair was longer, almost to his shoulders, and his body had thickened, his waist bulging a bit, like his father's. But his eyes gleamed with a secret thrill, as though he were about to laugh. She clutched the doorpost with one hand and struggled to breathe.

"Elazar, why—" she heard herself say.

"I divorced my wife," he said.

"What?"

"She was barren. The High Court says a man can divorce his wife after ten years, if they have no children. I waited ten years."

"You waited for what?"

"For you. I waited for you."

He stepped toward her. She could smell the sweetness of his breath. He reached a hand toward the doorpost, and touched his fingers to hers. Ten years drained through a crack in the floor beneath her feet.

"I waited," he said again. "I waited ten years, but I couldn't wait forever. Every night and every day for ten years I was thinking of you. And I kept my promise to you. That's why I did it. I can't imagine you weren't thinking of me the same way."

Rachel slid her hand off the doorpost. Elazar's hand fell away from hers, suspended in midair. "What did you do, Elazar?"

Elazar's face turned dark.

The deputy high priest, Rachel thought, in Zakkai's voice. *They have plans. They want me to join them*. She stared at him.

"What did you do, Elazar? WHAT DID YOU DO?!"

"Rachel, don't you understand? We can get married now! You and I and Yochanan can—"

"You're a murderer, Elazar! A murderer!"

"*I'm* a murderer? I'm not the one who showed up at the procurator's house with a knife."

"You murdered him!"

"Rachel, please listen to me. There are people in this city with daggers hidden under their cloaks, looking for Roman officials to kill. They think they're endangering the Romans, but they're actually endangering us. Do you know what could happen if the Romans decided to retaliate? They could destroy the city. They could burn the Temple. If that happened, it would be the end of this entire people, forever. Do you understand that? We need to find these crazed zealots before they find each other."

But Rachel was screaming now, wailing. "He was innocent, Elazar! Absolutely innocent! He thought there was a plan, but the only plan was yours!"

"I was only thinking of you, Rachel."

"Of *me*?"

"I only did for you what I would have wanted you to do for me," Elazar said. He tried to take her hands in his, but she beat them away. "You would have done the same for me, wouldn't you? I would have been grateful to you forever if you had done the same for me. I couldn't wait anymore, Rachel. I know you couldn't either."

Rachel couldn't answer; she was gasping for air as though she were drowning. Before she caught her breath, she heard a voice behind her.

"Mother?"

She looked over her shoulder and saw Yochanan.

He stood narrow and thin, still in his sackcloth robe from the night before, his feet still bare. His hair hung in dirty knots around his childlike face. With his eyebrows raised, he resembled his father.

"Yochanan," Elazar said.

Rachel turned back to Elazar. Her body became an immovable rock. "Go away, Elazar," she hissed. "I never want to see you again."

"Please, at least let me say goodbye to him," he begged.

Her voice seared the air. "Leave. Immediately. Don't say goodbye." She closed the door in his face. Then she turned and sank to the floor.

Through a fog she felt her son approach her. Suddenly his body was beside hers on the floor, her hand in his.

"That man was right," Yochanan said softly.

"What do you mean," Rachel said, though she could not make it a question. She was sobbing, with her back against the door.

"He was right," Yochanan repeated. Rachel had never heard her son's voice so low. He almost sounded like a man. "If Father had actually done it, we all would have been killed or enslaved. Maybe they would have burnt down the city and the Temple too. And Father would have done it. That man was right." He paused, a gap in time that contained his entire childhood. "Who is he, Mother?"

Rachel swallowed salt and thought of how to answer. *The only man I ever loved. The man who saved your life. The man who murdered your father. Your father.* "A person who lives in the past," she said.

"How did he know my name?"

RACHEL DID HER BEST to live in the future. Within a year she married again, and soon she had babies again—four little sisters for Yochanan, girls who grew up to give him many nephews to raise and teach when Yochanan's only son died, of the same illness Yochanan once had. Rachel didn't see Elazar again for many years, not until Yochanan had become the greatest sage of his generation, a leader, a master, an elder, a venerated old man—so old that he was lying in a coffin, being carried out of the besieged city by his nephews and disciples, with Elazar ushering him through the city gate. Because Rachel still needed Elazar, though she didn't know it yet.

CHAPTER

11

DEATH-FLAVORED SMOOTHIE

. . .

Leave. Immediately. Don't say goodbye.

Rachel would have, except that it was impossible. What made it impossible was Meirav, who had started sleeping at her house.

The move was subtle enough that when it happened Rachel hardly noticed it. Rocky stayed out late, which was a pleasure at first, because it meant he slept through the mornings, staying out of Rachel's way. A habit of centuries led Rachel to rise each morning at dawn, and the early morning hours were her private time with the past. So it was with slight alarm that Rachel went down to her kitchen one dim morning to find Rocky and Meirav, both fully dressed, throwing fruit into a blender. Rachel hung back by the kitchen threshold and observed them in silence.

"I don't see the appeal of a smoothie," Rocky was saying over the blender's roar. To Rachel's astonishment, he had shaved. "You're outsourcing your stomach's job to a machine. Who wants to drink pre-chewed cud?"

"Millions of people love pre-chewed cud," Meirav informed him when the blender stopped. Meirav's dark hair sprang out in wild uncombed curls. Her movements were sure and calm, commanding the room. Rachel watched with an uneasy pleasure. Could it be this simple?

"It's not just your stomach you're giving up on. It's your teeth too," Rocky insisted, and waved a spoon with intense energy. "It's like you're anticipating your future as a decrepit toothless invalid. If you're pre-masticating food, why not go all the way and just administer it intravenously? I mean, is the goal to eliminate various bodily functions until there's nothing left for people to do on their own but die? If you ask me, smoothies are a foretaste of death."

Meirav laughed. "You're very morbid before breakfast."

"I'm very morbid all day long," Rocky replied, and poured her a tall glass of something thick and purple. "Enjoy the taste of mortality," he said, and kissed her on the cheek. Then he noticed Rachel in the doorway.

She expected him to cringe. Instead he sang, "Good morning, Mom. We made you breakfast."

"Thank you," Rachel said. "I'd love a death-flavored smoothie."

Rocky looked startled, but then noticed Meirav's smile. "Sorry, I gave you yogurt instead," he said. "For a long life." He pulled out a kitchen chair for Rachel in front of an elaborately layered yogurt parfait. Rachel stared at him as she cautiously lowered herself into the seat. Meirav plopped down beside her, slurping through a straw. Rachel listened to the sucking sounds from Meirav's mouth and entered an aural gallery, a tunnel of noises that burrowed through centuries, every disgusting bubble and gurgle and burp and churn and squirt and gasp and trickle and pant that resounded through mortal bodies at every moment, a never-ending flow like cool water across Rachel's feet as she remained still. The vibrations from Meirav's slurping filled the little kitchen as though Meirav herself were pure bottled energy, a quivering liquid barely contained inside her suntanned skin. It was how Rachel had often thought of Rocky, a thick boy's body full to bursting. Rachel glanced at her smiling wrinkled son, then listened as he drummed four fingers on the table, trying to wiggle his way out of his skin. Meirav belched, and she and Rocky burst out laughing.

"You're taking the train to the city, aren't you?" Meirav asked Rachel. "We could go together. I'm catching the 7:45."

"Meirav has her own company," Rocky explained, with awe in his voice. "She does contract work for cybersecurity."

Maybe she does, Rachel thought. Or maybe you're a chump. "I usually take the 8:50," she demurred.

Meirav rested a bangled hand on Rachel's wrist. "What are you going to do, sit around for another hour with this clown?" she asked, and shot Rocky a smile. "Before you know it, you'll be drinking the smoothie of death."

Rachel glanced at Rocky. To her surprise, he was laughing again. "Don't try saying no to this lady," he told her. "You'll regret it for the rest of your life."

"And think how long that life will be, if you're not drinking Rocky's smoothies," Meirav added.

Before Rachel knew it, she was boarding the train with Meirav.

By the time they slid into their seats Meirav was already on the phone, leaking a groan as she glanced at the phone's screen before propping it against her ear. The call was in Hebrew—the new Hebrew, which Rachel only haltingly understood, though she knew who Meirav was talking to.

"Your mother?" Rachel asked when Meirav finally put down the phone.

Meirav sighed. "Yes. Not everyone my age still has one, so I should be grateful. But it isn't easy. There's a strange time when you become the parent and the parent becomes the child." She smiled at Rachel. "You and Rocky are so lucky. It's not often that you see such a healthy relationship."

Rachel ground her teeth together. Now Meirav was scrutinizing her, examining the sun-worn creases in Rachel's face as though she were peering into a mirror. At last Meirav leaned back, satisfied with what she saw, and said, "I want to know some things about Rocky."

Rachel narrowed her eyes and remembered her fears. "I'm sure Rocky would be happy to answer all your questions."

Meirav glanced at her phone again, then slipped it into her bag. The phone's disappearance made Rachel nervous. Now Meirav was facing her, her angled body closing off the route to the aisle. Rachel looked down at Meirav's knees and felt trapped.

"Maybe, or maybe not," Meirav parried. "I just wondered if there's anything I ought to know about him."

Rachel bristled. "And you think I'm going to tell you."

"Aren't you?"

Rachel braced herself against the vinyl seat. Twenty centuries flooded within her, carrying every soldier, officer, agent, enforcer, spy, and thug who had ever turned up at her door, searching for one of her sons.

"I'm not that kind of mother," Rachel said.

Meirav squinted at her. Then, to Rachel's surprise, she smiled and said, "You just told me everything I need to know."

Rachel breathed, sipping air through a narrow straw. It was becoming clearer to her why Meirav was here. Something Rocky was doing online was illegal, or more than illegal—bad enough that he couldn't merely be indicted or arrested, but rather had to be cultivated, manipulated, turned. And now Rachel was becoming a protector, an accomplice. She had no idea where this lure was leading, but it was clear she had to extricate herself immediately, and that was exactly what she couldn't do. Suddenly she thought of Rocky as a little boy, dragging himself home from school with a bloody nose and a swollen lip; she felt herself falling upon him, covering his little body with hers, choking on rage and regret. Now she avoided Meirav's glance as an old sorrow welled up within her, brimming at her eyes.

How had she raised such a person—so smart, yet so deeply, deeply stupid? What had she done wrong?

"I know a lot about Rocky already," Meirav said. "The arrests, the divorces, the patent litigations, the bankruptcy filings—"

"He told you all that?"

Meirav smiled. "They're public records. He didn't lie about any of it when I asked him. And I didn't lie to him about myself either."

Rachel eyed her. Was that normal, hunting through public records? Rachel often had trouble keeping track of what was normal. Of all the things that changed, nothing changed more than what was normal. But what was this about Meirav not lying? "What do you mean, about yourself?" Rachel asked.

Meirav sighed. "I don't want to bore you," she said, with a gentle roll of her eyes. "Ask Rocky if you like. But let's just say he and I are very similar. People like Rocky and I aren't like other people, and we keep getting punished for it."

Rachel examined Meirav, her bangles and her wrinkled skin and her wild hair. The woman radiated an unearthly confidence, a luminous quality that made Rachel lean back, afraid of being burned.

"I've looked at the protocol he's building on the blockchain," Meirav was saying.

Blockchain, blockchain, Rachel thought. It sounded familiar, but from what? Something Rocky had tried to explain? Long ago, she used to work hard at remembering the details of what her children were doing and dreaming, but after too many years of trying to keep up with the four elements and the bodily humors and the luminiferous ether and the music of the spheres, she had finally understood that all details expire, that none of it mattered, except that it mattered to her child. Rachel nodded, pretending to care.

Meirav said, "It's hard to explain to someone who doesn't know, but it's—well, it's an incredibly powerful tool, and it's also a work of art. If he can complete what he's doing, it's going to change a lot of industries."

This was implausible, except as a lure. "I thought he was mining money," Rachel tried.

"Yes," Meirav replied. "But while he was trying to mine more efficiently, he figured out something else, a way to embed information into this permanent record of transactions, with an interface anyone can use. It's got some bugs, but if it works, it could be a hack-proof way of creating a permanent digital record." Meirav took a breath, and glanced at the ceiling of the train. "My father used to work on archaeological digs," she said. "He wasn't an archaeologist, he was just a building contractor, but every building contractor in Israel has to report on remains they find when they dig, and he had a real sense of where to find things. He made some major discoveries, even if the professors got the credit. But in the future, the records aren't going to be underground like that. They're going to be digital, and we need ways to preserve them, ways that don't rely on governments or other institutions that might not be here in five hundred years. That's what Rocky's working on, even if he thinks he's just working on currency. It's breathtaking, really. It's like he figured out a way for information to never die."

Rachel wondered if this was supposed to be a good thing, then wondered if it wasn't simply a variation on what her father was already doing two thousand years earlier. But now Meirav had her hand on Rachel's wrist. Meirav's fingers warmed her skin, a heat that frightened her. "That's why I wanted to talk to you," Meirav said.

"What does this have to do with me?" Rachel asked, although she knew the unspeakable answer: everything.

"Because I want to buy Rocky's idea," Meirav announced. "I have some investors who would love it, and I want him as a partner."

This was deeply absurd. After thirty years of being ripped off, according to his own count, was Rocky really dumb enough to be ripped off again? Of course he was. "As a partner in your company?"

Meirav drew in her breath. "As a partner in everything," she said softly. Then she forced a grin. "Now is the part where you tell me that I'm making an enormous mistake."

Rachel hesitated. She looked hard at Meirav before answering. "No, but maybe Rocky is."

Meirav lowered her eyes. With quick movements she pulled her bag up from beneath the seat and slipped her phone out again, shivering a finger over its screen. It was a show, Rachel knew. Meirav's teeth dug into her lip. Suddenly Meirav looked up again, steadying herself against the seat. "I'm getting off at the next stop, to take the ferry downtown," she announced. A change of plans, Rachel thought, and enjoyed the brief frisson of triumph. "But I have one more question for you."

Before Rachel could refuse, Meirav asked, "Do you believe in God?"

Rachel was dumbfounded. Crazy children! "Why are you asking me that?"

"Because it affects what I think of Rocky," Meirav said.

No, this woman definitely wasn't like other people, Rachel thought. Or at least not other people alive right now. "It's a stupid question," Rachel finally answered. "Why would God care if anyone believed in him?"

Meirav laughed out loud, and rose to her feet. "See you soon," she sang, and sprinted for the door.

Rachel remained on the train, utterly bewildered. The conversation was so surreal that for a moment she wondered if she had dreamed it. Everything Meirav said about Rocky was impossible, far too good to be true—which meant that whatever danger she posed was likely immediate, and immense. Rachel leaned back and watched the tunnel blurring past her as she entered the bowels of the city. Rachel rarely prayed anymore; hundreds of years of evidence had demonstrated its pointlessness. But now she closed her eyes and whispered beneath the tunnel's roar: *Please, please protect my child.* Her phone buzzed, an answer.

You are almost out of time, it read. *Come now.*

Like a woman in a trance, she got off the train, hailed a cab, and returned to the unfinished tunnel.

Elazar was luminous, a glowing candle in the dark. He had shed his coat and wore a loose white buttoned shirt, and as he opened the tunnel's door for her, he was the same boy he had once been: a boy in a white robe with thin bristling wrists and hopeful eyes, waiting in moist darkness, luring her underground to a place where time stopped. He seized her arm, and her breath caught in her throat.

"Why are you still here?" he asked.

He had closed the door behind them. Now he stood facing her in the hurricane lamp's dim fluorescent gleam, brandishing a plasticized white envelope in one hand.

"What do you mean? You told me to come."

Elazar let out an irritated grunt. "I mean, why are you still here, in this life? Why am I the one calling you here, instead of you calling me?" He waved the envelope, its white plastic shining in the lamplight. "I have everything you need to leave right here. You can go right away."

"What's the rush?" Rachel asked. She had forgotten, in the intervening century since they had last been together, how exasperating Elazar was, how controlling, how paranoid—or perhaps, she thought now, how anxious, how traumatized. She reached for him, but to her astonishment he stepped away from her. She followed him deeper into the tunnel, to a muddy patch beneath a spiderweb of black wires, along a wall oozing moisture and regret. They stood facing each other, equals.

"Rachel, I hope you're joking. This is urgent. You cannot stay here. Not one more month, not one more week. If I could have made you leave yesterday I would have. You cannot wait."

"Why? Because of Hannah?"

"Yes, because of Hannah. Because of *this* Hannah."

He still liked to wound her; he enjoyed the power. Hannah after Hannah poured through Rachel's mind, a cascade of anguish. She stepped closer, edging toward him until his back was against one of the tunnel's grime-coated walls. She enjoyed the power too.

"That's ridiculous, Elazar," she retorted. "There's nothing urgent about this at all. Even if we really believe it's dangerous for her, scientific research takes years and years."

"Not with money. And not with a discovery like this."

Rachel tried to keep her voice even. "Elazar, I can't leave now. There's—there's a situation I need to address." Rocky rose in her imagination as the child he once was, a boy with a bloodied face and an endless future.

"The situation you need to address is your granddaughter's imminent death."

The words lacerated her. She swallowed, rallied. "Elazar, please. We don't know that. We absolutely don't know that."

"We know that."

Rachel glanced up, away from his angry eyes. Above his head hung a white sign with red gleaming letters: *This work site has gone 0 days without an accident.*

"We know that it's happened before, yes," she admitted. "But those other times, they—they were accidents, they were coincidences, they were guesses. They were meaningless."

"They were consistent," Elazar announced. His hands were at his sides now, the envelope pressed against his thigh. She could feel the energy in his hands, the tension in his chest, his body coiled like a spring. It still amazed her, how she felt his body in her own. "Rachel, we aren't like other people. But we are like other people in this one respect: we don't know everything either. Whatever's gone wrong with us, or gone right with us, it seems eminently clear that other people knowing about us is very, very bad, even if we don't know why. Though I don't think it's hard to guess why."

"Why?"

Elazar breathed, a long thick breath, and said, "So no one will ever make the mistake of wanting it."

"People already want it," Rachel objected.

"That doesn't matter. As long as they know for a fact that it's impossible, that it doesn't exist, they can dream about it until they die and it won't change how they live." Elazar's voice was trembling. "But if it *does* exist, if *we* exist, if they find out for a fact that it's possible for someone, even if only for the two of us—then suddenly no one's life will matter anymore. Because then the entire goal of everyone's life on earth will only be to attain this curse."

Elazar was glaring at her, his face tight with fury. But Rachel recognized what was suppressed beneath it: a vast, unbridgeable pain. She took hold of his shaking shoulders and spoke to him like a mother. "Elazar, for just one moment in your endless life, can you stop prophesying doom?"

Elazar ground his teeth. "I've had at least eighteen moments in my life when I wasn't prophesying doom," he said. "And in at least fourteen of those, I was wrong."

Rachel held him, stroking his neck as though he were a child. "Maybe you're wrong again," she said, with preternatural cheer. "It might not work the way we think. It's just as you said. We really don't know. We only—"

He jerked away from her. "So you're going to risk this child's life, just to prove a point?"

Rachel stood bereft, wordless.

"I didn't think so," he said. He sank to the floor against the wall, laying the envelope beside the lamp. Without thinking she followed him down, sinking with him into the earth. For a moment they were silent, the air thick with dripping rainwater and ghosts. Then Elazar turned to her and grinned.

"Beginning again is easier now than it used to be," he remarked, nudging her back to life. "You might even like it."

Everything that maddened her about Elazar still maddened her. That was oddly comforting. "You've been telling me over and over how much harder it is," she said.

"To get started, yes," he explained. "Much harder. You need all kinds of documents. You need to forge things. You need to lie. But you always needed to lie. The good part that's different is that now you can keep up with everyone you leave behind."

"What do you mean, keep up with them?"

Elazar smiled again, and sat up against the wall. "Tell me this, Rachel. Is it really true that you never saw your children again after leaving them? That you never even tried to see them again? You've said that before, but I never believed you."

Rachel thought. Surveying her memory took time, but Elazar was patient. "It's true, I never did," she said. "Once or twice it happened by accident."

"And didn't you try to talk to them when it did?"

"One time I tried," she answered. The tunnel's ugliness was aggressive, dank industrial incense wafting through rusted metal. How hideous the world had become, Rachel thought, a carrying case for the ugliest of memories. "I was at an airport baggage claim, watching the suitcases going around, when I saw one with my son's name on it," she confided. "A son I hadn't seen in nearly forty years."

Elazar was still grinning. "Tell me you didn't run after that suitcase, and I will never ever believe you."

Rachel tried to smile back, but couldn't. "I did," she admitted. "That time I did. I followed that suitcase all the way around that carousel to the other side, and I saw him. I still regret it."

"How could you regret that?"

"He was an old man," Rachel said softly. "Not just an old man. He was in a wheelchair, being pushed by a woman I didn't recognize—maybe a second wife? Or an aide? I don't know. I stood right in front of him to make sure it was him. It was. The eyes were his, exactly like my father's. But he didn't look back at me. He was just gazing into space, an empty shell. I told him that I loved him. Then I ran away before the wife could call the security guards." Rachel bit her lip. "Elazar, I don't want this. I don't."

Elazar shook his head. "You can't only think about endings," he said. "There's no point to that. Endings are something you and I will never understand." He took her hand in his, and the thrum of his skin warmed hers. "There must have been other times when you heard things about someone you left behind, good things, beginnings."

"Of course," she said. She remembered subscribing to synagogue newsletters in New York years ago, searching for great-grandchildren's birth announcements. Occasionally she spotted one, though she couldn't always be sure. Then there were the officially successful children, the ones whose stories reached her wherever she went. There was the daughter in Neapolis who, at thirteen, had the bizarre idea of tying moldy bread to her brother's leg where he had gashed it at the foundry. *We want the skin to grow back, Mama*, she had explained, *and everything grows on old bread, so isn't it worth trying? It certainly can't hurt!* Decades later in Rome, busy with new children, Rachel still heard legends about the woman healer of Neapolis, the miracle worker people traveled for days to see, the one who could cure any illness and who twice brought people back from the dead in the marketplace by breathing into their mouths and pumping their hearts for them with her hands. Rachel's thirty-fourth son wrote a monumental code of religious law whose manuscript copies soon appeared in every community from Babylonia to France; whenever she heard someone cite it during a long sabbath meal, the world gleamed with unearthly light. For decades Rachel bought multiple copies of the novels written by her sixty-third son, giving them as gifts to his half-siblings. She listened to recordings of concertos played by another daughter, a violinist, until the wax cylinders were damaged beyond repair. Rachel often fantasized that death meant encountering answers, a revelation of the purpose of being alive. But instead she had these smaller revelations, moments when the curtain between the potential and the actual was suddenly pulled back, bathing the world in light. Those moments were fleeting, incremental. In the congregational newsletters where she hunted for births, she more often recognized the names in the obituaries. The wax cylinders wore away, leaving only grooves in her mind. But the grooves in her mind remained, waiting to be played again. She never forgot a child.

"That part, the good part—that's the part that's gotten easier," Elazar was saying. "Obscenely easy, in fact. You used to hear about your children through other people three times removed, or read about them in newspapers, or hunt down rumors. But now there's no need for that. Now you disappear, you begin again, you create a few new identities online—and before you know it, you're tracking down your children. I'm not talking about spotting a few famous ones in the news. I'm talking about being able to follow everything all of them do, forever. You can see where they're living, who they married, watch their children taking their first steps. You can see what they ate for lunch. And if you're very, very, very careful, you can even still tell them what to eat, or who to marry." He smiled again, his eyes gleaming.

"That's terrifying," Rachel said.

"Why?" he asked.

"The responsibility is terrifying," she told him. "And it's also a lie."

"Why is it a lie?" Elazar asked. "I think it's the deepest truth I've discovered in the past two thousand years."

Rachel tried to find the words to explain, but Elazar wasn't waiting. "Every intelligent person alive today wants to accomplish something grand—invent something, create something, dramatically change the world," he said. "Some of the smarter ones actually do it. You and I weren't born thinking we could do that. We were born thinking it was our job to be servants of God."

"Were we wrong?" she asked.

"No. That's what parents are. Not only parents; everyone who provides new possibilities. That's exactly what they are, even if they don't think of it that way." Water dripped from the ceiling onto his hands. "Today a lot of people aren't content with that. They expect to complete something, to see how their works or their children 'turn out'—as if anything ever ended. But you and I know that we can only make beginnings. We can't even create anything ourselves, not really," he said. "All we can try is to help the people who do. Like Rocky and Meirav."

The name startled Rachel. "How do you know Meirav?"

Was that a stupid question? She had long accepted that Elazar had special powers; he was a priest, and even if his powers since then had become tawdry and manipulative, he was still a priest. But in the pallid light of the hurricane lamp, Rachel saw that Elazar was avoiding her eyes.

"Because she's my daughter," Elazar said.

Rachel leaned against the tunnel's wet wall, stunned. She heard Meirav's voice in her head: *My father always used to say, Don't worry, Meirav, I can still die, and then you can go to university for free!* She sucked in air, and tasted something sweet.

"She was only sixteen when I left. But I've been watching her since then. She's my favorite of all my children, which is saying a lot." He forced a smile. "Of course, I never really knew Yochanan, and I did like his mother best."

Rachel leaned back against the tunnel's wall and allowed herself to feel Yochanan beside her. In her mind she inspected him: his curls, the curve of his lip, his laugh. *Obviously I'm taking it seriously if I'm laughing about it!*

"Why is she your favorite?" Rachel asked. When Elazar didn't answer, Rachel dared to add: "Because of her mother?" A lump of irrational jealousy rose within her throat, flavored with absurdity and acid.

"No, no, no," Elazar intoned. "That woman was crazy. She was born in America because her father was some kind of diplomat, but she was from an old Jerusalem family that had been in the city for thousands of years. You know how that city makes people lose their minds. Imagine a hundred generations of inherited lunacy."

"Thousands of years?" Rachel repeated, and finally smiled. "Do we know them?"

Elazar laughed. "Probably, right? That must have been my fantasy when I married her. But she looked down on everyone, everyone. Nothing was good enough for her, nothing met her standards—to a demented level. She wound up in a mental hospital. She reminded me of my father, actually."

Rachel recalled kneeling before Elazar's father, inhaling smoke from her own burning hair. "But your father really was above everyone else," she said.

"Yes, and today he would probably be in a mental hospital too." He paused, as if acknowledging a presence. "Meirav is something different. Part of it was just the time of her birth. For almost two hundred years before her, all my children felt obligated to spit in my face. It wasn't just me, it was every parent I knew. I'm sure it happened to you too. If you were religious, your children became atheists; if you were a freethinker, they ran off to the rebbe. If you spoke Yiddish they spoke Hebrew; if you spoke Hebrew they spoke German. If you were a Socialist they became Communists, and on and on. It was so degrading. But Meirav is only fifty-two. She was the first child in over a hundred years who wasn't afraid to love me."

Rachel eyed Elazar with heartsinking pity.

"I don't only love her because she loves me," he pleaded.

"Did I say that?" Rachel asked.

"You thought it."

Rachel laughed, and was relieved when Elazar laughed with her.

"That isn't why," he insisted. "Meirav is—she's a free person. She does what she wants, not what other people want. Sometimes it gets her into trouble, but she isn't troubled by it. That's what amazes me about her. Nothing troubles her. All my other children inherited my fears, except for her." *What are your fears?* Rachel considered asking, but she already knew the answer: being alone. "She always reminded me of you." Then he added, "Rocky reminds me of you too."

Rachel snorted. "Whatever he's inherited from me, it hasn't served him well."

"Not yet," Elazar conceded. "That's why I sent him Meirav."

"What do you mean, you sent her?"

"Not sent. Guided, maybe. She already had reasons to be here. Let's just say I gave her more reasons."

This was absurd, Rachel knew. "But Rocky met her by chance," she protested. "No one arranged it. They were sitting together in a courthouse waiting room."

Elazar shrugged. "If they hadn't met there, they would have met somewhere else. For everyone but us, the whole world is a courthouse waiting room."

Rachel stared at him, aghast. "Elazar, this is cruel."

"How is it cruel?"

"You said you admire your daughter's freedom, and my son's

freedom." And mine, she thought. "But that's exactly what you're trying to take away, any way you can!"

Elazar held his palms in the air, a gesture that reminded her of Rocky. "So maybe it's a mistake. Maybe they'll be miserable together. But that's their business, and they were already miserable alone, so why not? I have a lot of faith in your children, Rachel."

A sickening thought wormed its way into Rachel's mind. "Have you—have you done this before?"

Elazar laughed. "No," he said. "At least, not intentionally. I've thought about it, many times. But I always wanted my children to have children, if they wanted them. And with yours and mine together, I wasn't sure they could. So I never tried. And until now it wasn't so easy. Now it's the simplest thing. You can find out exactly where they are, every minute of the day—even if they're fifty-two years old and sitting on the other side of the world. Now you can be with them forever. This is what I'm explaining to you, Rachel. You and I don't change, but the world does."

"Elazar, you can't follow your children around for eternity!"

"Of course I can. That's what parents do, whether they're dead or alive. Why, do you really think your parents aren't guiding you? Or that mine aren't guiding me?"

"Are they?" Rachel asked.

Elazar looked at her, and in his face she saw his father. "They are in my every breath."

The tunnel around Rachel was becoming crowded with ghosts. She was relieved when Elazar abruptly turned from her, reaching for something on the floor beside him. "I need to show you this," he said. He held up the large white plasticized envelope as details rattled from his mouth. "There's a metal box for it just down there, so it'll be waterproof and fireproof. I'll show you where I keep the key to the tunnel right outside, so you can find that too. Everything will be waiting for you here." He paused, embarrassed, and placed the envelope in her lap.

The envelope was unsealed. Rachel slid her hand inside it and pulled out a passport.

The passport was the same shape and color as her current American one, but embossed with Hebrew letters. On its cover was an image of a seven-branched candelabrum like the one Elazar's father once lit each day. Her hands shook as she opened it. Inside was an old passport photo of her, altered slightly, with a much fresher face than the one she had now. Instead of her current surname, the Hebrew text read *Bat-Azaria*, Daughter of Azaria. Her birthplace was listed as Jerusalem.

"It's eight years old already, which means you'll have to renew it almost immediately, in two years," Elazar explained. Two years, for him and for her, was almost immediately. "They just introduced some new biometric features that I couldn't replicate without you, so here you are in the last of the old version. Like we always are." He smiled. "I included a credit card for you too, and a phone," he told her, digging deeper into the envelope and flashing plastic. "There's also a bank account, with money to get you started. The language isn't the quite the same as what you remember, but after two months of TV you'll catch up. You've been living in America since you were a child, according to the documents, so no one will expect much. Just remember this address." He unfurled a piece of paper with words in what she still thought of as the new Hebrew script, the cursive that was under a thousand years old. His handwriting was beautiful. "It's your apartment in Tel Aviv. Not even in the same city as me, see? Your own life. But look where it is." She read the address, in the eternity cast by Elazar's shadow. *18 Son-of-Zakkai Street*. "I thought you would appreciate that."

"I don't understand how you did this," Rachel said.

"If I told you I would have to kill you," Elazar joked.

She tried to frown at him, but couldn't. She swallowed a sob.

"I had to do this for you, Rachel. You haven't burned for seventy years, so you don't know how much you need it. Without all this you'd be a beggar on the side of the road, or worse. Much worse."

"It wouldn't be the first time," Rachel murmured. But when he took her hand in his, her body throbbed with a cruel ache, the pain, deep and never-ending, of being too young.

"I'd happily live with you in this tunnel from now until the end of the world," Elazar said. "But I understand that isn't what you want."

"Elazar," she whispered, and ran out of words. Instead she overflowed, and cried as they clutched each other in the dim tunnel, both of them crying until they ran out of tears. Because the tears did run out, even if nothing else did.

THAT NIGHT RACHEL LAY in bed, listening to Rocky and Meirav's muffled laughter downstairs, and closed her eyes. Beneath her eyelids the room grew dark, then illuminated with an old light, an oil lamp in her sister's hands.

"Rachel," her sister whispered, touching her shoulder. "Come. Now."

Her sister's fingers on her shoulder made her imagine she was a small child. Time collapsed in Rachel's mind even then, a condition of being alive within it. But as she rose from the mat on the floor, she took her place again in the firm column of days in which she lived: she was a thirty-year-old widow, not yet remarried, waking up at midnight in her sister's house, roused from her sleep by her childhood companion because their mother was dying. She hurried silently to the next room.

Her mother lay on a stack of sheepskins, curled under three woolen blankets, though the night was warm. As it happened, it wasn't the last time Rachel would hear her mother's voice; two weeks still remained when her mother continued to speak, pray and insult her daughters in ways Rachel chose to blame on delirium. Two weeks later Rachel and her sisters would strip her mother's body, wash her, purify her, stand guard over her corpse until dawn, and then carry it forth from the city teeming with soldiers and angry boys, out to the cemetery on the mountain just east of the Temple, where her grandparents and great-grandparents and everyone before them were already buried, going back a thousand years. Yet for now her mother was still alive and had woken in the night, searching for her youngest daughter.

"Rachel," she rasped, as Rachel's sister slipped out of the room.

"Here I am," Rachel answered.

Her mother's body was swollen from illness, and the swelling made her younger, erasing her wrinkles and easing her face back to the one Rachel remembered, a young woman's face, plaintive and hopeful. Rachel sat beside her mother and did not know what to say. When she first met Elazar, her mother had transformed before her eyes from a loving, devoted, righteous woman into entirely the wrong kind of woman—a woman who stupidly bent her head and worked and prayed and buried her imagination deep in the ground beneath her feet, a woman who followed every rule because she didn't know better. But since Zakkai's death, Rachel could not bear her mother's presence. Her every gesture, even from her sickbed, reverberated through the air like the blast of a ram's horn in Rachel's face: *I knew so much more than you ever imagined*. Rachel looked down at the woolen blankets, afraid to meet her mother's eyes. She felt her mother's hand on her forehead as though she were a little girl.

"May God make you like Sarah, Rebecca, Rachel and Leah," her mother murmured, reciting a script. Rachel tried not to cringe. She was already the Rachel from her father's scrolls, already the youngest sister, already beloved and betrayed. But then her mother added: "May God grant you a long life, and many children."

"Many children?" Rachel asked. Rachel was widowed, mother of one, already old and angry. Was it a curse?

"I pray to God that you will have more children," her mother said softly. "When you do, remind them that God is with them, that someone is watching."

Rachel felt a river of sorrow well up inside her, pain mingled with regret. She was raising Yochanan; wasn't that enough? And besides, who could forget that God was with him? They were in Jerusalem and always would be, right across the valley from the everlasting House of God itself. How could anyone forget? But her mother was in pain, and dying people said all kinds of irrelevant things. Her father had collapsed while sputtering a verse about sheep. "I will," Rachel conceded.

"I am watching," her mother said. And breathed.

CHAPTER

12

IT GOES BY SO FAST

. . .

The children climbed up to the stage carefully, following a teacher's whispered prompts as another teacher leaned over an old piano, bumping out pediatric chords. There were many of them—a hundred kindergarteners in single file, the girls in little dresses, the boys in tiny collared shirts—and the line moved slowly, but eventually the risers in front of the row of microphones filled up with children of identical vintage, gathered together like the off-spring of some indifferent egg-laying reptile who had abandoned its young.

Seated on a metal folding chair beneath the stage for Ezra's end-of-the-year kindergarten show—she and Hannah had arrived early for front-row seats, making up for Daniel's absence while he finished a business trip—Rachel felt a creeping unease. This routine massing of children was still new for her. Years ago, no one forced children to assemble this way until they were older, and then only the boys, for wars. But now this parading of identically-aged children before their parents to sing forgettable songs had become a ritual, the children replacing the flocks of lambs once brought for sacrifice, reminding the adults of their obligations. The ritual induced visions. Rachel looked at the sea of small people as they began their forgettable song and suddenly saw all of these children old, very old. Their heads were gray or bald; their arms flabbed; the girls' faces sagged under clownish makeup; the boys' temples caved in, cadaverous. Their sunken eyes squinted behind thick lenses, gazing into a void. One by one they wandered off the stage, disappearing into the wings, until the assembly dwindled to nothing: empty risers, exactly as before. Everything fades, everything returns. Rachel shook her head, returning to the present. It was then that Hannah's son Ezra broke ranks, squirming to the front of the stage and yanking a microphone from its stand. He managed to shout, "I got the microphone! Hello, Mommy!" before a teacher dragged him away. The audience guffawed. Rachel recognized her granddaughter's boy, the one who lightened everyone's burdens, as one of her own. Elazar was right: it was time.

In the car afterward as she drove Hannah to the train, Rachel noticed her preternaturally rational granddaughter wiping her eyes.

"What's wrong?" Rachel asked.

Hannah turned to Rachel and smiled, her makeup smeared with an errant tear. "Nothing," she answered, and tried to smother a sob with a laugh. "I just—I look at Ezra up there with the other kids, and I know he's only five, but he's my baby, and I know I'm not going to do this again."

I can't take this anymore, Rachel thought. "Lucky you," she said aloud, and tried to make it sound like a joke. She imitated the little boy's voice: " 'I got the microphone!' " The boy, she knew, was another Rocky.

Hannah laughed, but barely. "He certainly knows what he wants," she sputtered. But in an instant she was gulping air, fighting tears again. "I've never told anyone this, but I still imagine him crying at night," Hannah said. "I wake up in the middle of the night because

I think I hear him crying, the way he did when he was a baby. Then I realize it's a memory, but it isn't any less real than when it really happened. Has that ever happened to you?"

Driving still felt new to Rachel, uncomfortable; she blamed it on her less-than-seventy years behind the wheel. There seemed no point in answering Hannah's question, certainly not while the car careened along tight turns through the nature reservation, the hilly forest on the east end of town. Rachel had more urgent things on her mind. She glanced up at the tall thick trees, plotting an escape—or more accurately, a rescue.

"Maybe it's because of work," Hannah was saying. "All day long I'm thinking about how to stop people from dying. My life is so perfect, right? I have no reason to be unhappy, none at all. But somehow everything that happens with Daniel and the children, all the wonderful things—it's as if there's this tunnel of sadness flowing through it. That's how I imagine it, like a secret passage underneath everything that's always flowing with this constant stream of sorrow, and no one can see it, but we all know it's there. And I just keep thinking that if no one had to die, that tunnel would dry up and disappear, and all these happy things wouldn't be so sad anymore."

Rachel gripped the steering wheel and hoped that Hannah would shut up. She scanned the sides of the road for a time before she spotted a turnout coming up, a little parking area on the road shoulder at the head of some trail. Hannah kept talking.

"At work I keep telling myself that that's why I'm here, that's what I'm striving for, just to get rid of that sadness. I feel like it's just out of reach, but I'm so close to it, and—" Hannah paused, tried, failed. "Anyway, it's very stressful emotionally and I never express it, I guess. So instead here I am, crying over Ezra's kindergarten show. Sorry, I know it's stupid. It's just that it . . . it . . . it goes by so fast."

Rachel yanked the steering wheel, jerking both the car and Hannah to the right, and then screeched the car to a stop beneath the trees.

"Gram, what the hell are you doing?"

Rachel killed the engine and sat for a moment in the stopped car, enjoying the odd silence beside the trailhead, at the gate of the forest. Then she turned to Hannah and said, "I need to talk to you. Can we please get out for a minute?"

Hannah's mouth crimped. "I have to get to work."

"No, you don't. I need to talk with you, and not in this metal box."

Hannah sat up, imperious, insulted. "I'm going to miss my train," she announced. She theatrically glanced at her watch. "It's really late, Gram. Whatever it is you want to say, how about if we just—"

"Hannah, get out of the fucking car."

Hannah leaned back, shocked. She was frightened now, Rachel could see. But Rachel did not linger. She was done lingering. She thrust open the car door and jumped out, slammed it shut, and started down the trail into the woods. She glanced behind her and saw Hannah stumbling out of the car, tapping out something on her phone with one hand as she raced to catch up with Rachel. Rachel walked faster, and then started running, tripping over rocks and branches as she made her way toward—she wasn't sure what, just somewhere where no one would find them. Her shoe snagged on something, a branch or a thorn, and she yanked it off, yanked the other shoe off, and ran barefoot along the path, her thick feet callused and impenetrable. At last, past three twists in the trail, she saw a boulder under a thick clump of old gnarled oaks. She sat down, panting, until Hannah caught up, her mud-spattered skirt and shoes jerking to a stop in front of Rachel. Her face shimmered with fear.

"Gram, are you okay? What's going on?"

"I'm fine," Rachel said, a reflex. Lying had become so natural for her, like eating or breathing, and just as necessary. But now she looked at her granddaughter, the young woman who looked more like her than anyone else had in two thousand years—the young woman who was almost the same age Rachel was when she was first widowed, when Elazar killed Zakkai, when her mother died, when she first understood that she was the adult, that Elazar wasn't her rescuer but her pursuer, that being loved was nowhere near as necessary as loving, that it was suddenly her task, her only task, to protect her children—and the flood rose within her.

"No, it's not true. I'm not fine, Hannah," Rachel declared. "I haven't been fine in a long, long time."

Hannah stared at her, her mouth slightly open, her forehead creased. She looked to Rachel like a little girl, confused and frightened. She sat down next to Rachel and waited. The forest rustled with birds and wind, ever changing. Rachel drew in her breath, braced her trembling hands against the rock, and spoke.

"I want to talk to you about your research," she began.

Hannah's face reverted to a sneer. "God, Gram! Really? You can't just—"

But Rachel wasn't listening. "You know how you told me I have the genetic deterioration of a teenager?"

Hannah raised an eyebrow, a shadow of her father. "Yes," she said. The word rose between them like an offering, a plume of incense.

"Why do you think that is?"

Hannah hesitated. "I don't know," she murmured, and then pounced. "I don't know yet, but I'm getting close. I think it might be an answer to something, maybe even an answer to everything. If I could get you to come to the lab, I could—"

Rachel dug her fingernails into the rock's surface, the rock that was older than she was. "You don't know, but I do."

Hannah eyed Rachel, her body still. "Why? Why do you have the genes of a teenager?"

"Because I am a teenager," Rachel said softly. "I'm eighteen years old, and I've been eighteen years old for the past two thousand years."

Hannah looked at Rachel for a moment. Then she laughed, a long, loud laugh. "That explains so much."

Trees rose around them, a curtain of leaves and tree trunks, hundred-year-old tree trunks, babies. Rachel shook her head. "Listen, Hannah," she said. "I know you want me to come to your lab." She watched as Hannah's smile faded. "But the only way I'll do that is if you can fix me—if you can change my genes, so I'm not like this anymore."

Hannah cocked her head. "You mean like gene therapy?"

Hannah's voice sounded normal, casual, as if Rachel had asked her to pick her up after work. Was this really happening? "What's that?" Rachel asked.

"Like you said, changing genes. You take out the mutation and deactivate it, or replace it with something else."

Rachel couldn't believe how simple Hannah made it sound. Was this what she had been waiting for, for two thousand years? "That's it," Rachel crowed. "That's what I need."

Hannah's eyes were on the trees, distracted. She was speaking as she always did, thinking as she spoke. "In theory it's possible, but it's only in Phase 1 trials for toxicity. Nobody does that except with terminal patients." She turned back to Rachel. Hannah was so small, Rachel thought, underneath these trees, these tall and silent trees that would outlive her. "Gram, I don't get it. Can you be serious for a minute? What are you really talking about?"

Terminal patients, Rachel seethed, boiling with envy. But no, it wasn't envy anymore! The excitement made her legs tremble. She leaned forward, pressing her bare feet into the mud. "Remember how I hadn't signed my will?" she asked Hannah.

Hannah nodded, a small, frightened nod.

"Yesterday I met with the lawyer and signed off on everything. I'm ready."

"What do you mean, you're ready?"

Rachel tried to laugh, and failed. "I don't even know what I mean," she pleaded. "All I know is that I want to die. To die for real." The sky seeped between the trees, deep and blue and silent, like it always did when she awoke, again and again and again. She turned again to her granddaughter, to her younger self, to herself. "Hannah, you're the first person in two thousand years who can help. Hannah, please," she begged. "I need you to kill me."

Rachel bowed her head before her granddaughter as though Hannah were Elazar's father, smelling her hair on fire. But she had forgotten that Hannah was a mother. Now Hannah was regarding her the way Rachel had so often looked at her own children, whenever they begged her for more stories or more playtime or for their dead father to come back: thinking of the kindest way to tell them that what they wanted was impossible.

"Gram, I'm not going to kill you," Hannah said.

"Why not?"

"Do I really need to explain this? First, I'm a doctor, and there's the whole Hippocratic do-no-harm thing. Next, I'm a person, and there's the whole I-don't-murder-people thing. Then on top of that—oh, I don't know, I guess there's the whole *you're-my-grandmother* thing. No, Gram. I'm not going to kill you."

"Can't you at least try?"

Hannah rested a hand on Rachel's, and spoke again in her mother voice. "Gram, you need help. More help than I can give you. You mentioned that you were on lithium. Maybe you need—"

Rachel flung Hannah's hand aside. Hannah jolted, alarmed.

"Hannah, whatever you're doing with my genes, with the pieces of me you stole, you have to stop it," Rachel said, trying to steady her voice. "You're in danger."

"How exactly am I in danger?"

Rachel breathed, paused, breathed again. "It's—it's happened before, whenever someone came too close. With—with—with other Hannahs, even," she stuttered. It surprised her, how much it hurt to say it. The burned girl rose before her, dissolving into smoke in a bright blue sky. "You're not the first Hannah, you know. You're the eighteenth Hannah in this family, going back to my mother, may her memory be a blessing."

Hannah grunted, an exasperated noise. "I know I'm named after your mother. You still didn't explain. What's dangerous about my work?"

"Everything," Rachel said. "I can't prove it, but—"

"Then how am I supposed to believe it?"

Rachel blinked, cringed. Children! "It's like anything else you believe. You believe in God."

"As a scientist I'm more of an agnostic."

"You can agnosticate all you want. It only means that your life is much, much bigger than you are, bigger than you can ever know. It only means that those seventeen other Hannahs are all within you."

Hannah smirked. "That last part is true, genetically speaking."

"Everything I'm telling you is true. I've been lying for your entire life until now."

Rachel dug her toes deeper into the mud. Hannah's gaze traveled up a tree trunk toward the sky. Rachel watched her granddaughter and could hear her thoughts, listened between the rustling leaves as Hannah weighed what she knew against what she loved. Then Hannah straightened herself on the rock and turned back to Rachel.

"Okay, Gram," she said. Her voice was level, stingy, cold. "I'd be lying if I said I believed any of this. But I'm listening. Explain to me how this happened. Explain to me how you got to be two thousand years old."

The mud was warm around Rachel's feet. She drew the warmth up through her body, like a plant drawing strength from the earth.

"When I was eighteen, I made a mistake," she said. "Like you, I was in love, and like you, I was stupid. I just wanted to save my baby boy. He was sick, and then he was dying."

Hannah had been marking time, but now her face shifted, a sudden recognition of something true. "What baby boy?" she asked. "You mean Dad or Uncle Jake?" Then her eyes widened. "You had a—a child who died?"

"There's a lot you don't know about me," Rachel said softly. "There are so many people you never met." And so many people I never met, Rachel thought, the children of the children, and their children too. "Long ago I was like you. I was a mother like you, a mother with a little boy," she said. "He was my baby, he was dying, and I wanted to save him. And I did, I saved him! But he still grew up, and in the end he died anyway. A lifetime in a breath. It goes by so fast, Hannah. It goes by so fast."

Hannah opened her mouth, confused, but Rachel did not stop.

"I know what you're trying to do, Hannah. It's beautiful that you're trying to do it. But I don't even know how to tell you how wrong you are."

Rachel was standing now, her feet sinking in mud as she reached for the girl who sat motionless before her, the girl whose face Rachel was now committing to memory, the girl whose still, small presence Rachel did not want to forget.

"You know how you were crying at Ezra's kindergarten show? That tunnel of sorrow that flows through everything?"

Hannah nodded, a tilt of the head that was barely a pulse.

"You need that tunnel, Hannah. Nothing means anything without it." Rachel heard her granddaughter's breathing, smelled the rot of the forest, breathed in the air her granddaughter breathed. "Not dying doesn't make it better. It only makes it longer." She closed her eyes and let the tears come, the world overflowing. "I'm so old, Hannah. I'm so, so old."

Rachel tried to preserve in her memory the tug of her granddaughter's arms around her waist, the weight of the young woman's cheek on her shoulder. She felt Hannah's body against hers and imagined her own arms stretching upward like a living tree, toes growing into the earth and fingers reaching for the sky.

CHAPTER

13

HOUSE FIRE

. . .

"Yochanan, you IDIOT!"

She couldn't help it, though later she couldn't forgive herself for it. Yochanan was already an old man, sick, and this time dying for real: dying in a nothing of a village after retiring from teaching in Yavneh, a beach town with nothing in it but Roman soldiers and, thanks to Yochanan, an academy of scholars studying the Torah. *For what*, Rachel wondered, *when everything is already lost?* It had been years since she had seen him. Ever since the destruction, since she had first witnessed the effects of the vow, she had been bewildered, terrified, afraid of herself. She looked now exactly like she had looked when she was eighteen years old. When she found out Yochanan was still living, she counted it a miracle. But when she found out how he had managed to survive and thrive, the rumors about her son that had infected everyone in Yavneh, she could not contain her rage.

He was confined to his bed by then, but she had begged permission to see him from his disciples, pretending to be a great-niece, offering facts about his family as proof. When she walked into the room, both of them were stunned: she that he was dying, and he that she had been reborn.

"Mother? But it's—it's impossible."

"My baby," she whispered. She barely recognized him. Yochanan was cadaverous; his skin stretched like parchment across his knobby bones. She struggled not to weep.

"I'm ill, Mother. Very ill," Yochanan said. His voice was labored, but familiar, each word carefully chosen, clipped and clear. "Time is already changing for me, folding on itself. You look to me like you did when I was a child."

"You'll always be a child to me," she said simply. She thought of explaining, though she saw now there was no need to explain, that explaining would only bring him confusion and pain, things his withered body had no more room for. She was stunned by how peaceful he was, and not merely because he was lying in bed. His voice was low and soft, his face eased into a sad smile, as though every last drop of anger had drained from his body, every passionate flame of his character quenched by a calm, steady, endless sea. It unnerved her. She still felt the fire. She remembered the rumors she had heard, and dared to speak.

"I heard what you did after you escaped the city in the coffin," she said, swallowing rage. She held his hand, stroking his shriveled knuckles to avoid crushing his fingers in hers. "Is it—is it true?" *How could I have raised someone so stupid?*

Yochanan looked at her, his face still peaceful, a man who knew he had done right. "Mother, I was thinking about the future. I can explain."

"Good," she said slowly, "because I need to understand this. I'm an old woman, Yochanan. Your time isn't my time, and maybe there's something you understand that I don't."

"But Mother, you aren't old anymore," Yochanan smiled. His grin shrunk him down to a child again, running through the city.

"And to me you will always be a boy," Rachel said. "Maybe that's all this is, a foolish boy's mistake. But you were never foolish, Yochanan."

"I wasn't foolish this time either," he insisted. In his voice she heard him half-grown, challenging the adults: *How could anyone know the day he's going to die?* "It was the wisest thing to do. The only thing."

Rachel clutched his hand. "Then explain. Is it true that after you were carried out of Jerusalem in the coffin, you were brought to Vespasian?"

"Yes, it's true."

"Vespasian, as in the Roman emperor Vespasian?"

"He wasn't the emperor then. He was just running the campaign to end the revolt."

"I know that, Yochanan," she muttered, snapping at her son the way she had once snapped at her mother, long ago. Another thought horrified her, as frightening as that first glance at her reflection in a cistern after she had burned: *Has my soul gotten younger too?*

"He knew I was coming," Yochanan said. "His spies were in the city. They arranged for me to see him."

Rachel breathed out, expelling anger and grief. "So it's true. You had an audience with the future Roman emperor."

"Yes," Yochanan said. A strange energy seemed to seize him. His voice sped up, the way it had when he was a young man, ready to prove a point. "And I already knew he would become the emperor, even if he didn't know it yet. When I rose from the coffin, I greeted him with *'Vivat Imperator!'* He laughed at me. But a few days later, he received a message announcing that Nero had died in Rome."

"Oh, Yochanan, you're a living oracle. Who needs the Temple when we have you?" Rachel tried to shield herself with sarcasm, but she could barely sustain it. The Temple in ruins was nothing compared to her child in ruins, lying before her, desolate.

Yochanan took a long, labored breath, then another, wincing with pain. His body was a smoking wreckage, a burn Rachel could feel in her own body. But his mind was the same.

"Everyone talks about the prophecy," Yochanan said, almost cheerfully. "But Vespasian didn't care about the prophecy. He cared what I could tell him about what was happening in the city, about the effects of the siege and the rebels' plans."

The bottomless double-crossings churned Rachel's stomach like foul meat. It made her long for Zakkai, for his insane, savage innocence. She sucked down bile, and came to the part she refused to believe.

"Is it true that when Vespasian heard that Nero had died, he offered to grant you any wish?"

"Yes," Yochanan said.

"While his camps with tens of thousands of soldiers were surrounding Jerusalem, while we were all starving inside the city and being slaughtered by the Zealots for any attempt at surrender, while we were waiting for the Romans to smash down the walls and kill or enslave whoever was left, while the Temple was still standing, while we hadn't yet lost the war? *That* was when the future emperor offered to make your deepest wish come true?"

"Yes."

Rachel could no longer see her son through her tears. "Yochanan, you could have saved the country. You could have saved the city. You could have saved the Temple. You could have saved the Holy of Holies, the House of God. And instead you saved—a story?"

IN THE DRAMATIC AND FRIGHTENING years before he left Jerusalem, Yochanan had been the opposite of stupid. As an adult he had his own academy, meeting with his disciples on the stairs of the Temple mount each day to study Torah, perfecting their moral aim like bowmen perfecting their shots. Life for Yochanan was all obligation, a devotion to the future at any cost. "If you're planting a tree and someone says to you, 'The Messiah just arrived,'" Rachel once heard him teach, "finish planting the tree and then go greet the Messiah." He hated the Zealots with an anger that scared Rachel: anyone who took up arms against Rome wasn't a hero fighting for freedom, but a death-seeking fool who cared nothing for his children. He preached it endlessly, going from house to house and begging every able-bodied man to surrender to the Romans and make peace; the Zealots were idiots to think they could beat the greatest army the world had ever seen, an army which had already surrounded the city with elaborate camps on every side. But it was only when the Zealots took control of the city, barred the gates so no one could defect, and burned up the food stores—someone had the idea that this might convince more people to fight—that Rachel, already widowed again and a grandmother of twelve, began to agree with her son, even when half her grandchildren joined the Zealots. When the Zealots stormed the Temple and strung the old high priest Hanania up by his neck, Rachel sent a blank scroll and, for the first time in fifty years, returned to the tunnel.

She was old then, or so she believed. Her hair had turned light and brittle, her skin had creased after years of sun, and her body was crimped and worn from children, and aching from hunger. But the water in the tunnel was cold and fast as it ran against her thin bare feet. As she climbed she felt a quickening within her, washing years down through the cut stone into the pool below, as if they had never existed. Before she knew it, his light loomed around the corner.

She had braced herself for him to look older, imagining him as his father once was, fat and bristling. She had forgotten the hunger. He emerged around the corner like a shadow from his lamp, thin and flickering, in a filthy robe stained with brown blood. His hair was still thick, but matted and lighter; his beard was patchy over his gaunt face, skin stretched across old bones. He smiled at her for an instant, before his face melted into a quiet agony. He fell into her arms, and she couldn't stop herself from crying.

"Elazar," she said, "your father, your father."

"It was inevitable." His voice was deeper than she remembered it, heavy in his throat. "He knew he was doomed." He pulled away from her and composed himself. For a moment Rachel remembered how he once had stood before her, the cocky young priest who couldn't stop smirking. "The Temple itself knows," he added, his voice thick with misery. "A few times at night I've seen the bronze gates open by themselves."

"From the wind?" Rachel murmured.

"The wind? It takes ten men to close them! The priests say that our Father himself is abandoning the house, that we're about to be banished from our Father's table." Rachel listened and heard the words between the words, the father who had abandoned the house, leaving his son behind. She clutched his hands.

"Are you in danger?" Rachel asked.

"No," he said, with a sad smile. "I'm not that good a person. The Zealots took over my house, and I give them whatever they want." Rachel did not ask what they wanted. "Unfortunately I'm not much like my father."

"I remember," Rachel said. "But you are powerful, Elazar."

Elazar cringed. Rachel imagined, for a brief hallucinatory moment, that he was still a teenage boy. "I don't expect you to forgive me," he mumbled. For the first time Rachel realized that that was exactly what he expected.

"I'm not here to forgive you," she said. "I'm here because I need you. Yochanan has been trying to convince people to make peace with the Romans, and the Zealots have him on their list of traitors. Since your father died, men have come to the house looking for him."

Elazar leaned against the tunnel's damp wall, his gaunt body spent. "I can't do anything for him, Rachel. I—"

"Just listen, Elazar." She tried to think of a way to explain it that didn't reveal her overwhelming failure as a parent and grandparent, the horror her life had become. There was no way. "My grandson is one of the Zealot leaders," she began.

In the cool tunnel her face burned, but Elazar merely shrugged. "One of my sons is, too."

"Your son?" She hadn't seen him for fifty years, she remembered. For the first time, she thought: *It goes by so fast*. "How many children do you have?"

"None anymore, except the Zealot," he said. He cleared his throat, hiding a sob.

"That's not true. You have Yochanan."

"Rachel, don't do this to me," he whispered.

"Please listen, Elazar. Yochanan went to my grandson and asked what he would have to do for the Zealots to—to let him leave the city." She did not use the words her daughter had used: *defect, betray, surrender.* "My grandson told him that the only way out is if he's dead."

"Dead," Elazar muttered. "So you want me to protect his body? I can't even do that, Rachel. I—"

"No, Elazar. There's another way. My grandson told him that dead people are allowed out of the city for burial—only important dead people, people whose followers the Zealots want on their side. They would allow the person's body to leave the city in a coffin. Do you understand?" Elazar watched her, unblinking. "But the Zealots never agree on anything, and I can't imagine how it could work unless we bribed the right people, convinced them not to open the coffin, and then convinced them to open the gate." Since the siege began, hunger had fatigued her, but the tunnel's thick wet air blew life into her lungs. "I need you, Elazar."

Elazar's body had been limp, the tired figure of an old man. But now he straightened. His face was wide and wild as though he were a boy searching the tunnel for ancient letters. When he seized her hands, a power gripped her that she had not felt for fifty years.

"Bring him in a coffin to the Dung Gate tomorrow morning," he said. "I can take care of everything else. Trust me."

In that moment she did.

BEFORE DAWN THE NEXT MORNING, Yochanan's disciples, including several of his nephews, brought a plain pine coffin to Rachel's home. Yochanan had been up all night waiting for them, studying and praying. Rachel also could not sleep. She sat beside him, reading the scrolls over his shoulder until Yochanan fell silent, and raised his eyes to hers.

"I keep thinking about Father," he said.

Which father, she wondered. The thought lodged in her mind like a grain of sand, the irreducible understanding that he would never, ever know.

"If he were alive he would be furious with me," Yochanan said, and watched her, waiting. It was heartbreaking how even old children still needed approval, still needed someone to say *Yes, you're right*, or more so, *Yes, you're right, and even if you're wrong, I and the world forgive you*. But it wasn't Rachel's job to forgive.

"If you were going to leave the besieged city in a coffin," Rachel answered, "I think he would have preferred if you were actually dead."

Yochanan tensed his mouth into a sad grin. "I hated him for so many years. But now that I'm old, I think he was just young. He made a young man's choice."

"Yes," Rachel said. "And yours is an old man's choice."

Yochanan laughed. "Then I've been an old man since I was twelve years old." He looked at her, and in his eyes Rachel saw the boy he once was, the boy who ran to her with his forehead bleeding, the boy who lost the story. "Mother, am I making a mistake? Who was right, him or me?"

"I won't live long enough to know," Rachel said. "But maybe you will."

AN HOUR BEFORE SUNRISE, amid his disciples' chanted verses, Yochanan climbed into the coffin. The hunger had made all of them into living corpses, but Rachel shuddered in sudden revulsion when her son closed his eyes. His gaunt old body lay drained and silent. The lid came down before she could say a word.

When dawn broke, the disciples assembled around the coffin and raised it to their shoulders. Rachel was surprised by how easily they carried it. Her son's body was whisked out of her house as if floating on water, carried on the current of everyone he had trained to take his place. She had no trouble playing the part of the mourning old mother; she trailed the coffin wailing aloud. They followed the path through the city she had run so often as a girl, through the alleyways and the marketplace and then down to the plaza in front of the southern stairs of the Temple mount, except now the streets were empty, hunger making it too hard for anyone to leave their beds at dawn. At last they came to the Dung Gate, with its twin pillars of teenage Zealot guards. Between them stood Elazar.

His white robes looked brighter, as they were when he and she first met; she imagined that he had taken pristine ones from his dead father. The Zealots crossed their spears as the coffin approached the locked doors. She watched as Elazar spoke to the two guards, passing them each something she could not see at a distance. The guards raised their spears and stepped forward, until they were blocking the coffin about four cubits before the gate.

"Who's in this coffin?"

"Our teacher, Yochanan son of Zakkai," Rachel's nephew said. "He died early this morning. We cannot keep his body in the city overnight."

Rachel imagined she heard a sound from within the coffin, but no one else seemed to notice. The guards were younger than her grandchildren. One of them yawned.

"Open it up so we can see," one guard said.

"Our teacher of blessed memory taught us the laws of purity regarding corpses," one of the disciples tried. "We cannot—"

"Fine then. Let's just stab through the coffin and make sure no one inside it is alive."

"And defile our teacher's corpse?"

"Stand back," Elazar announced. His voice was unlike Rachel had ever heard it before: a heavy rolling bellow, like his father's on the holy days calling out to crowds of thousands. "Stand back and let him pass." The two guards glanced at Elazar. Then they unbolted the city gates and thrust them open.

Before the coffin could come closer, Elazar slipped along the wall and into an alley. When the coffin reached the threshold Rachel glanced into the alley, but he was already gone. The coffin passed through the doors quickly, the men carrying it almost running, with Rachel following behind. By now Rachel was weeping again, wailing like she had when Yochanan was a sick little boy, unable to understand why she was crying, her eyes blind with tears. But when she reached the doors, one of the guards thrust his spear across her waist.

"Not you," he said. "You stay."

The gates closed before her, and her son was gone.

RACHEL STAYED.

Not alone, because no woman is ever alone; every woman has her own unchosen assortment of parents or children or siblings or nieces or nephews or cousins or uncles or aunts, her own babies or elders or someone else's, a clutch of needy people always hanging on her neck. But the siege went on and on, and the weight on Rachel's neck became ever lighter. Her three oldest daughters starved to death. Six of her grandchildren followed; a seventh, a teenage boy, left the city on a rebel sortie to attack an enemy camp, and never returned. And then, one hot summer morning, battering rams smashed down the city walls.

Rachel woke to the sound of screams, and bolted upright on the old sheepskin her youngest grandchildren had sucked on as they starved. To her horror, her house was empty: her last living daughter, the mother of the Zealot, must have fled with her younger children in the night, thinking the old woman might hold them back if she tried to say goodbye. Afterward Rachel would tell herself that they had surely escaped the city somehow, that the half-stripped woman she later saw in the upper marketplace, bound and tied to ten others, was surely not her daughter but someone who happened to resemble her, some other unfortunate woman who would soon find herself on an auction block in Rome, which was, after all, perhaps a better fate than the women and men whose bodies Rachel tripped on as she ran as fast as she could through the bloodstained streets. For an instant there seemed no point in continuing—not in running through the city, nor even in breathing. She might have offered herself up to the soldiers then, or run into one of their spears. But she remembered Yochanan and kept running, searching for a way out.

She thought of the tunnel; of course she thought of the tunnel. But so had half the city, including the Zealot warriors; the mouth of the tunnel was stuffed with corpses, and the pool ran with blood. There was nowhere to go. Then she thought of Elazar and his dead father, of the power of the vow, and hurried toward the Temple.

It was nearly impossible to enter the outer court. Thousands of people had gathered there, knowing that nowhere else in the city would God protect them anymore, that at least this one last place of divine favor remained. Rachel pushed her way through the crowds, mostly women and small children and old men, until she passed through the outer gate and no longer had to push, for the crowd pushed her, driving her toward the eastern colonnade of the outer court where she had first met Elazar. The Temple court looked like the morning of a holiday, thousands upon thousands of people gathered to beg forgiveness. If somehow she could reach the inner court, Rachel thought illogically, if she could fight through the crowd and reach that place where she had once climbed the fifteen steps and stood at the threshold before the altar, she still might be able to find a priest, press her face to the floor, make a final vow so she could escape the city alive and live to see her son again. Or if all else failed, at least she might find Elazar.

When Rachel realized this was hopeless, it was already too late. The bowmen and catapults around the ramparts had begun their attack, a hailstorm of stones and flaming arrows falling like burning rain. Rachel was trapped in the panicking crowd, the towering Temple visible high above the screaming people around her, arrows whizzing in all directions in front of the shining edifice—some fired by Roman soldiers, others by Zealots inside the inner court. Moments later, soldiers on the outer court's colonnades began throwing lit torches at the Temple itself.

The Temple did not burn, not at first. It melted. Silver and gold plating on its surfaces heated until the precious metals shivered and slid down the massive limestone walls, solid becoming liquid. Only then, as she watched the tops of the gleaming walls melt in the hot wavy air, did Rachel see the flash of a torch soar across a patch of blue sky and disappear inside one of the golden apertures near the roof. For an impossibly long time the walls continued dissolving, thin curls of smoke from the priests' courtyard around it inscribing the sky like incense. And then the House of God erupted in flames.

The massive bronze doorframes groaned and crumpled inward as the planks of the cedar doors slowly transformed from wood to ash, until the doorway stood open like a vast mouth, vomiting fire and smoke. The fire spread quickly, and the crowds near the gate to the inner court were consumed by the flames. Soon Rachel saw flaming people climbing up onto the parapets surrounding the outer court, screaming as they fell into the city below. Others rushed toward the gate to the inner court, scrambling over piles of burning bodies to plunge themselves directly into the furnace, final sacrifices to purge their sins. The flames grew and swallowed the priests' quarters, fire flowing across melting silver and cedar beams and rendering whoever remained inside into ash. As the colossal Temple vanished behind a towering column of thick black smoke, Rachel smelled the burning flesh. At that moment she knew with total certainty that life in this world had ended.

As the fires spread to the surrounding buildings, the crowd around Rachel pushed toward the inner court, then pushed back again as flaming wooden beams collapsed onto waves of people, fire spreading from one person to the next as people pressed against one another, unable to escape. Heat smothered the crowd from above, the air wavy and thick with ash. All around her people were gasping, slipping and disappearing beneath one another, and the ground rose and fell with bodies underfoot. Rachel's corner of the crowd pushed toward the eastern gate, a wooden door on the outer court—locked, her father had taught her, until the arrival of the Messiah. If it were opened, it would lead to the deep valley on the mountain's edge, a precipitous ravine facing the cemetery where her parents were buried. The door had never before been opened, but today it was a gaping maw of smoke and flame, the wooden doors on fire and the metal doorframe dripping molten gold. The people around her pushed out of the fire's way, climbing over one another to the colonnades beyond the flames' reach. But Rachel saw that flaming gate and understood that there was no longer any purpose in being alive, that the door had been opened for her. She ran through it, her body catching fire as she leaped to the valley below.

WHEN SHE AWOKE, she knew she was dead. It did not occur to her that death involved no waking. She opened her eyes and found herself lying pressed into the ground, one cheek hot against limestone and her breasts and belly pushed against her threadbare robe on the burning dust. When she scrambled to sit up, she saw the mountain she was on, a bare rock-strewn hillside bereft of people. Its emptiness frightened her. In her entire life she had never left the city, and the strange silence on the hilltop only made her more certain that she was dead. She shakily rose to her feet. Before her was another empty hilltop, nearly identical to the one she stood on. To her right and left stood more empty hilltops, each as desolate as the last. It was only when she turned fully around that she saw the city in the distance, its entirety on fire, a massive burning pillar of thick black smoke rising up to a clear blue sky.

So she wasn't dead, she understood. She had survived—which was like being dead, only worse. Surely something had happened that her memory had erased, some mindless journey from there to here. Perhaps she had jumped through the gate and hit her head, became a temporary idiot, and then wandered for days. Not much later she became even more certain she was alive. It was summertime, the sun was high in the sky, and she was overcome with thirst. She heard a noise nearby and suddenly saw a ram, a large and majestic animal, stepping through a thorn bush near the hilltop's edge. In the city she had often seen rams being led up to the Temple for sacrifice; as a girl she had looked into the animals' eyes and imagined that they understood their importance, their essential part in the world's maintenance and repair. The ram on the hilltop lifted its head and stared at her blankly, its eerie eyes devoid of meaning. The animal defecated, then turned and headed back down the hill.

She followed its horns until she came to a well. So there were people nearby, she thought with relief. In the distance she could even make out a low stone wall, with a row of tents behind it. She pulled at the well's rope and desperately hauled up a full bucket. But as she bent down to plunge her mouth into the water, she saw a reflection in the water's surface: the soft, smooth, uncertain face of an eighteen-year-old girl.

She dropped the bucket, barely noticing as it plummeted back into the well. She reached up, frightened, and felt her bare head, noticing suddenly that her hair was uncovered outdoors, for the first time since she had married fifty years before. With growing horror, she pulled a handful of her hair around to her face and saw it: thick black hair, the same hair she had when she was a young girl. As she dropped the hair, she looked at her hand, her thin, uncertain, ungnarled, unwrinkled young girl's hand, and stopped breathing.

By then the Roman soldiers from the garrison down the hill had arrived on horseback behind her, the captains pointing their spears at her as the others bound her and took her back to their camp for the entertainment of the officers. Seven years passed before she managed to steal enough money to escape, to make the journey to her still-living son, the famous Yochanan.

"YOCHANAN, YOU IDIOT!"

Yochanan sat up in his bed, taking her hand in his. "Mother, don't you understand? When Vespasian asked me what he could give me, I knew exactly what to ask for. I asked for permission for the Torah scholars to be protected near their garrison in Yavneh.

That way, no matter what happened to Jerusalem, there would still be people who could teach the Torah in the future. That way the Torah would be safe."

"But you could have saved the Temple!"

"I don't think I could have done that. If God wanted to destroy the Temple, God would destroy the Temple. God destroyed the Temple before."

"The Romans destroyed it! And you could have stopped them!"

"I did what I could. I did what was possible."

"You're like a child! You saved your favorite book!"

"Yes! Because nothing matters but the story!"

Rachel pulled back from her son, and buried her face in her smooth, unwrinkled hands. She pressed her palms against her eyes and saw the flames again, saw her whole life in flames, saw her own body burning, her skin sliding off her flesh like molten gold, saw her tiny son almost dying in her arms—and then pulled away her hands and saw her son, her old, old son, dying before her. She held her breath.

"We saved you, Yochanan," she said, measuring each word. "Your father and I, we saved you, when you were a baby and almost died. We saved you again when you were old, we put you in a coffin and carried you out of the city."

"You and Father," Yochanan said, and coughed. He didn't ask her to explain. Yochanan must have thought she meant it figuratively, that Zakkai's ghost had haunted her. Or maybe he thought she meant a divine Father, some ridiculously abstract concept of a world that preceded him? Yochanan turned everything into a metaphor. "You taught me what mattered," he said. He took her hand again, as if he had become the parent, comforting her. But his breathing was labored now. He leaned back on cushions like a philosopher at a symposium, drinking wine and wisdom. "That's why I saved what mattered most in the world," he rasped. "I saved the future."

Children! "Yochanan, you don't understand," Rachel said. Her voice sounded like a teenager's, angry and desperate. She was younger than her son. "I gave up my own death for you, with a vow in the Temple," she whispered. "And now the Temple is gone, and I'm never going to die, Yochanan. You're dying, but I'll be here forever, in an eternal life."

"Then maybe you'll find out if I was right," Yochanan said.

He smiled, breathed, and fell into a deep, deep sleep.

SHE COULDN'T WATCH HIM DIE. When she left the room, his oldest disciples rushed in to hear his last words, waiting until he arose with a cough and noticed their presence, succumbing to their demand for a final teaching. Rachel heard him speaking from behind the doorway's curtain.

"May you fear God as much as you fear other people," her dying son said.

"Not more?" one follower asked.

"No," Yochanan told him. "Because a person about to do something wrong always says, 'I hope no person will see me.' If only they feared God nearly as much."

And if God isn't present, Rachel wondered, if God has pushed open the doors of his house and departed, and burned down whatever remains, if nothing at all is left, then what? Does one enter an empty world, running through an empty city with no one waiting and no one watching, delivering a message to a future that doesn't exist? What then was the purpose of being alive?

Rachel heard her son's death rattle from behind the curtain: a gasping, heaving sound. She heard it and could not cry. Instead she looked down at her shaking young girl's hands that once held her father's scrolls, and ran out the door.

She ran down the hill, away from the village, away from every living thing, away from the world. Houses and shanties quickly thinned around her until the dirt road opened onto a stubbled plain, devoid of anything but rocks and olive trees and clusters of sheep. She would run until she ran into the sea. Ahead of her, a young man—no, a boy, she saw as she raced closer, a teenaged boy, gangly and thin-wristed, with a sparse beard and pauper's robes—stepped away from the sheep he had been watching and into her path. She veered to the side, hoping to avoid him on her drive toward oblivion. Until she heard him call her name.

"Rachel!"

She skidded to a stop just past where he stood. She turned around slowly, a strange electricity coursing through her aching legs. When she faced the boy, she saw his smooth skin, his thick black hair, his bare pale wrists, and his odd green eyes.

"Elazar?"

He leaned back, and the fear in his face startled her. His voice shook. "I thought—I—I hoped it was only me," he murmured.

Rachel glanced at the dirt, the rocks, the sheep, the sky, and remembered the house on fire. Had nothing changed? But everything had changed.

"He's dead, isn't he," Elazar said.

It was unbearable to hear it. Rachel felt her skin burning again, seared like molten gold. She doubled over and gasped for air. When Elazar held her she had no strength left to push him away.

To her astonishment, his hand against her back steadied her. She breathed more slowly, each breath a tiny foothold out of the pit. And then he said something that comforted her: "I hope you didn't watch him die."

Rachel raised her head and saw the boy from the tunnel. Years evaporated like water. "I couldn't," she said. She looked again at Elazar, not remembering, but feeling in her body his fingers along her neck, cold currents against her feet, his mouth on her breast, her baby's shriveled weight in her arms, cool air on her shaved scalp, wet smears of ink on her fingertips, blood from Zakkai's body dripping on her sleeves, Elazar's hand pressing on hers against the doorpost of her house, the shifting weight in her son's coffin. What had been the point of the vow, if it had only come to this?

"I couldn't bear it either," Elazar said. "And as a priest I'm not supposed to approach the dead." She thought of correcting him, reminding him of how irrelevant it was: there was no more reason to remain ritually pure, no more Temple in which to serve. He needed no reminding. He paused, a catch in his throat. "But I knew it was coming. Last night I said goodbye."

Rachel gulped dry air. "You—you were with him?"

"I live here," Elazar said. "I'm his youngest student."

"Elazar," she whispered. "Why?"

He cast his eyes to the ground. "I'm not the best or the wisest, I know that. But I'm surely the most devoted. I followed him. I followed the story."

All the anger Rachel had borne for the past seven years ignited within her, flaring in her body like a pillar of fire, a fire so all-consuming that she no longer knew who it was for—Elazar, Zakkai, Yochanan, the Romans, God, herself—and it no longer mattered. She had become a vast and towering rage that scorched the entire world.

"There is no more story, Elazar!" she screamed. "Don't you understand? There is no more story! We've lost everything, everything! The story is over!"

Elazar stood before her, a young boy and an old, old man. "In that case," he said softly, "maybe it's time to begin again."

CHAPTER

14

HER TIME

. . .

Rachel hadn't expected it to look like this. She had imagined something like her seventieth son's chemical laboratory, the one he built in the storage room in the back of her husband's tailor shop: two narrow tables cluttered with old metal pots and glass jars and little burners, something always boiling and smoking and filling the room with acrid fumes, incense that might have once cleansed her soul but that instead made her struggle to breathe. But Hannah's lab was completely devoid of smoke. Instead, as Rachel noticed while being led in by an unshaven man-child in a toothpaste-stained shirt, the series of small rooms were full of computers, along with countertops holding humming plastic boxes that might have also been computers. The tables and chairs looked surprisingly cheap. A basketball hoop was tacked to one wall above a wastebasket. Rachel sidestepped a wad of gum on the floor and stood still. She looked around at all these impossibly young people staring at their screens and felt a rush of awe she had not felt since the day she knelt in the sanctuary before Elazar's father: mortal wonder and dread.

"Gram!"

Hannah rose from her cheap chair. Rachel trembled in her granddaughter's presence. If Hannah felt the import of the moment, she didn't let on. She craned her neck around the room. "Guys, this is my grandmother," she announced. "She's offered to help us out, so be nice!" The gaggle of half-adults at the computers nearby tittered a bit before resuming their glazed stares at screens. Their ease made Rachel nervous. "Come, I'll take you down to phlebotomy," Hannah said, and grandly took Rachel by the hand. The two of them walked on together.

"Most of the clinical stuff happens at the outpatient center next door," Hannah explained. "We hardly ever take samples here; it's only for special cases, when we need to follow up or the samples are really sensitive or something like that. You definitely qualify as a special case." She waited until another woman passed them in the hallway, and then ushered Rachel into a little room.

Rachel sat down in the throne-like chair with its enormous armrest, next to a rack of test tubes. To her surprise, Hannah closed the door behind them and leaned against it, facing Rachel.

"Gram, I wanted to bring you here myself, because I wanted to give you one more chance to say no."

Rachel grimaced. Was she being tricked? "I already signed all those papers."

Hannah waved a hand. "I don't care about the papers. I care about you." She paused. "I want to be sure that you understand why you're here."

Rachel stared hard at her granddaughter's face, her wide eyes, her smooth cheeks, her wet pink pearl of a lower lip. She was like a baby, impossibly young. Rachel pushed down compassion. She knew how to deal with children. "Of course I understand," she said, and dug her fingernails into the armrest. "I hope you understand too. You and I have a deal."

Hannah bit her beautiful wet lip and visibly swallowed, caught in Rachel's glare. Finally she offered a tight, curt nod. She looked down at the counter next to Rachel and aggressively flipped through papers, an act. "The staff are going to come in and collect some samples to get us started," she said, rattling off protocol. Then she looked up, and met Rachel's eyes. "And then we're going to—" She paused, her lips trembling as Rachel stared. "Then we're going to—to see what we can do for you."

What we can do for you. Rachel watched in wonder as her granddaughter hid her face, and blew out the door.

WHEN RACHEL RETURNED the next day—"just a quick follow-up," Hannah had called it, "just a few more tests," though there were many, several hours' worth—Rachel was astounded by how familiar the lab seemed. Not from the previous day, since she was now mostly at the outpatient center, but from long before that, from a world seared into Rachel's soul. Everything involved elaborate rituals, and familiar rituals too: the intricate purifications of specially designed vessels, the delicately worded vows she had to sign, the elite caste of select people imbued with arcane knowledge, the consulting of body parts as oracles, the long silent waiting for judgment, the obsessiveness involving blood. On her way to the lab that morning, Rachel had summoned Elazar to the tunnel. He had been begging her to leave again when she finally confessed.

Outside it was pouring. The rush of water rattled the tunnel's empty pipes and made the dark space come alive. Rain made other people sad or irritable, Rachel had noticed recently, but childhood memories welled within her, and water falling from the sky still brought her a surge of hope. She shivered with the thrill of it, the thrill of what was to come.

Elazar was drenched. His jacket flowed with rivulets of rain, and his dark hair was plastered against his eternally crumpled forehead.

She threw her arms around his neck and felt cold water slide across her skin.

"Every time I see you here, I feel sick inside," he said. "You should be long gone by now, Rachel. You have no idea what kind of damage you could be doing."

But Rachel no longer cared. She took his hands like a little girl. "I told Hannah," she announced. "I told her everything."

Elazar smirked. "So what?" The rain outside made him giddy too. "I've told people hundreds of times. Haven't you? 'Hey, kid, guess what: I can't die!' It does feel good to tell people, I'll give you that. But it's meaningless. They never believe you."

Rachel clutched his hands, shaking with excitement. "No, Elazar. This time it matters. Hannah and I, we made a deal. A vow."

"A vow?" The word burned in the air between them.

"Yes, a vow." Rachel heard her own voice rising. She couldn't help it. "A contract. An exchange. I'm going to give her what she wants. And then she's going to make me die."

Elazar looked at Rachel for a long time before laughing out loud. His laughter filled the tunnel like thick smoke. Rachel found it hard to breathe.

"It isn't funny," she finally said.

"You're right," he said, choking on laughter. "You're killing your granddaughter, which is not funny at all." He gasped for air, tears running down his cheeks. "You're right, technically it's not funny. But you have to admit there's something hilarious about it. She's dying to live forever, and you're dying to show her how."

Rachel dropped his hands. She stepped back, just slightly, and clenched her fists. "Don't you understand? I'm not killing her, I'm saving her. That's exactly why I'm doing this. To protect her."

It still hurt him, the dropped hands, the slight step away. He squinted at her, shrunken. Her power over him amazed her. "How?" he asked.

"She was already going to use whatever she had from me, no matter what," Rachel told him. "If that's dangerous, which we don't know—"

"Which we like to pretend we don't know."

"—which we *don't know*, then she's already in danger. But this way, at least there's a chance that *I'll* die. And if that happens, then there's no secret for her to discover, nothing miraculous to prove. And then she'd be safe." Probably. Maybe. Possibly. Rachel was blind, groping the curtain of darkness before her for some hidden pattern, some shape behind it. She listened to the rain she couldn't see.

Elazar shook his head. "What makes you think it will work? You're acting like we haven't spent the last two thousand years trying. Have you forgotten all that? All those sorcerers, witch doctors, alchemists, healers. Centuries of quacks—"

"This is different," Rachel said. The tunnel rattled, a crazed, joyous sound. Even Elazar's face seemed brighter, water gleaming on his furrowed brow. Real hope was so alien to Rachel that it was frightening, trembling and luminous. "Hannah knows how to do this. She already saw the problem in my chromosomes. She *saw* it. No one before has ever seen it, not even close. This is real. She's going to alter my genes or something. She already knows what to do." She looked at her watch, a gesture that made Elazar snort. "I'm going there right from here," she said. Her voice was louder than she wanted it to be. "It will probably take a while, weeks or months even, and this is only the beginning. I just—I just wanted you to know."

Elazar snorted again. "This is nonsense, Rachel. It's impossible."

"Why should it be impossible? You and I are impossible. But here we are."

"Here we are," Elazar said sadly.

She felt the air between them shift, something in him yielding. She prodded him at his weakest point. "High priests used to have this power," she said. "Did it ever occur to you that Hannah and people like her are the new high priests?"

Elazar looked at her with heavy eyes, his thick wet hair dripping on his temples. "Rachel. What's the point?"

"I need to do this, Elazar."

"But why?"

She hesitated. She had never tried to say it before, to give words to the bottomless darkness surrounding her, a shard of a girl caught in the world's throat. "I just can't bear it anymore," she said slowly. "Being alive. Losing everything again and again. Every year, every day, I still expect it to get easier. But it doesn't. It never does. Instead it just changes. Constantly changing, constantly in motion. Everyone else thinks they're moving toward something. But you and I are the only ones who know we'll never get there, that nothing is ever over. I feel like I'm always falling. I've been falling without landing for two thousand years."

"Maybe you've been flying," Elazar said.

Something in Rachel crumpled. She pressed her back against the tunnel's wall and heard her mother's voice: *Don't you dare believe a word he says!* And then another voice, gentler, wiser: *Don't believe in yourself until the day you die*. And then only rain.

"Listen, Rachel. I can't make you do anything," Elazar said softly. "I can give you every passport in the world, arrange everything you need, tell you everything I think you should do, and you'll never do any of it. You'll only do what you choose." His damp face glistened in the dim light. "That's exactly what's magnificent about you. That's exactly why I chose you. That's exactly what I've always loved."

He looked down at the tunnel's floor. Water was draining in from the entrance, flowing in little channels past their feet. She leaned in and held him, pressing her cheek against his soaked shirt.

"I need to go now," Rachel said.

"Come back soon, please. Don't leave without saying goodbye."

His body was trembling, but Rachel was still listening to the rain falling, eager for what awaited her. She kissed him and hurried back out into the rain, on her way to the new temple.

THE STAFF AT THE OUTPATIENT center on her third visit two weeks later warned Rachel that she might feel lightheaded, after they carefully removed from her body what appeared to be several quarts of blood. She put on a show for them, sinking into the chair and asking for candy. But when she reached her house, she had the thrilling thought that they were right: perhaps even before Hannah had upheld her end of the bargain, mortality was already sinking its talons into Rachel's flesh. She was lightheaded, and imagining things. It otherwise made no sense for a rental truck to be parked in her driveway, or for Rocky and Meirav to be hauling a pile of enormous cardboard crates into her house.

She left her car on the street and walked up to them as they lifted one box at a time, hefting either end in a perfectly synchronized dance. Rocky was sweating, and exhilarated. They barely noticed her until she spoke.

"And here I was hoping that you were moving out," she finally said.

Meirav laughed. Rocky lowered the box to the asphalt, shaking out his hands. "Dreams do come true," he intoned cryptically.

This was annoying. "What's in those?" Rachel asked.

"A mining rig," Rocky said.

"A what?"

Rocky pushed one of the crates with his foot. "I explained it to you already, Mom." To her surprise, he didn't sound exasperated. His voice was level, mature, content. "Come in, we'll show you."

Bewildered, Rachel followed him and Meirav down into the basement. Her dead husband's desk and the bins of toys that had cluttered the room were now stacked in a corner to make space for a series of tall metal and plastic machines, ensnared in a thicket of black wires. Only a few had been set up, and there was no strange blue fluid around their bases, but she immediately recognized it. The only thing missing from the picture she had seen online, besides the fluid, was Elazar.

"Where do you even buy something like this?" she asked. It already looked monstrous. And there were still a half-truck's worth of crates outside.

"Normally you'd have to get all the components separately. But this one came as-is," Rocky told her, beaming. "I bought it off that Spanish guy. That Arab guy. Whatever he was. I guess he needed to unload it. Great price too. Total fire sale."

Elazar was dumping his machines? "Did you—did you meet him?"

"Nope. He just left the key at the storage place. Thus providing further evidence for your theory that he doesn't exist." He poked Meirav, like the child he once was.

"Rocky showed me the photo of him online, though," Meirav said. "I told Rocky he had to trust that guy. He looked just like my father!"

"If your father was about thirty years younger," Rocky interjected.

"And twenty pounds thinner," Meirav smiled.

"And a twenty-first-century cryptocurrency miner," Rocky parried.

"And alive," Meirav added, and laughed. "Otherwise they're exactly the same."

Rachel leaned against the wall and tried to stop the room from reeling around her. Rocky noticed her alarm, and assumed it was his fault. "Before you ask, Mom, yes, this is the thing that needs cooling fluids and all that. But don't worry, we're not going to leave it on or anything." Rachel nodded, as though this was her main concern. "And it's not going to stay in your house. We're just testing it to make sure it runs okay, and then we're done."

"What do you mean, you're done?" Rachel asked.

"We're bringing it to Rocky's new office next week, when his lease begins," Meirav said with a smile. "There's a basement space there with a generator. He's going to need to expand, but this is a good start."

"New office?"

Rocky grinned, and looked like a little boy. "Meirav found me some investors," he sang.

"What he means is that I'm his investor," Meirav announced.

"*Primary* investor," Rocky corrected. "It's a new startup, so here we are, starting up. It's not even for mining currency. It's for this new protocol I've been working on. It's a set of algorithms that bakes different kinds of data into the blockchain so that anyone can—"

Meirav swooped in and took Rachel's hand. Her fingers were warm and sweet. "Don't bore your mother to death," she scolded Rocky, and turned to Rachel. "Trust me, it's a good thing. A really good thing. He doesn't even need this rig, honestly. It probably makes more sense to get shares in a larger system. He just wanted a little extra independence on top of what I'm giving him."

"Plus it was a total fire sale," Rocky repeated.

"I guess we all want a little extra independence," Rachel murmured, then looked at her son. He was radiant. "Congratulations, Rocky."

Rocky colored, and grinned. It had been years since she had seen him so happy. He waved a hand. "Anyway, Mom, sorry to park it in your house. It'll be gone next week. And so will I."

"What's all this stuff?" a little voice said.

Rachel turned to see her great-grandson Ezra standing on the basement steps, wearing his superhero cape. "What are you doing here?" she asked, and glanced at her watch. "Shouldn't you be in school?"

"They had some stupid early dismissal," Rocky explained. "Teacher meeting or something. Hannah forgot it was happening, so I went to pick him up. He's been watching TV upstairs."

Rocky had picked him up? This was even more astounding than Rocky moving out. Rachel had the sudden feeling that she had become a spectator in her own house, in her own life. I'm superfluous, she thought. She smiled.

Ezra had already flown down the stairs. His eyes widened. "What IS all this stuff?" he asked again.

"Computers," Rocky said.

"That's a LOT of computers," Ezra murmured, awed.

"Actually it's just one big computer," Rocky clarified. "If you want, I can show you how it works."

"Yes yes yes!" Ezra shouted. "The Amazing Jumping Man says YES!" And then he leaped toward the machines.

Rocky caught him mid-pounce, spinning him in the air until the boy screeched with laughter, not even noticing that his grandfather had parked him safely on the stairs. "The only thing is, you can't turn it on yourself," Rocky told him once he stopped giggling. "It gets really hot if it runs more than a few minutes, so we have to be careful. Got that, Amazing Jumping Man?"

"Got it," Ezra snapped back. He composed his little face into an expression of utter reverence. "Show me!"

"Help us get all these parts inside and then we'll fire it up," Rocky said. "There's a few smaller boxes you can handle. Jump to it, kid."

Rachel watched as Ezra flew out to the driveway, Meirav and Rocky trailing behind him.

WHEN SHE MET ELAZAR in the tunnel that night, she gathered her anger together and presented it to him, a bouquet of pique. Even the anger was exciting. In the last week she had felt herself becoming younger, the proximity of death bringing a rejuvenating hope. She wanted to seize Elazar and eat him alive.

"Why are you dumping your property on Rocky?" she asked. Even her voice sounded different to her, not bitter but gleeful. "Whatever that thing is, aren't you going to need it?"

She had been so eager to confront him that she hadn't noticed how different he looked: lighter somehow, the circles around his eyes diminished. His face gleamed with a genuine joy. "Oh, the mining rig," he sang. "That wasn't my property, technically. There's a whole pool of owners. I just owned the controlling share."

"You're all about the controlling share."

Insults slid off Elazar's back like rain. "I've been so blessed, I just wanted to share the bounty God has given me."

"I don't think God gave you a currency-mining server."

"His mercy endures forever," Elazar intoned, and shrugged. "I just thought, maybe it's time to unload things I don't need. Give them to someone who needs them more."

Suddenly Rachel understood. A hundred memories ran through her mind from the times she had prepared to burn: cash planted in other people's drawers, safes unlocked, grown children kissed goodbye in their sleep. "You're leaving," she breathed.

Elazar glowed. "Oh no, Rachel. It's much better than that. I have amazing news. Your granddaughter is going to kill me!"

"What?"

"I signed up for one of the studies her lab is running. Don't worry, it's off-site. I won't ever meet her."

"What study?"

"Some study of gene therapy and toxicity. They edit your genes or something like that. Does it matter? It's so dangerous that it's only for terminal patients."

"Aren't you the opposite of a terminal patient?"

Elazar's eyes sparkled. "Not according to my medical records." Rachel groaned as Elazar grinned. "I gave them what they wanted and they took me. They said it was extremely high-risk."

Rachel frowned. "High-risk for her."

"Yes, I still think that. But you're already putting her in danger. If she dies, it's not my fault. And this way, at least I have a chance. Just like you."

Rachel controlled her flinch. How could she still care what he thought? "You said it was nonsense."

"Yes, I still think that too. But I decided that I'm willing to try nonsense. If you're not going to be in this world, I don't want to be here either."

A hollowness opened around Rachel. "There's more to life than me, Elazar."

"I don't think so." Rachel was astonished to see his eyes fill with tears. "Rachel, I want to say goodbye."

Rachel looked at Elazar as though he were a child, full of quiet pity. "Elazar, please," she said. "It may not work. And even if it works, it will probably take weeks or months, won't it?"

Elazar shook his head. "Maybe, but I don't care. I don't want to see you that way. And I don't want you to see me that way. Both of us have watched more than enough people die."

The tunnel was silent. Rachel felt Elazar's utter terror in her own body, as hundreds of years of hope and fear drained into the ground beneath their feet.

"Let me hold you once more, Rachel," he pleaded. "Just one more time."

She said yes.

He took her clothes off slowly, gently peeling away each layer as he revealed her shoulders, her back, her legs, her breasts. She felt the current rush across her feet, a river of sorrow and love and gratitude. She looked at Elazar, forever beautiful and forever hers, and understood in that moment why no one wanted to die. She took him in her arms and kissed him like she was eighteen years old.

He breathed in her bare body in the dim light, running his lips along her neck as he whispered in her ear. "If I could do it all again, Rachel, I would still follow you. Until the end of the world."

The lab and the outpatient center attached to it were just beginning to feel ordinary to Rachel when Hannah began to be thrilled.

"It's really exciting, Gram," she gushed as Rachel put on another sacral gown, preparing for yet another nameless scan. Hannah's voice rasped as though she'd caught a cold, which she probably had. Rachel had noticed that the pretense of purity at the lab and the clinic only went so far. The place festered with hidden corners of dirt, unemptied trash bins, used tissues. "I've run a lot of experiments and seen a lot of things. But nothing like this. There's a lot we still have to analyze, but we're very excited. Cautiously excited."

Rachel sat on an exam table beside whatever machine was supposed to probe or inspect her, ready to lay herself down like a sacrificial goat. "I'm excited too," she said, with an edge in her voice.

It was a test. There was something in Hannah's demeanor, a hesitation, that made Rachel deeply suspicious. Rachel had begun to contemplate the possibility that she had been betrayed. But now she watched her granddaughter and noticed a heaviness in her movements. The young woman bent over the table, leaning against it as though bearing a pack on her shoulders.

"You look tired," Rachel said.

Hannah shrugged, and forced a smile. "I've been here pretty late most nights, working on this," she admitted. "It's exhilarating. And tiring too, I guess."

Hannah looked more than tired, Rachel thought. She looked older. Maybe even ill. "You're working too hard," Rachel said carefully.

"It's catching up with me, for sure," Hannah conceded. "I'll go home early today. I've barely seen the kids all week."

"Good idea," Rachel said.

Hannah sat down on a stool near the exam table and caught her breath. For a moment Rachel forgot why either of them was here. Hannah seemed to forget too. Rachel's aggressively perfect granddaughter closed her eyes for an instant longer than a blink, and leaned against the wall behind her.

"Gram, how did you do this for all these years?" she asked.

Rachel glanced around at the room's whirring machines. "I never did anything like this," she tried.

"I don't mean the science. I mean—I mean—just life," Hannah said. "Working, raising children, building a business, living with everyone, getting through every problem, never a moment alone. I feel like I'm only just beginning, and I'm already exhausted. I can't even imagine. How did you get through it all, for so many years?"

"By knowing that nothing lasts," Rachel answered.

Rachel did not know what would happen next. And she finally felt alive.

Someone's house must be on fire, Rachel noticed as she turned onto her street. Not because of the fire engines—there weren't any, and no distant sirens either—but because of the smell. And as she got closer, the smoke. Soon she was in front of her own house, except that it couldn't be her own house, because this house was on fire. Smoke was streaming out of several of the lower windows.

The front doorway had no door, just a gaping open mouth of smoke with a bleeding man lying on the floor within it, a man whose thick squirming body looked strangely familiar. She lunged out of the car and rushed to his side.

"Rocky, what happened?"

"Door fell on my leg," he grimaced. "I can't get up." Rachel knelt down next to Rocky and saw that the blood was mostly from several large gashes in his left hand, which clutched his thigh. Rocky waved his right hand and shouted, "Ezra's upstairs!"

"WHAT?"

"He was sick at school, so I brought him home! He was playing in the basement and then he went up to nap. He's sleeping upstairs!"

Rachel peered into the house in horror. The smoke made it hard to see. She yanked her phone out of her pocket and pressed it into his bleeding hand. "Crawl out as far as you can and call 911," she said. "I'll get him."

"Mom, no! You can't—"

"Rocky, I love you," she said. "It's my time." She bent down and kissed him. He was a baby again, all possibility. "Marry Meirav. Make something magnificent. I'm watching."

"MOM!" Rocky screamed.

But she was already running inside.

THE STAIRS WERE ON FIRE, at least along one side. Rachel didn't care. All that mattered was making it up to the little room with the little window, the room where she had once tucked Rocky into bed every night. She reached the upstairs hallway just ahead of the flames, diving to the floor and rolling to put out the sparks that had already touched her clothes. Then she raced for Rocky's old room, yanked the door open and slammed it behind her.

Ezra was standing in the middle of the room, blinking and coughing, red-faced and bewildered. When he saw her, he grabbed her around the waist and burst into tears.

"I'm sorry, Gram! I did it! I'm sorry!"

"Did what?"

"I turned on the computers! I left them on! I'm sorry, I'm sorry, I'm sorry!"

In another life there would be time to consider this, to back through the multiple curtains of responsibility and blame that covered the void, to imagine that the fire wasn't simply waiting for her as it always was, as it always had been, as it always would be. But not now. She crouched down and held Ezra's little face to hers.

"Listen to me, Ezra," she said. "I need you to remember this for the rest of your life. This is not your fault. It's my time. Tell your mother that, okay? Your grandfather too. Tell them it's my time. Promise me."

"I promise." The little boy was sobbing.

She glanced behind her and saw the smoke seeping around the edges of the door. She knew how fast the flames would come. She clutched the boy to her chest, kissed his head, inhaled his smell. But she was out of time; already she was inhaling smoke. She cranked open the tiny casement window. There was no way she could squeeze through it. Even Rocky, eight years old when they bought the house, had been too big to fit—which was exactly why this had been his room. But Ezra was so little. And so, so young.

"Now jump out the window. I know you know how."

Ezra's wet eyes bulged. "JUMP?"

"I'll watch you jump. You're the Amazing Jumping Man."

He shook his head, still sobbing. She lifted him and perched him on the windowsill, seating him with his legs swinging in the outdoor air.

He twisted his head toward her. "Gram—"

She kissed him again. "I love you, Ezra. Don't forget. Keep jumping. I'm watching, always. Ready? One, two, three!"

For a five-year-old, the numbers were a magic spell. She watched as his dark curls took flight, heard the crunch of the bushes below, looked out on the front lawn as he scrambled off the bushes and raced toward his crawling bleeding grandfather.

And then she turned to face the flames.

CHAPTER

15

DAYS OF OLD

. . .

Rachel had forgotten how peaceful it was to hold a baby in her arms. She remembered well the agony of days and nights with newborns, the formless chaos and endless demands. But it had been more than half a century since she had had a baby, and she had forgotten the peace.

For years she wondered if Elazar had planned it, if the fire was nothing more than his malevolent plot to save her life. If that was true, he was biding his time. There was no sign of him for so many years that she even thought he might have succeeded in dying. Then, last year, she had seen him—a younger him, a happier him, a him so different from the one she knew that she couldn't be entirely sure it was him at all—in a news photo: an announcement about a team selected to train for an international mission to Mars. She had mourned and rejoiced, her mourning and joy indistinguishable. His presence was hard to bear. His absence made her love him more.

She had met Nir on her post-army trip, backpacking in Peru. She was amazed by how fresh everything felt in this version, how unexplored. She had thought she had been everywhere, seen everything, and was astonished to discover entire new continents. She had also never tried drugs. She wasn't surprised that they had no effect on her. What surprised her that warm night at the Incan ruins in Pisac, among the dozen other Israeli tourists who had taken leave of their faculties by the floodlights near the ancient terraces, was a young man with tan skin like hers and thick curly black hair. He wore glasses and a T-shirt whose Spanish words she didn't understand, and was scratching with a pen inside a little notebook. The pen and the notebook were more than strange: it had been at least five years since she had seen anyone use a pen. It was like watching her father dip his quill into her mother's ink. She was sitting with her back against a terrace wall outside the national park's official borders, discovering yet again that the drugs did nothing, when she noticed him watching her.

"You're not stoned," he said.

"No," she answered. "I guess it's just not for me."

He nodded. His brown eyes gleamed behind his glasses with a weird childish wonder. "I'm the same," he said. His voice was too quick, too eager. She liked it. "I know I'm supposed to be smoking my brains out. But I spent the last three years half-asleep. Now I just love being awake. Being alive."

Something within Rachel quivered to life. She had avoided dating during her army service; the last time she had done this, she had worn dresses, stockings, girdles. She leaned over and touched the young man's shoulder. "What are you writing?" she asked.

"Nothing," he muttered, and quickly shut the notebook. But she had already seen his sketch of her, crosshatched in deep black ink. She was shocked to see herself so young.

"It's beautiful," she said. I am beautiful, she thought, in quiet awe. The world was full of unexpected light.

Nir's backpack buzzed. He fished out his phone, red-faced and relieved. "Ten new messages in the last three minutes," he muttered. "And over there it's not even six in the morning."

"Crazy girlfriend?" she asked.

He shook his head. "My mother texts me constantly. And my sister. And my four brothers. Even my grandmother texts me. I went halfway around the world and they're still following me." He laughed, but Rachel could see the effort he poured into putting the phone down without reading the texts. He tried to distract her. "Enjoying the big trip?"

The question was inane. "Amazing," she said, like she was supposed to say. There were always things she was supposed to say.

To her surprise Nir smirked, and gestured at the wall behind them. "We're supposed to be wowed by these ruins," he said. "But I'm from Jerusalem, and my grandmother is from Aleppo." Rachel nodded, remembering both. "The guide yesterday told me these terraces are six hundred years old and he thought I'd be impressed." He paused. It was sweet, his fear of saying the wrong thing. "But maybe you are. You're American, right?"

"Not really," she murmured. "Not anymore."

"But you must still have family there," he pushed.

She sighed. "It's ancient history."

He laughed. "For an American."

Rachel was tired of being coy. "Before I left America, my family's house burned down," she said.

Nir hesitated, confused. Then his eyes widened. The innocence was captivating. "With—with people inside?"

Rachel wanted to begin anew, without lying. "Yes, with people inside," she said simply. "That's why I left. I don't have a family anymore."

For a long moment Nir sat still, silent. Then he smiled, and offered her his phone. "Would you like a new one?"

Several years passed, years full of things Rachel had never done before—university courses, exams, laboring in a lab, more exams, medical school, the exhilaration of learning new things, things that mattered, things that made her want to ask more questions and then ask even more—before she finally said yes. Now she nursed their newborn baby on a quiet evening in their tiny apartment, overwhelmed with peace.

Nir had run out to pick up a few necessities, a strange thing that young men now seemed to routinely do for their wives and children, along with dozens of other tasks she had never seen any man do, like vacuuming a rug or emptying a dishwasher, the equivalent of cleaning out ashes from an oven. She marveled at it. Nir had even let her give the baby whatever name she wanted, no matter how weird or unfashionable. "You have too many people to name him for," he told her. He was right.

She marveled more at the actual baby at her breast. The baby was tiny, a smear of dark fuzzy hair and large brown eyes, and he was terrifyingly familiar. From the moment he was born Rachel felt the jolt of recognition, as though something deep and ancient had risen up from a vein sunken in the earth. It was wondrous, and frightening. As he suckled he steadied her, and her body flowed with milk and peace. But when he slept, his little mouth detached from her, and she succumbed too easily to her fears. She distracted herself by scanning her phone with her free hand, searching.

She searched for Elazar, as she often did, searched and searched but could not find him. Instead she fell back on an old favorite, photos someone had posted years earlier of Rocky and Meirav, hoisted high on raised chairs. When she tired of that she searched for a name she only rarely encountered beyond a few repetitive profile pictures and outdated listings, a troubling void in the virtual universe. But this time something new came up: a photo of a familiar woman leaning casually against an institutional white countertop, a faux-serious pout on her no-longer-young face, followed by a clickbait headline on which Rachel, stroking her baby's little head, eagerly clicked.

Why Hannah Mendelsohn, Badass Biologist
Who Developed the First Effective Anti-Dementia
Treatment, Wants Everyone to Die

Hannah Mendelsohn doesn't know you, but she wants you to die.

Not now, but someday, when you're old and satisfied, even if you're sure you'll always want more. "Dying is what gives life its meaning," Mendelsohn asserts.

If that sounds obnoxious coming from an energetic 43-year-old biologist and mother of two, consider this: Nine years ago, before she began the work that led to Memagen, the anti-dementia treatment that comes to market this month, Mendelsohn was hard at work on defeating death. A recipient of a grant from Google, she and a team of colleagues were toiling away at expanding the human life span.

She laughs about it today. "Grant money makes people do really stupid things," she says.

While Mendelsohn was researching life extension, a beloved grandmother died violently, running into a burning building to save Mendelsohn's child. That marked the beginning of the end of Mendelsohn's interest in immortality.

"She was very much against my research," Mendelsohn said of her grandmother. "She had told me that she wanted to die. Her death was basically a suicide. I'm not a very spiritual person, but after she died I thought I could feel her judging me." Then came Mendelsohn's own bad news: lymphoma.

Her illness proved treatable, but harrowing. "After my diagnosis I couldn't do anything at all professionally for over a year, even after the treatments ended," Mendelsohn says. It forced her to do a lot of thinking, specifically about death.

"My fears while I was sick were pretty universal: not accomplishing as much as I'd hoped, not getting to see my children grow up," Mendelsohn recalls. "But those are really dynamic things. Every stage of a project or year with a child is really different from the one before. And it's exactly those changes that make those things matter," she says. "I realized I wasn't afraid of dying. I was afraid of no longer changing. I wanted to keep changing, keep making and seeing things change. And if you back up a bit, you see that none of that can happen without the arc of our lives, without one generation replacing another."

When she returned to work, Mendelsohn decided to focus exclusively on cognitive deterioration. The result is Memagen, an entirely unprecedented

The baby stirred in Rachel's lap, then opened its mouth and wailed. She put her phone down on the couch and brought her breast to the baby's lips.

Nir came into the apartment and dropped a pack of diapers on the floor. He joined her on the couch, caressing her hair.

"Reading anything interesting?" he asked, pointing at her phone.

"Nothing new," she said, and smiled.

"Of course not. Everything new is right here." His face glowed as he kissed the baby's head. "It's so exciting, isn't it? Here we are, at the very beginning."

Rachel looked down at the baby and saw, in the tiny body at her breast, everything that awaited him. In weeks he would smile; in months he would crawl. He would stand, he would walk, he would run, he would grow, he would learn, he would labor, he would love, rage, dream, move through his own tunnels of joy and sorrow, bear both the light and the curse, suffer and die, and she would endure it all. But it was worth it, it was worth it, all of it was worth it.

The baby leaned away from her, removing himself from her body as he always would, again and again and again until he was buried in the earth. She held him up to face her in the room's dim light.

"Yochanan," she whispered, "I am watching."

ACKNOWLEDGMENTS

. . .

Historical portions of this book are drawn in part from Talmudic sources on the first-century sage Yochanan ben Zakkai, on the Jewish revolt against Rome, and on the destruction of Jerusalem in the year 70 CE, as well as from *The Jewish War* by Flavius Josephus and from Jacob Neusner's scholarly biography of Yochanan ben Zakkai. I am indebted to Michael Wex for his comparison of Hillel's maxim "What is hateful to you, do not do to your neighbor" with the Golden Rule, found in his playfully titled *How to Be a Mentsh (& Not a Shmuck)*, and to Ilana Kurshan for her interpretation of *terumat hadeshen* (the ritual clearing of ashes) in relation to family life, found in her radiant memoir *If All the Seas Were Ink*. I also thank her for checking the manuscript for continuity with traditional texts; any remaining errors are mine alone.

I was fortunate to have early readers, including Sarah Hurwitz and Roberta Schwartzman, who offered me much-needed encouragement at the beginning, and even more fortunate at the end to have incredibly detailed and invaluable comments from Gretchen M.

Grant. As ever, I am grateful to my agent and my editor, Gary Morris and Alane Mason, for their dedication to my work; and to my siblings Jordana, Zachary and Ariel for their lifelong devotion, and particularly to my sisters for their reading and feedback.

This book is dedicated to my parents, Susan and Matthew Horn, who taught me what to do when it doesn't go by so fast, and to their fourteen grandchildren, including my personal favorites: Maya, Ari, Eli and Ronen, whose inspiration for this book is perhaps best left unexamined. And to Brendan Schulman, for twenty years of adventures in our life together, and hopefully a hundred more.

ETERNAL LIFE

Dara Horn

READING GROUP GUIDE

ETERNAL LIFE

Dara Horn

READING GROUP GUIDE

DISCUSSION QUESTIONS

1. Rachel lives through many experiences and circumstances throughout the millennia. What are the parameters of her life? What rules does she use to govern her eternal existence?

2. Elazar and Rachel confront one another about the separate lives they lead. When Rachel makes a comment about the wives Elazar has had, he defends himself, saying, "Don't talk that way. It was real for them" (p. 12). Do you think Rachel and Elazar's eternal lives make living somehow less "real," or more separated from reality?

3. Is Rachel what you expect from someone who has lived for more than two thousand years? Why or why not?

4. What problems does the twenty-first century pose for Rachel? How is her predicament different from past centuries?

5. Chapter 2 opens with a rumination on Rachel's regret (p. 6). What are her regrets in life? Does Elazar have the same regrets as Rachel?

6. The temple exerts a strong influence on Rachel as a young woman. How do religion and notions of faith change throughout her life?

7. Zakkai questions a translation of the Torah, believing that the word "urim" means "cursed," not "light" (p. 52). What is the significance of this translation, and how does it tie in with Rachel's predicament?

8. *Eternal Life* moves back and forth through time from the modern day to Rachel's life growing up in Jerusalem during the Roman occupation. In between, her life takes many forms and iterations.

Do you think she changes fundamentally from who she was as a girl? In what ways? In what ways does she stay the same?

9. When the high priest Hanania tells Rachel she can save Yochanan if she makes the eternal vow, he recommends that she avoid doing so. "You are young. . . . You will have more children," he says (p. 70). Do you find the adage "time heals all wounds" to be applicable to Rachel's life? How or how not?

10. *Eternal Life* has certain parallels with the legend of Faust, who makes a bargain with the Devil's accomplice Mephistopheles. In exchange for knowledge and magic power, Faust promises his eternal soul to the Devil. In what ways do Rachel and Elazar's lives parallel the legend of Faust? How does their story cast it in a different light, or subvert it?

11. Rachel confronts Yochanan about allowing the temple to burn, and he explains that he made a choice to save the Torah scholars instead (pp. 205–6). What are the implications of his choice? What does it say about the things that remain eternal?

12. Elazar is hesitant when Rachel tells him Hannah might be able to put an end to Rachel's eternal life. "High priests used to have this power," Rachel tells him. "Did it ever occur to you that Hannah and people like her are the new high priests?" (pp. 214–15) What does Rachel mean by this? What does it imply about the modern roles of science and religion? Do you agree with Rachel's perspective?

13. What does the article on Hannah's career imply about her understanding of mortality? Do you agree with her sentiments?

14. By the novel's end, Rachel has started yet another new family. What do you imagine for Rachel's future?

SELECTED NORTON BOOKS WITH READING GROUP GUIDES AVAILABLE

For a complete list of Norton's works with reading group guides, please go to www.wwnorton.com/books/reading-guides.

Diana Abu-Jaber	*Life Without a Recipe*
Diane Ackerman	*The Zookeeper's Wife*
Michelle Adelman	*Piece of Mind*
Molly Antopol	*The UnAmericans*
Bonnie Jo Campbell	*Mothers, Tell Your Daughters*
Jared Diamond	*Guns, Germs, and Steel*
Andre Dubus III	*Townie*
Donna M. Lucey	*Sargent's Women**
Anne Enright	*The Green Road*
Amanda Filipacchi	*The Unfortunate Importance of Beauty*
Maureen Gibbon	*Paris Red*
Stephen Greenblatt	*The Swerve**
Lawrence Hill	*The Illegal*
Ann Hood	*The Book That Matters Most*
Dara Horn	*A Guide for the Perplexed*
Blair Hurley	*The Devoted**
Nicole Krauss	*The History of Love*
Maaza Mengiste	*Beneath the Lion's Gaze*
Claire Messud	*The Burning Girl*
Daniyal Mueenuddin	*In Other Rooms, Other Wonders*
Neel Mukherjee	*The Lives of Others; A State of Freedom**
Richard Powers	*Orfeo*
Kirstin Valdez Quade	*Night at the Fiestas*
Jean Rhys	*Wide Sargasso Sea*
Mary Roach	*Packing for Mars*
Akhil Sharma	*Family Life*
Manil Suri	*The City of Devi*
Madeleine Thien	*Do Not Say We Have Nothing*
Vu Tran	*Dragonfish*
Rose Tremain	*The Gustav Sonata*
Brad Watson	*Miss Jane*
Constance Fenimore Woolson	*Miss Grief and Other Stories**

*Available only on the Norton website

Don't miss other award-winning titles by DARA HORN

www.darahorn.com

"[An] intense, multilayered story. . . . [Horn's] writing comes from a place of deep knowledge."

—*New York Times Book Review*

"Rare and memorable."

—*Wall Street Journal*

"Nothing short of amazing."

—*Entertainment Weekly*

"Not merely a striking success as a whole but a technical tour de force."

—*Commentary*